IRVINE WELSH

Irvine Welsh is the author of eleven novels and four books of shorter fiction. *Trainspotting* (1993), his first novel, was a phenomenal bestseller and has since become a cult classic of the 1990s, described by the *Sunday Times* as 'The voice of punk, grown up, grown wiser and grown eloquent'. The film of the novel was directed by Danny Boyle and released in 1996, and has been ranked tenth by the British Film Institute in its Top 100 British film of all time. *T2 Trainspotting*, based on the novel *Porno* (2002), is a sequel to *Trainspotting* and reunites the original cast. Welsh currently lives in Chicago.

IRVINE WELSH

The Blade Artist

VINTAGE

3 5 7 9 10 8 6 4

Vintage
20 Vauxhall Bridge Road,
London SW1V 2SA

Vintage is part of the Penguin Random House group of companies
whose addresses can be found at global.penguinrandomhouse.com

Penguin
Random House
UK

First published in Vintage in 2017
First published in hardback by Jonathan Cape in 2016

penguin.co.uk/vintage

A CIP catalogue record for this book is
available from the British Library

ISBN 9781784700553

Printed and bound in Great Britain by Clays Ltd, Elcograf S.p.A

Penguin Random House is committed to a sustainable future
for our business, our readers and our planet. This book is made
from Forest Stewardship Council® certified paper.

For Don DeGrazia

'Man is the only creature who refuses to be what he is.'

Albert Camus

CONTENTS

1

THE BEACH

As he elevates her skywards, the bright sun seems to burst out from behind Eve's head, offering Jim Francis a transcendental moment that he pauses to savour before he lowers the child. The hot sand will soon punish his bare feet, he thinks, turning away from the solar flare, and he'll have to watch she doesn't burn. Eve is fine for now though, her bubbling, machine-gun giggles urging him to continue the game.

The glorious thing about working for yourself, setting your own hours, is that you can always take time off. Jim appreciates being here on the deserted beach, so early at sunrise this July morning, with his wife and two young daughters, while everybody else sleeps off their Independence Day celebration hangovers. The beach is absolutely deserted, bar some squawking seabirds.

When he'd first moved to California, they'd stayed in Melanie's two-bedroomed apartment in the small college town of Isla Vista, close to where she worked at the university campus. Jim loved the closeness to the ocean, and they'd regularly walk the coastal trail, from Goleta Point to Devereux Slough, sometimes only seeing the odd beachcomber or surfer. When first Grace then Eve had come along, they'd moved to a house in Santa Barbara, and the treks were curtailed in favour of shorter jaunts.

This morning they rose early, the tide still low, parking the Grand Cherokee up on the Lagoon Road. They walk in old sneakers, as the beach is littered with tar balls, produced by the nearby Ellwood Oil Field, the only point of attack on mainland American soil during World War II. Ambling down towards the ocean, they passed the low sandstone cliffs that separate the University of California's Santa Barbara campus from the Pacific, towards the still, richer blue of the lagoon. The tide pools, and the crabs left stranded in them by the outgoing sea, mesmerised the girls, and Jim was reluctant to move on, sharing in their wide-eyed joy, which took him back to his own childhood. There would be more crabs to see later at Goleta Point though, so they roamed further, setting up camp under the cliffs, beyond which sat the university and Isla Vista. The storms in the night have combined with the holiday weekend and the college off-season to leave the beach bereft of human traffic.

The uncharacteristically severe weather has been easing off lately, but the unruly sea has created large sandbanks. If you aren't inclined to wait for the tide coming in, those have to be negotiated before you get to the ocean. Jim has kicked off his shoes and picked up Eve, knowing that his three-year-old shares his habit of impatience, while Melanie has smoothed out the beach towels and is sitting with five-year-old Grace.

Paddling in the sea, Jim hoists Eve up, once again enthralled by the stream of chuckles this induces. Because

2

of the sand dunes he can't see Melanie and Grace, but knows that Eve can. High in his outstretched arms, she has her mother and sister in her line of vision as she gurgles and points their way each time he raises her above his head.

Then something changes.

It's the kid's expression. At the next skywards swing, Eve lets her hands fall by her side. She is looking in the same direction, Jim chasing her eyeline to the top of the sandbank, but there is confusion on the child's face. He feels something thud inside him. Pulling her to his chest, he walks quickly up the dune, his bad leg heavy in the sand. But when Melanie and Grace come into his view, far from slowing down, he strides forward in greater haste.

Melanie is both relieved and scared to see Jim rising from the sand, in the hazy overhead sun bursting through the clouds, Eve in his arms. Perhaps they would go now, the two men who had emerged onto the beach from the gravelled paths that wound down from the cliffs above. She'd been vaguely aware of them, but had scarcely given it a thought, thinking they would be students, until they had come over and sat right beside her and her daughter. She had been applying suntan lotion to Grace's arms and had started to do the same to herself.

— You need a hand puttin that stuff on? one of them asked, a crooked smile under his dark shades. It was the tone that chilled her; not leering, but cold and matter-of-fact. He wore a black tank top from which heavy muscles coiled out, and ran a hand over a close-cropped skull. His accomplice was a smaller man, with blond straggly hair spilling into piercing blue eyes, and a warped grin of rank malevolence.

3

Melanie said nothing. Those men were not students. Her previous employment had involved working inside the prisons they stank of. She felt paralysed by a terrible sense of cognitive dissonance, as she'd advocated freedom for such men in the past. Men who seemed plausible, reformed. How many of them would turn wrong when they got back into the community? While Melanie wasn't easily fazed, the situation dripped with badness. Her knotted gut pulsed insistently, telling her that they were more than just pests. And Grace looked at her in appeal, urging her to do or say something. She wanted to somehow convey to her daughter that doing nothing in this situation was doing something. Melanie had looked onto the cliffs, down the beach, and there was nobody. This spot, usually so popular, now eerily deserted.

Then Jim, striding swiftly across the sand, Eve clinging to him, pointing over at them with a chubby finger.

— What's up with your fuckin tongue, bitch? the black tank top snaps. His name is Marcello Santiago, and he is used to being answered by the women he speaks to.

Suddenly Melanie is really scared. Jim approaching them, *Oh God, Jim.* — Look, leave us alone, my husband's here, she says calmly. — You have the whole beach, we're just out with our kids.

Marcello Santiago stands up, looking towards Jim, who has advanced over to them, still holding Eve. — We reckoned we might share your picnic, he grins at him.

The blond man, who is called Damien Coover, has also risen, and he stays close to Melanie and Grace.

4

— What's wrong, Daddy? Grace asks fretfully, looking up at her father.

Jim nods at Melanie. — Take them and go back to the car, he says evenly.

— Jim . . . Melanie appeals, gaping at him, then Damien Coover, but finally regarding the girls and standing up and yanking Grace to her feet.

She moves towards Jim, who transfers Eve into her arms, his eyes never leaving Santiago and Coover. — Go back to the car, he repeats.

Melanie feels the proximity of the girls, glances at the two men, and then moves up the beach towards the small parking lot on the bank above. She looks back and sees that her bag is on the towel. Her cellphone and Jim's are inside it. It's open. She sees Coover register this. Jim does too. — Go, he says a third time.

Coover watches as Melanie and the kids depart up the beach. Her body is taut and toned in her bikini, but a stoop of terror has made her habitually graceful movements pensive, fractured and ugly. Nonetheless, he manages a pointed leer. — That's some hot pussy you got there, brother, he laughs at Jim Francis, and his friend Santiago, who has been balling and unballing his fists, joins in, a low mirthless sound.

There is nothing in Jim Francis's reaction: just stony evaluation.

So Santiago and Coover are compelled to contemplate the silent man facing them, dressed only in his green khaki shorts. A bronzed body, muscular but pitted with strange scarring, connotes this man as miscast in that family of blonde

5

Californian females. He is of an indeterminate age: at least forty, possibly around fifty, which would make him a good twenty years older than the woman he's with. What, Santiago wonders, does a man like that have in order to get such a hot piece of ass? Money? It's hard to figure out, but there is something about him. He looks back at them, like he knows them.

A database of encounters past, of bar-room and penitentiary faces, starts to roll through Santiago's head. Nothing. But that look. — Where you from, buddy?

Jim remains silent, his gaze sliding from the dark lens of Santiago, onto the blue eyes of Coover.

— Starin me down . . . Coover's voice goes high and he reaches into the duffel bag at his feet and pulls out a large hunting knife, brandishing it a few feet away from Jim Francis. — You want some of this? Get the fuck outta here while you still can!

Jim Francis flashes an odd look at the knife for a couple of seconds. Then he stoops, his eyes never leaving Coover, and picks up the bag and towels, turning slowly, following his wife and children up the beach. They notice that he walks with a slight limp.

— Gimpy asshole, Coover barks, sheathing his blade. Jim halts for a second, sucks in a slow breath, then walks on. The two men share a mocking laugh, but it is one underscored with a sense of relief that the man who was facing them has just departed. It is more than his strong build and the attitude he carries that he would fight savagely, and to the death, in order to protect his family. There is something about him, that scar tissue on his body and hands, as if he's had substantial tattooing covered up; those thin but extensive cicatrix configurations on his face; but most of all, those eyes. Yes, Santiago considers, they indicate that he belongs in a different world to the one inhabited by that woman and those kids.

Jim gets to the Grand Cherokee, parked on the gravelly lot behind the beach, fifty yards from the tarmacked road. There is another vehicle positioned there, a beat-up, four-door Silverado pickup truck. For a second he panics as he can't see Melanie or the girls, but it's only the rising sun, burning away the cloud cover, reflecting on the windows of the car. They are safely inside and he joins them, to find Grace asking questions. Who were those men? What did they want? Were they bad? He straps her in the back with Eve, and climbs into the front passenger seat. Melanie starts up the Grand Cherokee and drives past the Silverado, knowing that it belongs to the two interlopers.

— We should go to the police . . . Melanie whispers, content that Grace is now distracted with a toy. — I was so scared, Jim. Those guys were trouble . . . She drops her voice. — I was thinking of Paula . . . I dunno what would have happened if you hadn't come by . . . I couldn't see you because of the dunes . . .

— Let's get the girls home, Jim says softly, his hand falling on her knee, feeling a steady tremble in it, — then I'll see about the police.

Home is only a short drive down Highway 101, and a further mile to their Spanish colonial-style house in Santa Barbara, a few blocks from the ocean. Melanie pulls the

7

Grand Cherokee into the front yard and Jim lets them all disembark, then heads into the second garage which he has made his workshop, emerging a few moments later and taking the vehicle back onto the road. Melanie says nothing, but as the car turns out of the driveway, she is once again uneasy.

2

THE DELIVERY BOY 1

The blood leaked out of the man's smashed head. Finally all was silent and still. Stepping away from the body, I looked up at those stark, forbidding walls. Above, a full moon shimmering in a bloated, mauve-and-black sky, its reflection dusting the metal rungs cut into the side of the stone. After that terrible ordeal, I was spent, and there was no power in my small, frail legs. I thought: How the fuck am I ever going to get back up there?

3

THE CONSIDERATIONS

Jim returns a couple of hours later, to find Melanie playing with the girls at the rear of the backyard, beyond the wooden decking, under a group of mature fruit trees. She has set up an elaborate game around the huge red-painted doll's house that he worked on for the best part of a year. The girls love it because, inside the structure, Jim has assembled an intricate series of pulleys, ramps and ball-bearings, which set off various calamities for the doll figurines that live there. On the lawn, an unfeasible number of candy wrappers and toys lie strewn about: Melanie's attempt to salvage something from the abandoned beach excursion.

She rises and moves over to him. — Did you speak to the police?

Jim stays silent.

— You didn't, did you?

Jim lets go of some air he's been holding in. — No. I just couldn't do it. It's not in my DNA to talk to them.

— When psychopaths put women and children at risk, normal citizens report that sort of thing to the police, Melanie snaps, shaking her head. — You know what happened to Paula, for fuck's sake!

Jim raises an eyebrow. The circumstances with Paula — the two guys, students, whom she knew — were different. But he isn't going to argue that detail.

Realising she's come over more patronising than intended, and that it's rankled with Jim, Melanie rubs his arm reassuringly, while mouthing his name in urgent appeal. — Jim . . .

Jim squints in the sunlight filtering through the big overhanging oak tree, sucking in another steady breath. She watches his chest expand. Then he exhales. — I know . . . it was stupid. I just couldn't do it. I drove around to see if those guys were still about, but there was no sign. They'd gone; the beach was deserted.

— You *what*? Melanie gasps. — Are you kidding me!

— I wasn't going to confront them. Jim shakes his head, his mouth tight. — I just wanted to make sure that they weren't harassing somebody else. That's what they would be getting up to, hanging around the campus, causing bother. Then I would've . . .

— What?

— I'd have called campus security.

— That's exactly what I'm gonna do right now, Melanie announces, and heads indoors for her cell, which is on the kitchen breakfast bar.

Jim follows her inside. — Don't . . .

— What . . .

— I did do something, he confesses, watching her features slide. — Not to them. To their car. I stuck a lighted rag in the gas tank and blew it up. So it's probably best that the

11

cops, or even campus security, don't know that we were around.

— You . . . you what . . . ?

As he repeats his explanation, Melanie Francis thinks of those assholes, with their arrogant, bullying threats, and considers how they would react to seeing their vehicle destroyed. She looks at her husband and starts to laugh, throwing her arms around his neck. Jim smiles, looking over her shoulder, through the window and out to the yard, where Grace is making Eve a daisy chain.

4

THE WORKSHOP

Guns n' Roses' *Chinese Democracy* blasts out from a large sound system at a volume that almost pushes Martin Crosby right back out of the heavy reinforced door he'd slid open in order to enter the small studio. A traditional stack stereo system and its huge dominant speakers are crammed into a window- and sky-lit space that's barely big enough to contain a kiln and an easel, with some paints and building materials stacked on the floor. He can't see Jim Francis at his work-bench but the heads of the Hollywood actors and pop stars lined up on shelving are recognisable to Martin, in spite of the implausibly creative mutilations the artist has subjected them to. A blockbuster star has his razored face crudely stitched back together. A cable-series icon has been cursed by a massive tumour growing out the side of his head. A pop princess has cruelly lost an eye.

Then, suddenly, the music stops and Francis is at his shoulder holding a remote, making Martin jump. The artist says nothing to his agent, as is generally his way. Martin Crosby, himself a calm, taciturn man, who prefers to listen as he peers out from over silver-framed spectacles, has plenty of ungrateful clients, some who see his role, at best, as a necessary evil. Yet he's never had one as – *hostile* wasn't the

13

right word, that would almost be an improvement – as *unmoved* as Francis. He's just driven two and a half hours on the choked interstate to offer support for his artist and his forthcoming exhibition, and all he gets from Jim Francis is, — So what you brings you up here, then?

As Martin explains, rubbing at a beard shaved to the same bristle-length as his hair, Jim Francis merely says, — All going okay. I'd best be getting back to it, and he points to a small fridge. — Help yourself to a bottle of water, as he picks up the handset and what to Martin is charmless, overproduced rock music fills the air and assails his eardrums. He goes to speak but realises the futility of doing so as Francis walks to his sculpture in the corner, hunching over another head, moulding it violently with his big calloused hands, and ripping at it with a selection of knives.

Yet it is *almost* worth coming up, just to see Jim Francis at work. It really is a sight to behold. Most sculptors are heavily orientated towards the physical, but it seems to Martin that Francis's controlled rage is scored by the music's chopping, ripping guitar work and raw vocals, to the extent that he actually lets the sound guide him across the clay. It is as if the band is composing this head, and they are using Francis as a conduit. Attached to the wall at his side are magnetic strips, which hold all types of knives. Most are the traditional thin stainless-steel blades he's seen other artists use for clay sculpting, but there are some larger ones that look like hunting knives, while others appear to be a surgeon's operating instruments. He recalls Francis once said in an interview that he likes to use utensils not traditionally associated with sculpting.

Jim Francis is a strange one, no doubt about that, Martin considers, though this quality is hardly unique among his client base. Artists are artists. Martin had wanted to talk about next month's opening, to make sure all the pieces would be ready for exhibition, and how best to set it up. This wasn't easy. Francis has an email account but never responds to Martin's overtures, nor does he return his texts. The phone conversations, when he deigns to pick up, are an exercise in gruff minimalism. The last time they'd spoken, Jim Francis had just said, in that gravelly accent of his, — Remember to invite Rod Stewart to the opening, before hanging up.

So Martin has come up from Los Angeles, and so far it is odds-on that it will prove to be a waste of a day. This really isn't acceptable. In his mounting frustration, Martin shouts at the artist's back, but the music is too loud and something makes him shy about physically touching Jim Francis, even the minimal contact to indicate that a conversation would be welcome. He sees his chance when the track changes and Axl Rose's scream briefly fades. — JIM! . . .

The artist swivels round and grabs the handset, switching off the music. He looks calmly at Martin.

— I appreciate that you're very busy and I greatly admire your work ethic, but we have some major decisions to make about the exhibition. I really need some undivided time with you. I've driven up from LA –

— Okay, Francis snaps in agitation, then seems to thaw a little, — give me an hour and we'll go and grab a late lunch. Go through to the house and Mel will get you a coffee or a beer or something, and he slams the music back on at a

15

volume that makes Martin Crosby keen to comply. Closing the door behind him, Martin moves into a small anteroom, then the main house itself. The studio was probably an old garage, in some way part of things here, but not in others. A bit like Francis himself, he speculates.

Martin has only met Jim Francis's wife, Melanie, once before, at the opening of a show. Again, she is as friendly and engaging as his client is brusque and distant. Her blonde hair is held back by a red band, and she wears grey sweat-pants and a red tanktop. An exercise mat had been placed on the floor in front of a giant flat-screen TV, and weights and elasticated resistance cords attested, along with a thin layer of sweat on her brow, to her recent exertions.

Melanie gets some cold bottles of water for them both, and sits Martin down on the couch. She lowers herself into a padded armchair opposite, folding her legs into a lotus position. — Jim can be pretty intense when he's working. I admire his single-mindedness, I get too easily distracted, but it isn't always fun to be around. She shakes her head in cheerful affection, letting Martin know that this observation isn't intended as a slight to her husband.

It is closer to an hour and a half when Jim Francis emerges, by which time Martin has grown hungry, although Melanie's agreeable company has distracted him. Francis nods at his wife. — Won't be long, he says, then turns to Martin and briefly raises his eyebrows. To end up with a woman so outgoing, vivacous and good-looking, and far younger than her husband, Jim Francis must possess some kind of charm, but Martin Crosby has always struggled to find it.

They get into Francis's station wagon and journey in silence to downtown Santa Barbara, stopping at a beachside cafe called the Shoreline. They head for a table in a tent-covered *al fresco* area looking out onto the Pacific, and Martin notes that Jim Francis seems more relaxed. He spies a couple with a big, wrinkled oriental dog, greeting them by shaking the man's hand, kissing the woman's cheek, then aggressively petting the enthusiastic animal. — Neighbours, he explains to Martin, as they take their seats. Francis smiles easily at the approaching young waitress. — How's things, Candy?

— I'm good, Jim, she sings, dispensing a flashbulb smile.

Martin joins his client in ordering an egg-white omelette with spinach and feta cheese, and a side of fresh fruit. He fires up his Mac, displaying representations of layouts, and different floor-plan options where paintings could be hung and sculptures mounted. Martin starts to explain the natural and placed lighting and the different effects they would have on the various pieces. — I thought if you could spare an afternoon or morning to drive down and see the space, he begins, before Francis silences him with a firm tap on the first set of configurations on the screen. — This one's fine, he says.

— Well, it does have certain advantages, Martin agrees, pointing at the image, — but the problem is that there's the brick wall here and no window –

— It's fine, Francis reiterates, looking over to a nearby table where a group of Independence Day revellers are drinking off hangovers with bottles of Corona beer turned upside down, tipped into outsized glasses of margarita.

17

— Well, uh . . . okay, Jim, I guess it's your call. Martin Crosby smiles tightly. — I like the understated classical pillars to mount the head sculptures, giving it a kind of last days of ancient Rome effect –

— Aye, sound. Did you ever hear back from Rod Stewart's people? Francis interjects, as the server arrives with the omelettes.

— Nothing yet. I'll get Vanessa to chase it up, Martin says in increased despondency, watching Francis throw some hash browns towards the scavenging gulls that loiter on the sands outside the patio area. To his eyes, his client seems to derive an inordinate amount of pleasure from the act of feeding those aggressive birds. He is particularly taken by one that hangs in the air on the thermals, careful to chuck food its way, enjoying its excited screeches, oblivious to the patent disquiet of the cafe's other patrons.

Later, when Martin Crosby is driving back to LA, his assistant puts a call through to him on his car speakerphone. It isn't Rod Stewart, or any of his representatives. It is a woman with the same sort of accent as Jim Francis's, and she claims to be his sister.

5

THE CALL

He hadn't heard Elspeth's voice in several years. Yet he recognised it straight away on the phone, without checking caller ID. Not that it would have come up, as they had long since lost touch. Their mother had died a few years back, after Jim had moved to the USA. Jim returned for the funeral, but had headed back to LA immediately afterwards. He had changed his number since then, without bothering to tell her. How had she got it? Elspeth was resourceful. His younger sister, ten years and four months between them. His brother Joe, just over a year older than him. And why was she getting in touch? It had to be about Joe, he was a heavy drinker. The drink took their father. It would get Joe too. — Elspeth . . .

— I googled you. Got your number from your agent. Took me a while to work out it was actually you . . . the Jim thing. Anyway, it's not good news . . . Her voice wavers. — I'm really sorry . . . he can sense her crippling hesitancy, — . . . but Sean died yesterday. He was found in his flat.

Sean . . . what the fuck . . .

— That's all I know right now, Elspeth says, a sad, fretful pain in her voice. More than the news, which provides only shock, her tone moves Jim Francis, as he and his sister hadn't parted on good terms. — I'm so sorry . . .

19

Jim's brain is scorched by the questions that pop into his head, jostling for his focus. He sucks air through his nose, filling his lungs. He thinks of June, the woman by whom he'd had Sean, and another boy, Michael. She'd presented the firstborn to him with an almost defiant pride. *See? See what I can do?* He'd felt some strange kind of personal vindication that had been beyond his expression, but little else. Then he'd gone to the pub and bought drinks for everybody and got hammered. A vision of baby Sean's face, then June's, and all the boys in that pub, suddenly sears into his consciousness. And then there's Elspeth's, his sister, now silent on the phone line. How proud she was then, as a young girl, to be an auntie. They all seemed to belong to a different life, one lived by somebody else. He looks at his tanned countenance in the mirror on the wall. Melanie is hovering behind him, her own face tense in the reflection. When Grace and Eve had come along it had been so different. He'd felt himself as something small, yet part of an infinite cosmos, and swarmed by an internal kaleidoscope of emotion, he'd cried and squeezed her hand.

— Are you still there? Elspeth's voice on the line.

— You got a number for June?

Elspeth slowly enunciates the digits, which he taps into his iPhone with his free hand.

— Obviously I'll be over. Will you phone me if you get any more details?

— Of course I will.

— Thanks . . . he coughs out, then lowers the landline receiver onto the cradle.

— It's Sean, he says to Melanie. — He's dead.

— Oh my God. Melanie clasps her hand to her mouth. — What happened?

— Found dead back in Edinburgh. Jim's voice is flat and even. — I have to get over there, for the funeral, and to find out what happened, obviously.

— Of course, Melanie gasps, wrapping her arms around him. He is tense; she feels like a sweater hanging on a bronze statue. — What did they say?

— He's dead, that's all I know.

She lightens but maintains her grip on him. His bearing reminds her of when she first tried to hold him, when they got together, that terrible stiffness in his body. — I feel so bad, I never knew him, or Michael.

Jim is silent, as still and immobile as one of his pieces of sculpture. Melanie can feel his tension seeping into her, hardening her. Breaking off her grip, she lets her arms fall by her sides. — You won't get involved in anything over there, will you?

Jim shakes his head dismissively. — What's to get involved in? I just want to find out what happened, go to his funeral, he says, then adds, in a different voice, — see whose tears are real, whose are crocodille, and he moves through to the small office, sits down in front of the computer and goes online.

— Jim . . .

— You say you never knew him. Neither did I, Jim mutters, his dark brown eyes clouding. — When he was younger he was just a distraction to me. An irrelevance. Then I was in

21

the jail. I did everything wrong with him and his brother, he says, seeming to Melanie to grow almost conversational in his tone, like he is talking to someone else. It disconcerts her, and he picks up on it, sinking his voice. — When I had kids I said I'd never be the way my old man was with me. And I kept my word; I was worse, he allows, almost bluntly, as he pulls up the American Airlines page on the screen. Then he turns to her and says, intently, — But I'm different with the girls.

— Of course you are, you're a great dad, Melanie says, probably a little too urgently. — It's different now. You were too young, you –

— I was addicted to violence, Jim coldly confesses, tapping in information and pulling out his credit card. — But I've got that nonsense under control now, cause it doesn't take me anywhere interesting. Just jail. Done too much of that.

— Yes. Melanie looks at Jim, squeezes his hand. She tries to find him, this man she's married, whom she'd taken with her back to the States. All she can see is a Scottish jailbird she'd met years ago called Francis Begbie.

6

THE DELIVERY BOY 2

They came by the house on Friday nights for card school, when my ma was at the bingo. There was Grandad Jock, Carmie, Lozy and the much younger man, 'Handsome' Johnnie Tweed, the only one of them who ever gave me money. He'd take me aside and crush the odd quid note or ten-bob bit into my hand, and tip me a wee wink, so I knew that this was just between us. They were an arrogant, entitled quartet, prone to swaggering around in long Crombie overcoats and trilbies. I was fascinated by them all, so was my brother Joe.

My dad would be pished, with my uncle Jimmy. He was always rat-arsed. My ma would throw him out, sometimes for years. When he came back he'd be sober for a while, but that never lasted. Then he went away for ages. They said he was working on the rigs, but I knew he was in the jail or kipped up with some dozy hoor. Then he returned once more, and stayed long enough to give Ma my wee sister, Elspeth.

I eagerly anticipated those Friday nights, even if they had a strange edge to them. Grandad Jock would be nursing a beer, which he rarely finished, and sipping at a whisky. One only. He'd look at his two sons: drunk, sprawling, flatulent and loud-mouthed, and even as a kid, I could feel him seethe with disappointment. I suppose it was something that we shared.

My ma hated him and his trio of mates. Gangsters, she called them. Back then, in the late seventies, they were among the last men on the dwindling docks. All of them, bar Johnnie, had been there since the war and were nearing retirement. The older three, through being in a reserved occupation, had missed all the fighting. I always thought it ironic that cunts thought of as hard had used their job status to shite out from swedging the Nazis. But personal gain was their real motive. — They took everything that was meant for the working people, I mind my mother once saying to me. — Stole fae their ain. The war stuff, it was meant for everybody, no just they thieving ratbags.

That was a wee bit disingenuous. I'd look around at all the stuff in our house compared to the scruffs' hooses. We had everything, until the old man pished it away. And you knew where it all came from. I never heard any talk from my ma of sending it back.

But she tried to keep me away from Grandad Jock and his mates. I was thirteen and in first year at school when they started to take an interest in me. That they didnae give a fuck about my brother Joe, fourteen months my elder, was good. It made me feel important.

Not a lot did back then.

I struggled with reading throughout primary school, and was put in dumbo classes in secondary. Letters and words on a page meant nothing, they were just a smudged code I couldn't crack. I would, many years later, be diagnosed as dyslexic. But back then the teachers and snobby kids laughed at me for being slow and stupid. I raged inside, with such force that I nearly made myself sick. Sitting there, at my desk, my breathing tight, almost passing out with fury. Then I learned that letting that rage out was the way to stop the laughter: to stop it by turning it into blood and tears.

So it felt good to be valued, by Grandad Jock and his pals; those bold, sly men, whom people seemed to fear and respect. Johnnie Tweed, though, I could never figure out. He was more ages with my dad, and I always thought he should have been his mate, rather than my grandad's. As his nickname suggested, 'Handsome' Johnnie was a good-looking guy with big white teeth and a shock of dark bath-brush hair, cut in a short crew. He smelt of strong aftershave, cigarettes and alcohol, like all the men did when you were a kid, but there was always something a bit more fragrant about Johnnie.

I hated school, and worked part-time as a delivery boy at R & T Gibson, a grocer's in Canonmills. I'd ride the big, black metal-framed bike, with boxes of groceries stuck in the huge basket at the front of it. I'd pedal this heavy monstrosity along busy streets, my skinny wee legs pumping hard just to keep it upright. I also stacked the shelves in the shop. The owner of the store was not called Gibson, but Malcolmson: a high-voiced, excitable cunt. Malcolmson was always bossing me around, along with Gary Galbraith, the other schoolkid who worked there.

One Saturday morning Grandad Jock came into the shop with Carmie. Willie Carmichael was a colossal, silent man with hands like shovels, and was forever by Grandad Jock's side. Jock wore this trademark lopsided smile, which I now associate with the word snide. He stared deeply at Malcolmson, who shuffled around uncomfortably as they talked, his voice growing higher. — *The Leeeeth dockers, aw aye, Jock, we've got tae keep the Leeeeth dockers happy!*

My grandad's cuntish smile never left his pus. He and Carmie took Malcolmson aside and whispered something to him. I kept out the way, stacking tins of pineapple chunks onto the shelves, but I could see Malcolmson's eyes get bigger and wider and Jock's and Carmie's get all narrow and slitty. After, Jock said to me, — *Make sure you work hard and behave yirsel for Mr Malcolmson here, boy, right?*

— *Aye.*

Then they left the shop. Malcolmson said fuck all for a while, but later looked at me in a strange kind of awe and fear. Then he told us that Gary Galbraith would be doing most of the deliveries and I would be stacking shelves, inside, in the warm. This was good news for me, but not for Gary. It was fuckin Baltic outside on that bike. But there would be just one delivery that I would have to make three times a week: a box of fruit and veg to the Leith dockers. I had never seen my grandad or any of his friends ever eat a single piece of fruit, or a vegetable that wasn't a tattie.

A nutter called John Strang, thick glasses, slicked-back hair, was the boy on the gate. He was known as a violent psycho, who had done time in Carstairs, a facility for the criminally insane. The stanes were cobbled, which didn't matter too much going in, but when I came out, after visiting their howf, the box was full of heavy bottles of spirits, which you could hear rattling and clanking together. Of course Strang said fuck all; he was obviously being looked after by Jock and the others, but

26

just going past that magnified gape was unsettling enough. Then I would cycle back to the shop and dump the bottles into the skip at the rear of the building. Johnnie would later come by in a van to pick them up. I knew this was their way of operating, as I waited behind the bushes one night, down by the Water of Leith walkway, and saw him appear.

But I liked going down to the dockyards to meet my grandad Jock and his mates. You could tell they were a group apart and that the other dockers had no time for them. They hung out at this brick outbuilding by an old dry wharf, which they had commandeered as their HQ. It was right at the eastern side of the docks, bordered by a big wire fence and a set of industrial units, well away from the other dockers. I think this arrangement suited all parties. The 'howf', as they called it, was obviously meant to be an old storeroom; it had a wooden table and chairs, and a rack containing some cleaning materials. There was a light, no windows, the place ventilated only by air bricks at the top and bottom, and sealed off by a big wooden door, which was left slightly ajar when we were inside.

I'd sit with them, drinking tea from a mug, keeping warm by a Calor gas stove they always had on in the winter, listening to them chat. They sounded weird to my young ears, often talking in riddles, using words and ways of expressing themselves I couldn't decipher. It was as if it was a different language, some kind of a code. They were like relics from another era.

They might have known fuck all about the Jam being top of the charts, but they knew about people, and their frailties. — See yir brother Joe, he's scared ay you, Grandad Jock said to me once down the howf. — He kens he's weaker than you.

27

I was floored by this revelation. Joe constantly bullied me: battering me, making my life hell. But I recognised a strange credibility in my grandad's statement. There was a panic in Joe's eyes when he beat me, like he was almost anticipating a retaliation that never came. But, armed with this insight, I resolved that it would now arrive. And he wouldn't be expecting it. This old bastard Jock, who could smell a man's vulnerability like a shark does blood in the water, he saw everything. He understood it all.

When I was younger I used to tell everybody this story of Joe and me, the story of the game-changer. The way I told it, though, I made it out that it was my dad that took me aside and told me to batter Joe's face in with a brick as he slept. That was how I wanted my father to be, to have that kind of will to power. But it wasn't my dad. It was my grandad. It was old Jock.

The main thing, however, was that the face was Joe's and the brick was in my hand. He wept all night, blood leaking into his pillow. I was scared, but exhilarated, almost tripping on my own sense of might. We both knew the score from then on in.

7

THE SISTER

The plane journey was a glorious, tortuous blur of knowledge. The audiobooks blasted into his ears through headphones, now supplemented by the Kindle. It was a magnificent liberation. He could enlarge the text, enhancing his focus on individual words without the proximate jumbled distraction crowding them out. He had learned how to modify the typefaces; some fonts were easier to read than others, and this experimentation yielded fruit. In tandem with the actors who read him the text, he had taught himself how to recognise words on a page. Gradually, the searing frustration of failure had been replaced by the buzz of learning. The sneers of teachers, the giggles of classmates, the mordant shame and the violent, incandescent rage, they belonged to another person, in another age.

Yet the name was still on his passport: Francis James Begbie. This, despite him using 'Jim Francis' professionally, and his wife mostly referring to him as Jim. It had been an easy development: by minor coincidence, Melanie's surname was the same as his first name, and she was often referred to as 'Frankie' by college friends. Nonetheless, she was flattered when he told her that he wanted to be known as Jim, and when Grace arrived, they would all take the surname Francis. — I don't want her growing up a Begbie, he'd said emphatically.

But whatever he was called, he hadn't believed that he would ever come back to Scotland. It simply wasn't on his agenda, and he vowed that his mother's funeral would be his last visit. He wasn't close to his brother and sister, nor his sons, whom he imagined would just do what they would do. What he hadn't really thought about any of them doing was dying. And his visceral reaction hadn't surprised him, but what did shock him was how deep it went.

As for friendships, those that existed between unreconstructed men of violence could thrive in camaraderie and even genuine affection for a while, as long as a pecking order was steadfastly adhered to. When it broke down, however, the results were devastating and few relationships could survive them, assuming both parties managed to. But in any case, his old friends lived lives that no longer had any appeal to him.

He'd spoken to June, quickly sensing through her anti-depressant-fuddled and muffled weeping that her principal agenda was to get him to pay the funeral costs, which he readily volunteered to do. She'd told him the bones of the case; that after an anonymous tip-off, Sean had been found bleeding in a flat in Gorgie, having suffered multiple stab wounds. The police reckoned he'd been assaulted there, but nobody else was present and the neighbours heard nothing to indicate a struggle. The flat was rented by a landlord to a well-known drug dealer who was currently serving a prison sentence. There was no evidence of a drug transaction, and as far as everyone knew, the dwelling had been empty a long time prior to Sean moving in.

As the flight dragged on it grew tiring, and the connection from London Heathrow was late. Now he emerges back into Edinburgh, cold and fatigued, wearing a light leather jacket, and wheeling out the mid-sized red case he'd stuffed mainly with T-shirts, socks and underpants. Winds from the North Sea blast him as he exits the airport terminal building. It had been a mistake not to bring more appropriate attire. He pulls out his iPhone, as a message from the phone company pops into his text box, outlining the extortionate rates he will pay while abroad. It is followed by a more welcome one from Melanie:

Love u!!! XXX

He texts back:

Arrived in one peace! Love u!!! XX

He looks in dismay, realising that he spelled *piece* wrong. Then, to his surprise, when he gets to the taxi rank, he finds he knows the cabbie, instantly recognisable by his distinctive corkscrew hair. And the driver knows him. — Awright, mate? It's Franco, ay? Sick Boy's auld mate!

— Terry. Franco, as he will always be known in Edinburgh, pulls a tight smile back. Juice Terry is one of the city's characters, and it is comforting to see an old face. Last he'd heard Terry was still making stag vids with his old friend Sick Boy, and driving a cab in his spare time.

31

— Read aw aboot ye. Yir daein well, Terry grins, then his face creases. — Listen . . . ah heard aboot yir laddie. Really sorry, mate. Young boy n aw.

— Thanks, but ah'd sortay lost touch with him.

Terry quickly mulls over the response, trying to work out whether it's genuine, or stoic bravado. — Ower fir the funeral, aye?

— Aye.

Driving Franco to the requested address in Murrayfield, and a street that is a mishmash of low-rise dwellings, Terry leaves him a card. — If ye ever want a cab, gies a shout, he winks. — Ah dinnae huv the 'For Hire' sign on that much, if ye git ma drift.

Franco takes the card and puts it in his inside pocket, exiting the cab, saying goodbye, and watches Terry speed off. Through a descending, eerie morning mist, he looks across at the imposing rugby stadium. Then, wheeling the red case behind him, he walks down the short driveway of the pebble-dashed house where his sister lives wth her husband and their two sons. He knocks on the door and Elspeth opens, hair piled high on her head and held there by an almost implausible range of pins and clips. She immediately embraces him, hugging him tightly, — Aw, Frank . . . I'm sorry . . . come in, ye must be exhausted . . . .

— I'm fine, he purrs, patting her back. They break their grip and Elspeth takes him indoors to the welcome heat, offering him a beer, which he rather curtly refuses. — Dinnae touch that stuff.

— *Sorry*, she says, making a bit of a fuss about the apology, then corrects herself. — Ye still teetotal?

— Nearly seven years.

Elspeth fixes herself a gin and tonic, though it's still morning. — You look really well, she offers, sitting down beside him.

Frank Begbie can't say the same about his younger sister. She seems heavier, bloated around the face. — Pilates, he smiles.

— You're joking!

— Aye, Mel does aw that. I just go to a boxing club four times a week.

Elspeth laughs in a manner that sheds years from her. — Ah couldnae see you doing Pilates, but California, ye never know!

— I suppose stranger things have happened.

As if acknowledging the truth in this, Elspeth states, — So you're an artist now, aye?

— So some people say.

Her eyes narrow as she raises the glass to her lips. Takes a sip. — Aw aye, I read a piece aboot ye in *Scotland on Sunday*. All those Hollywood stars, wanting to be pals with you. Elspeth raises an eyebrow. — You ever met George Clooney?

— Aye. Met him once.

— What was he like?

— I liked him, Franco concedes. — And because of that I don't think it's good manners to talk about people when they aren't around.

33

There is a pomposity in his response that rankles Elspeth. — Since when did *you* start caring about good manners?

— It's never too late.

Elspeth seems to consider this, as if contemplating, then biting back a stinging retort that was forming on her lips. — I'm really sorry about Sean, she begins, then her expression sets sternly. — But we should put our cards on the table. Just soas we both know where we stand.

Franco raises a single brow. — Fine by me.

— Ye kin fool some ay them wi your big rehabilitated act, Elspeth smiles scornfully, — but ye cannae con me. Ah know you. Ah ken what you are. She looks at him, waiting for a reaction.

None is forthcoming. Her brother seems not so much to have failed to take any offence as to have not heard what she actually said.

— But we're still family, she sighs. — So you're welcome to kip in our spare room till after the funeral.

— I'm much obliged.

Elspeth's eyes narrow. — But one step out of line and you're out the door. Ah mean it, Frank. I've the boys here.

Frank Begbie feels something familiar rise inside him. He wants to stand up and tell her to fuck off, and just get out of that dull, ordered suburban home, with its bland, beige decor and furnishings. But he sucks air into his lungs and looks at the two china dogs on the mantelpiece. They were his mother's, they came from the old place. Then he turns and nods slowly at her in the affirmative. — I understand.

34

Elspeth seems disconcerted at this compliant response, and visibly swallows. — Sean came round here a few times, you know.

— Aye?

— It was good at first, lovely tae see him, she smiles, before grimly shaking her head, — then when he went down-hill, he was only here tae cadge money.

— I'll pay you back.

— It's no about that. Elspeth lifts her glass. — I didnae want him hanging around Thomas and George. They're good boys. But they looked up to him, because he was older and their big cousin.

Frank tries to take all this in. Sean, his nephews, this house here in Murrayfield. It is acceptable enough, though nowhere near as impressive as his own home in California, he reflects with some satisfaction. When he was a kid in Leith, Murrayfield appeared to be a millionaires' playground. Now, to his critical eyes, it seems – at least this part of it – just another drab, shabby neighbourhood and nothing what-soever to aspire to. But his head is crackling with static and a huge yawn rips from him. — Listen, ah'm a bit jet-lagged. Would it be okay tae get my head down for a bit?

— Of course, Elspeth says, and she leads him through to the spare room.

Franco strips to his underpants and gets beneath the duvet. Enjoying the luxury of stretching out flat after the cramped plane, he drifts off into an unsatisfactory sleep full of disjointed dreams. A few hours have elapsed when he is woken by noises coming from downstairs. Punching Terry's number into his iPhone, he then does some stretches, followed by a bit of shadow-boxing in the full-length mirror and 150 pushups, before taking a shower.

The boys, George and Thomas, aged ten and nine, have returned from school. They regard him in blank fascination. After an exchange of pleasantries about flights and America, George ventures, — Mum said that you were in prison.

— George! Elspeth hisses.

— Naw, it's okay, Franco smiles. — Yes, I was.

— Wow . . . you must have done some bad things, right?

— Some bad things, Franco concurs, — but mostly stupid things. That's why people go to jail. But you lads seem far too smart for that caper. So how's school?

The boys are both keen to recount their days, and as he chats to them, Franco is confounded by how much he actually likes his nephews. Even Elspeth seems to lighten, and he shows her pictures of the girls on his iPhone. — They're beautiful, she says, but almost in accusation, her tones hinting at the inevitability of him somehow destroying them.

Greg, Elspeth's husband, arrives home from work. He has put on a bit of weight and his hair has thinned. — Frank! Great see you. He extends a hand and shakes Franco's firmly. — Obviously sorry about the circumstances, he glumly corrects himself.

— Aye, you too, and thanks, Franco manages, thinking how Greg looks like the classic British middle manager; tired, harassed and beset with the crippling awareness that he's gone as far as he's likely to, and that the next big life change

will be long-off retirement or worse, not-so-long-off redun-
dancy. — How's work?

— You do not want to know, Greg shakes his head.

You do not want to know how much I do not want to know,
Franco thinks.

But Greg, like his sons, is friendly, and keen to make
conversation. — Merger talk in the air. Never good, Frank.
He stares out the window. Dropping his breath, he repeats, —
Never good.

After dinner (Franco is disconcerted to find himself calling
it that too, instead of tea) the boys go to their rooms, and
Greg gets more serious, nursing a whisky, as Elspeth loads
up the dishwasher in the kitchen. — I really admire you,
Frank, the way you've turned your life around through art. It
must be so rewarding.

— Money's good but, ay.

— I always fancied writing the great Scottish novel . . .
Greg wistfully intones as he points to a bookcase. — I took
a creative writing course once . . .

Franco tracks Greg's gaze, taking in the spines of the
usual suspects, finding that he's read most of them. — They
ey said ah was good at art at school, but I could never see
it. I once drew this picture wi a black sun. The teacher
went radge; 'A black sun, Francis Begbie?' But I liked the
idea of a black sun, like a black hole in space. Sucking
everything intae darkness: where we came from, where we're
headed.

Greg nods, but his grin crumbles as the desolate weight
of Franco's words hits home. He rallies, and ventures

37

admiringly, — To have that kind of creativity . . . I wish it was me! Meeting all those stars . . . Have you ever met Jennifer Aniston?

— Best blow job ah ever had.

Greg raises his brows, glances towards the kitchen, and lowers his voice. — Wow, you're joking, right?

— Aye. She wisnae that good.

— Ha ha ha . . . Greg chortles, falling into silence as Elspeth reappears.

Frank has been looking at the CDs displayed in a big cabinet. Underneath there are several board games stacked on a shelf that grab his attention. He rises to inspect them. — Monopoly . . . an Edinburgh yin! Never knew they did that. Fancy a game?

— No, Elspeth says with stony finality. — Do you remember the last time we played Monopoly as a family? At my ma's that Christmas?

Franco is suddenly taciturn, as the boys come through from their rooms. — What happened? George asks.

— Never you mind, says Elspeth.

Franco recalls how they had placed a bottle of the Famous Grouse whisky in the middle of the board, the idea being that when somebody landed on Free Parking, they would have a nip. He seemed to land on it a lot. Then Joe had cheated, claiming he had rolled a ten instead of an eleven, thus positioning himself on Park Lane, intending to add it to the Mayfair he already had. Frank had picked up the bottle and sent it crashing down over his brother's head, to the shock of Elspeth, June, Joe's ex Sandra, and their mother,

Val. They'd taken Joe to the hospital, where he had received twelve stitches. This recollection makes Franco change his mind. He pulls out Mousetrap. — No seen one ay them for years, he says, opening the box.

— You used to hate that game, Elspeth recalls. — You eywis said that it was a lot of work to go round the board, just to set the thing off, and it didnae always work.

— I quite fancy a wee game, but, for auld times' sake, Frank suggests. — This is posher than the one we had. I don't mind of the man in the bath, and he looks at the plastic accessories, which George and Thomas are already eagerly assembling on the board.

8

THE INCIDENT

The next morning Franco rises early, looking out of his window to the end of the street and the small bridge, which crosses over the Water of Leith, leading to the rugby stadium. It is strange that the river winds all the way out to Leith and the Firth of Forth, down by the docks. Once again, his perception of the neighbourhood shocks him. With its cheap, shoddy, pebble-dashed dwellings, this is one step above a council scheme.

Picking up his US cellphone, he notes that the battery is running down and realises that through packing in haste, he's only brought a US charger. Nonetheless, he calls Melanie, taking a chance that she might be up late. She answers immediately. — Hey, you!

— Hey, honey, how's things? Franco feels his accent bland out. — How are my girls?

— We're all good. It's just tough to know what to tell them. I settled for 'an old friend of Daddy's is ill', I couldn't think of anything else.

Franco considers this, acknowledging, — Good move; it's probably for the best.

Melanie spills into an anecdote about Grace, and then Frank tells her that they'd been playing Mousetrap. When it seems as if his phone is going to give up, they say their goodbyes, and he goes to the kitchen to make breakfast.

Elspeth is surprised to come through and find him in her domain, making an egg-white-and-Swiss-cheese omelette, sporting an apron depicting the body of a fat woman in her underwear. She has never seen him so much as boil a kettle before. — New talents, she remarks.

— Can I interest you guys in any of this? he says, that slight American affectation still in his voice.

Elspeth declines, but Greg, trying to smooth down a tuft of hair as he enters, enthusiastically takes up the offer. Bolting back his food, Franco then briefly vanishes, only to re-emerge in a zipped sweater, ready to go outside.

— So where are ye off tae this early? Elspeth asks.

— Thought I'd take a wee stroll intae toon, then maybe head doon tae Leith, see if there's any old faces kicking about.

Elspeth remains silent, issuing him with a spare key. He can see that trademark intense activity buzzing behind her eyes as she processes the potential ramifications of this.

When Franco departs, Greg comments, — Your brother is like a completely different guy! Had a great chat with him about his creative process.

— You see the best in people, Greg, Elspeth says coldly. — You don't know what he's really like.

Franco sets about trying to piece together Sean's last days. His first port of call is the flat in Gorgie where his son met his demise. It is tucked down a sunless, tenemented side street at the back of Tynecastle Stadium. Canals of moss

41

grow between its cobblestones and a deathly stillness and silence pervades. The stair door is on an entryphone system, but he pauses, disinclined to start harassing neighbours for information, until he's learned more about the broader facts of the case.

The rudimentary details garnered from June badly needed supplementation. Heading up to George IV Bridge and the Edinburgh Library, he reads the newspaper reports of the incident. Then he calls Gayfield Square police station, on the assistance number listed in connection with the case. To his surprise, the receptionist immediately puts him through to the officer responsible for the investigation. The policeman introduces himself as Detective Inspector Ally Notman. Expressing sympathy for Franco's loss, he says that he wants to see him personally, asking when he can come in. Franco tells him he could be down there within the hour, to which Notman is agreeable. Following this call, he expects the power bar on his iPhone to indicate the charge is spent, but it hangs on resolutely.

He walks through the city with a peculiar, detached buoyancy. When he comes to the top of Leith Walk, his pulse kicks up further; this is the gateway to where he is from. Despite his positive reception on the phone, it is a strange feeling walking voluntarily into the Gayfield Square police station. On his last visit, many years past, he'd been dragged through those doors into a holding cell, semi-drunk, raging and covered in the blood of Donnelly, another rival, after a knife fight outside the Joseph Pearce pub across the street. This had taken place in broad daylight. What, he wonders, had he been thinking? *Fucking kamikaze pilot.* He stops, steps back from the glass station doors, looking from the step of the Georgian square back over to the pub. It would have been less hassle to have simply walked into the station and plunged the desk sergeant.

Now the officer greeting him has a welcoming smile, this continuing sympathetic treatment further knocking Franco out of kilter. The detective he'd talked to earlier is summoned and promptly appears. DI Ally Notman is a tall, dark-haired man, thin, but with an expanding drinker's waistline. Notman shakes Franco's hand, conveying condolences at his loss, as he ushers him into a quiet room. Only then does the detective dispense with the soft soap, going systematically through the details of the case. — Sean suffered multiple stab wounds to the chest, stomach, abdomen and thighs. The lacerations on just one arm indicate that he was only able to put up token resistance, probably due to his extreme intoxication. The blow that killed him was a wound that severed the femoral artery in his leg. He would have bled to death inside a minute. Notman raises his dark eyebrows, looking for a reaction from Franco.

— Seems like the boy who did this was in a rage, and got lucky, Franco considers. — It's no exactly the work ay a stone-cold assassin.

Notman keeps his face poker-straight, though Franco thinks he can see a flicker of acknowledgement in the cop's eyes. Then the detective shows him a copy of the toxicologist's report. — This indicates that Sean was heavily drugged.

Franco scans the document; amid the technical jargon the words *heroin, ecstasy, cocaine, amphetamine sulphate,*

43

cannabis, valium, amyl nitrate and *antidepressants* jump off the page. *Whoever came intae that flat and plunged the poor wee cunt never exactly had their work cut out.* — And some, Franco observes. — What was he no on?

— As I said, it's unlikely he would have known much about the assault in that condition.

It was extreme liberty-taking, Franco decides. — Any suspects?

— Our investigations are ongoing, Notman says blandly. — We'll obviously keep you and your ex . . . Sean's mother . . . informed of any developments.

— Sound, Frank Begbie says. He knows the drill. The polis wouldn't be going the extra mile to find the guilty party here. To his dismay, he now finds that he can scarcely blame them. Sean, like himself, had probably long been lost, and would have gone on creating havoc around him. Why indulge people like that when they would simply take each other out if you left them to their own devices? Despite our limited and grudgingly unenthusiastic lip service, the truth is that we've moved beyond democracy, universality and equality in the eyes of the law and, *de facto,* embraced a hierarchial, elitist world view. Those at the bottom aren't important, as long as they only threaten each other, rather than those at the top, or revenue streams like tourists. His own children, Sean, Michael and River, his ex-girlfriend Kate's son (whom he'd practically forgotten about as he had commenced his long stretch just before the kid was born, splitting with her when he was inside): they are of no consequence to him. How can they be compared to Eve and Grace, born to an

44

educated mother in advantaged circumstances? You always bet on the sleek thoroughbred rather than the Clydesdale. If he differentiates his own offspring in this manner, how can he condemn the polis for their lack of interest, when some poor tourist is probably getting their bag nicked up the town?

— One thing, Franco says, — who found him?

— Somebody made an anonymous 999 call to the ambulance service, said there had been a bad accident, then hung up.

Frank Begbie thinks about this. The caller is obviously implicated in some way. A straightpeg would have called the cops, as well as the ambulance service, and not described what happened to Sean as an accident. — Could it have been the caller that did him?

— It's possible. Or a friend or accomplice who witnessed the murder, and knew both him and person who did it. Perhaps had an attack of conscience later, Notman says, — but we don't know.

Franco ponders this, feeling that it's about as much as he's going to get from the cops.

— You seem to have turned your life around. I hear that you're doing well for yourself in the art world, Notman half smiles.

— Can't complain. I've had a wee tickle, Franco says, now fully realising that they would do fuck all about Sean. And he's also worked out that their main reason for agreeing to see him so readily was to tell him that he should do fuck all as well.

45

— I appreciate that you must be upset, Mr Begbie, Ally Notman states, his tone now professionally grave. — But it goes without saying that you have to leave this to us. Are we clear on that?

— I'm happy to let you boys do what you do best, Franco smiles, then adds darkly, — and leave me to do what *I* do best.

Notman's face drops.

Franco breaks into a beaming smile. — Which, of course, is painting and sculpting.

9

THE DANCE PARTNER 1

They found themselves at the club's outside veranda area to the rear of the building, drawn by the dance beats spilling from the sound system, courtesy of a DJ in the corner. After the drab, near-deserted interior, this proved to be an oasis: people were dancing, sitting at tables drinking and smoking, or loitering in small groups. Melanie and Jim immediately registered that they were two of the very few non-Latinos present; another white couple gyrated with some style and proficiency, while two black men leaned on the banister, alternately looking down into the street then turning back to appreciatively scan the crowd. At Melanie's prompting, she and Jim took some seats positioned against the wall and opposite the bar area. As they looked out onto the polished wooden dance floor, the table's red cloth brushed against their legs.

They hadn't been settled long when two strikingly beautiful women, dressed to kill and with matching attitudes, strutted out onto the patio. One was entrancing and sleek, with a slender figure and almost implausibly angular curves. She has to be a model, Melanie thought out loud. The other, with her smouldering lips and long black hair, had a lioness prowl that drew a reaction from everybody present. Jim and Melanie were not the only people to exchange glances; something was going on, with the innuendo of much more to follow.

Seconds later, behind both of the strutting interlopers, a young man in a light blue suit walked in. He was handsome and lithe, slick but easy in his movements. Smoking a cigarette, he surveyed all with an air of haughty, but jovial, disdain. When his eyes fell on first the two black men, then Jim and Melanie, he cracked big smiles, as if acknowledging new guests. Then he waved over to the DJ, and joined the two women at a table, where they ordered a bottle of white wine.

Melanie had tried not to stare, but something about this trio absolutely sparkled. The aura from them resonated across the space, and they emanated a total connection to the music and the atmosphere. They seemed important, but for a deeper reason than how they looked. It was as if they belonged there; had an almost divine purpose in the proceedings.

As half an hour elapsed, Melanie and Jim were disappointed that the impressive trio had not joined in the dance, as almost everybody else seemed to be up. At Melanie's urging, she and Jim rose and struggled through the steps, being met with kindly, if slightly pitying looks. Then the DJ put on a song with a faster beat, and the blue-suited man rose, nodding to the thin, model-type woman, who was sipping her drink. Taking one deep puff of his cigarette, before crushing it into the ashtray, he took her hand, and they walked towards the dance floor. At first she appeared only half interested, but his look seemed to ignite her, and they started to dance to the music.

Melanie could feel her heart begin to race. She looked at Jim, who was totally transfixed by the duo. They instinctively made for their seats, to better appreciate the performance. It was a remarkable one, as the dancing couple seemed to embody sound into human movement: rhythm, flair, style, grace, and an incendiary passion. Neither Jim nor Melanie could take their eyes from them. The man ran his hands softly through the woman's hair, caressed her face, and then suddenly, as the beat violently exploded, grabbed her waist, thrusting her body down, her head lashing back.

Melanie felt her mouth open wide, her spine tingle and her palms sweat. Then, under that hanging tablecloth, Jim's hand was on her knee, then crawling like a tarantula up her thigh. Despite this, she couldn't avert her gaze from the couple on the floor. Every beat of music was scored by the flash of a hand, the twist of an arm, the swivel of a hip, while each crescendo was powered by a spin . . . then two . . . then three . . . then four . . . followed by a pause, and Melanie could feel Jim's fingers, up her skirt, inside her panties, probing at her wet pussy for her clit. And almost at the same time her hand was inside his zipper, undoing the top button on the waistband of his trousers, fastening around his brick-hard cock. She could hear his breathing, slow and ragged, as they remained fixated on the dancing couple. Jim's inhalations grew shallower still, mirroring her own, as they got off on the dance and the style, jazz and sex appeal of the incandescent duo.

The entire crowd, couple by couple, cleared the dance floor as the stars' performance built in intensity. It was seemingly reckless, yet at the same time partnered with a technical perfection on every beat. A circle formed around them, as people just watched and clapped. This blocked Melanie and Jim's view of

the couple, and they too would have risen from the table had
they not both been gripped by their own eye-popping climax.
When the song finished, the entire room cheered, whistled and
clapped. Melanie and Jim sat in a stupor, realising something
significant had just happened. He whispered in her ear, — Do
they do salsa dance classes in town?

— Yes, Melanie said. — I'm sure we'll find something.

It had to be Harry the police department sent along. Lonely,
sad-eyed Harry Pallister, whom she'd first encountered in
seventh grade at Goleta Valley Junior High School. Melanie's
thoughts flashed back to those days. Some boys she could
scent lusting after her, their pheromones filling the air. And
with some of them, she'd reciprocated their ardour. But Harry
lurked in the shadows pining silently, occasionally catching
her with his sad, longing stare. Then, when Melanie began
freshman year at Santa Barbara High School, as she stepped
onto the campus of that Spanish colonial building, flushed
with excitement, the first familiar face she saw was Harry's.

Her joy evaporated.

Now he stands on the front porch, and even with the sun
behind him making her squint, Melanie can see his thin,
sincere face, that quietly martyred expression of his, as if the
world was too much for him, but he was nonetheless valiantly
and uncomplainingly fighting on. Then, as now, it seemed to
be the harbinger of great disappointment. — A bit of news,
about those men you called about.

Already she is wishing she hadn't made that call about
being menaced by those guys. Why had she? Jim had gotten

revenge, of a sort, by blowing up the vehicle. She knew the real reason had been the rape ordeal suffered by her friend, Paula Masters, at the hands of two other men. The culprits weren't drifters, they were students, but that didn't matter. Men dangerous to women were just that. — Hey, Harry, come in, she forces herself to sing, stepping into the house. He follows her, looking blankly at the art on the walls, into the lounge and, at her behest, sits down on the sofa.

Harry digs into his leather document case, producing two photographs, placing them on the table in front of her. — Was this them? The two men who harassed you?

There is no mistaking the duo. The criminal mugshots make them look even more like who and what they are; they could have been taken yesterday. The dark one, silent and menacing: the fair one, his face still set in that sneer. Melanie swallows, wishing she'd taken Jim's advice. Why, why, why had she made that call? But all he'd done was blow up their car . . .

She nods in acquiescence. — Have they been causing more trouble?

Harry acts as if she hasn't spoken, going back into his document case, pulling out a typed sheet of paper. From where she sits, Melanie can't make out what it pertains to, far less its specific contents. He lets the silence hang as he reads it. She interprets his behaviour as some kind of dominance statement.

Melanie had never been frightened to embrace who she was. She saw no need to apologise for her beauty or her wealthy background. She simply acknowledged that her family's liberal values had bestowed on her a magnanimity and concern for others who navigated life in less ostentatious comfort than her, understanding that this relative affluence had also given her the breathing space to indulge her calling. Aware that her good looks got her both positive and negative attention, she had learned, with a calm assertiveness, how to deal with jocks and nerds and everything in between. You didn't get sucked into the agendas of others. Ever.

But Harry's mute longing had always grated on her. Like he was just hanging around, waiting on Melanie to validate his life with a smile or a 'hello' or even an 'I love you'. Now he is silent again.

Melanie urges him to speak. — Harry?

— You said they were threatening, he coughs, taking out a small notebook from his trouser pocket.

She is getting it now. Harmless Harry with the notebook. They're never harmless, 'the polis', Frank, no, Jim called them, commenting in glacial reserve after the first time she had introduced them, at an opening of her work. Harry had come along, as a guest of a mutual high school friend whom she resolved to have a quiet word with. What had Harry smelt off Jim? The criminality? The danger? Or even the art? Whenever she'd caught sight of him that evening, he wasn't stealing the usual disconcerting glances at her. He was scrutinising Jim. Perhaps trying to fathom the attraction for women like Melanie, good-looking, intelligent and rich, of men whom he obviously reckoned were programmed to disappoint. Trying to discern their advantage over ones such as him, the loyal foot soldiers who only wanted to look after a woman. To provide for her. To save her. Melanie pondered how scary in their own way such men could be, without even knowing it. Often more so than many criminal psychopaths. Now Harry's slow stare, his slightly awkward, goofy demeanour, as he asks her about the confrontation with those two troubling, troubled souls. — And Jim, how did he react?

— He was very *calm*, Melanie says, stretching out the word to relax herself. — He got me to take the kids to the car. Then he kinda faced those guys down, and followed us.

After some more scribbling, and another silence, Harry asks, drumming his pen on his notebook, — What did he say to them?

Melanie knows that this isn't about those guys. She draws in a breath and feels the friction slip into her voice. — I don't think he said a goddamn thing to those assholes. Why would he? Who were they?

Harry fastens his bottom lip over his top one, makes a smacking sound with his mouth. — A body was fished out of the sea. It got snagged on the rigging of Holly, the offshore oil platform, and was found by a maintenance worker. Otherwise the current would have taken it right out into the ocean. It was this guy, Marcello Santiago, a gang member and career criminal. He passes over one of the photographs again. The darker man, the one with the muscles, who had chillingly wanted to apply her suntan lotion. — He had a bad record, multiple felonies, including violence and rape. His associate, Damien Coover, with whom he was recently seen, and who is currently missing, is a known paedophile. You were lucky Jim was with you and the girls. Those guys are bad news. Well, in Santiago's case, used to be.

Melanie gazes at Santiago's picture. Her blood is gelid in her veins. The air-conditioning thermostat clicks on, blasting cool air into the room. She shudders. — He's . . . dead, she gasps. It was a silly thing to say, given that Harry has just explained that his body had been washed out to sea, but she is in shock.

But through that, Melanie is aware that she's handed over some power to the police officer. To his credit, Harry pretends that he didn't hear her stupid, inane remark. Instead, he looks down at his notebook. — Jim came back with you and the girls, yes?

— Yes, Melanie says, flinching. Then she goes into a shivering spasm, just as Harry looks up.

— Are you okay?

Melanie takes a deep breath and nods. — It's scary to think that they were so close to the girls . . . She looks back at the pictures on the table, regaining her composure. — What do you think happened?

— Well, we don't have the official pathologist's report yet, but initial examinations indicate multiple stab wounds.

— Oh my God, Melanie says, then maybe too quickly asks, — Do you think this guy's murder was gang-related?

— Santiago's dead, Coover's vanished. Perhaps Coover killed him after some petty dispute and tried to make it look gang-related by taking him out to sea, but he never figured on Holly . . . but you never really know with those guys, though. Harry tapped the pen on his notebook again. — They might have been high, had an argument, hell, whatever . . . that strip of the beach is normally busy, but after Independence

Day . . . The full forensics report is due soon, he offers, then his tone changes. — But listen, Mel, it's obviously not my job to jump to conclusions. I'm telling you this in confidence as a friend, he says, then pauses, looking hopefully at her.

Melanie is grateful, without knowing just how indebted he expects her to be. — I appreciate it, Harry.

— But I'm also being candid because I know that I can discuss this rationally with you, given your experience of men like those . . . and he pauses again, as Melanie feels a ringing in her ears, — . . . through your work.

— Thanks . . .

— Anyway, those guys are no great loss, Harry says cheerfully, folding up the documents, — two very dangerous individuals, and he rises to his feet.

Melanie stands up too. — Yes, that was apparant by their behaviour.

— There's another theory, he nods, scrutinising her reaction, — that Coover might be dead as well. So while these guys are dangerous, they were maybe not as dangerous as whoever took them out. If anybody did.

— Right, Melanie says. She can feel her mind starting to tumble, and knows that Harry is trying to read her again. She attempts to switch her thoughts to Devereux Slough, the marine life and those nesting terns that so interested Jim.

— So how is Jim? Harry sings breezily.

— Back in Scotland. A family bereavement, and she heads through the hall to the front porch, compelling him to follow. Hoping, for once, that he would be distracted with his eyes on her ass.

— Sorry to hear it. Anybody close? She hears his disembodied voice behind her, thin and metallic.

Melanie opens the front door and turns to face him. — Thankfully, no, she says, unflinchingly. It was easier to say than it should have been. But she has told Harry more than enough. — Now if you'll excuse me, I have to pick the kids up.

— Of course, he smiles, sauntering out. — Good to see you. I'll keep you posted, and he gives her a little salute before he heads off down the driveway.

10

THE BROTHER

The best way to go to Leith is on foot, right down the Walk from the city centre. Franco had been determined to savour every step of the descending trek, but stopped at a couple of cut-price electrical stores. Neither had a UK-to-US power adaptor, or a UK lead for the iPhone. Instead they had tried to sell him almost every other electrical or phone-related product or service imaginable. He'd declined, and headed back outside.

The rain has started to fall, so he jumps on a bus down Leith Walk. By the time he gets to Pilrig it has eased off, so he disembarks after a couple of stops, striding to the Foot of the Walk, along Junction Street, down Ferry Road, to Fort House. The imposing building, a monument to sixties municipal architecture, is now eerily empty, but they haven't yet pulled it down. He looks at the huge walls that surround the scheme, and casts an eye over the flats. There was the Rentons' old house, Keasbo's, Matty's . . . but there really is nothing left any more. A melancholia descends upon him, and he heads towards the Firth, following the cries of the gulls. He soon finds himself traversing through a saturated new-build housing development at Newhaven. It has rendered the area unrecognisable to him.

Elspeth had no number for their brother Joe, just an address he'd left her when he'd turned up around a fortnight past, drunk and looking to borrow cash. It seemed a long shot that he'd still be at the same place. Joe was an established couch-surfing jakey, staggering from one insecure Housing Association tenancy or the beneficence of an old pal on to the next, burning down organisations and friendships as he went.

This area had been designated part of the new Leith for urban professionals, but the flats had been constructed with poor building materials, and with no social amenities around the recession had rendered them unsaleable. The developers cut their losses and handed them over to the Housing Association who rented them to breadline council tenants, often those evicted from the big schemes for antisocial behaviour. So the few young professionals who had been misguided enough to purchase such properties found themselves trapped in an embryonic ghetto.

To Franco's astonishment, Joe is still at the address and answers almost immediately, cheerlessly opening the door, then going back inside, urging him to follow. His brother regarded him in such a perfunctory manner, it was as if Franco had just nipped out for a packet of cigarettes, rather than to California for six years. Joe Begbie, wearing a parka, slumps onto the couch, and swigs at a plastic litre bottle of flat-looking cider, seeming relieved when Franco refuses a slug.

Franco casts his eyes around the small, barren room. The walls are painted white, and are grubby around the light switches. The beige carpet, sticky under his feet, is discoloured with different spillage. The place is littered with empty food cartons, beverage cans and overflowing ashtrays. It seems an advertisement for how a middle-aged man shouldn't be living.

— That Sandra, Frank, ye were right aboot her. You had that cow sussed, Joe offers, eyes red and sunken, as he augments his cider consumption with a nip of whisky from a bottle of Grouse.

He makes to pass it to Franco who again waves it away, as he thinks of Sandra and chips. He's always associated the two after a teenage sex incident up the old goods yard. — Kick ye oot, aye?

— Fuckin evil bitch, Joe hisses, his eyes burning. — Poisoned the kids against ays n everything. He shakes his head, then his face suddenly fills with cheer. — Still, good tae see you again. Kent you'd be back!

— Just for the funeral. Then ah bolt.

Joe's face crumples into a scowl as he lowers the whisky onto a wooden coffee table, the periphery of which is discoloured by cigarette burns. — Dinnae tell ays yir no lookin for the cunt that did Sean! Ah've been lookin!

— Aye, fae that couch?

— Ah've been lookin! Joe protests. — It's no that easy . . . you dinnae ken what it's like roond here now . . .

— Aye, life kin be hard, Franco blandly concedes.

— Ah've nae snout.

— A tragedy. You have my apathy.

— You stoaped?

— Aye.

— Snout?

— Aye.

— Yuv stoaped smokin?

Franco shakes his head. — How many weys dae ye want ays tae say it?

— Hmmph. Joe fixes his brother in a piercing stare. — Any money in this art game, then?

— Ah dae awright.

— Aye, ah read aw aboot that, right enough. Aye, you're daein fine! Shoes, Joe says bitterly, nodding at the polished black leather on Franco's feet. It seems to set him off as he suddenly explodes, — You cannae say thit ye didnae make mistakes, Frank!

Frank Begbie retains his composure, hauls in an even, steady breath. — Mistakes are what other people make. People that tried tae fuck ays aboot. They made mistakes. Usually, they peyed for them n aw.

This is enough to turn his brother's volume down. — California. How's that workin oot for ye, Frank?

— Fine enough.

— Ah'll bet it is. Joe's eyes dance, or rather something behind them does. — How's it the likes ay you git tae go tae California? he slurs, then snaps suddenly, — Big hoose, ay?

— Five bedrooms. A big outbuilding converted intae a workshop, or studio, as I like tae call it, Franco almost sings, as a sweet taste fills his mouth.

— Near the sea?

— Naw. Well, about three-quarters ay a mile away.

— Big hoose, but, Joe's accusatory tone continues.

— Aye, though there's a lot in the neighbourhood that's bigger. N you? Still livin oan other people's couches, mate?

— Aye, this is ma mate Darren's place, ay.

— Cannae be much fun, Franco nods, looking again around the room, the walls of which seem to close in a little more each time he regards them. — Mibbe ah'm just no pickin up on the glamorous side.

Joe is irate, looking at Frank in fury. — Come back ower here tae lord it ower everybody –

— When you're slumming it, I suppose it must look like the rest ay the world's lordin it, Franco says.

— Ye goat a sub? Joe asks, in a completely different tone. Franco had realised early into the conversation that external kindness or scorn made zero difference to Joe's mood. It was purely determined by the units of alcohol flowing through his system, and the fractured, internal narrative his fuddled brain was jumping through.

Franco rises, fishes out a crisp tenner from his pocket. Places it on the table. — See ye behind the goals.

11

THE SECOND SON

He had walked past the old Leith Academy school in Duke Street, now converted into flats, recalling sitting beside skinny, ginger-headed Mark Renton in the English class. How he struggled to understand the words on the page, and he knew that the teacher, Hetherington, a bullish, rugby-playing man with a beard, and leather elbow patches on his checked jacket, would ask him to read again. In his mind's eye he saw the teacher scanning the room, making his eyes big, as young Frank Begbie's insides packed densely and seemed to fall through him. — Francis, if you could read next . . .

The anticipatory glee of his humiliation filled the room. Then, next to him, Mark Renton, whispering, — Julie visited the cinema with Alice.

— Julie visited the cinema with Alice . . . Franco repeated.

— Very good, Francis Begbie. But I'd appreciate it more if Mark Renton would keep his mouth shut. The next line, Francis.

The squiggles danced before his eyes on the page, reverbing. — Sh . . . sh . . . sh . . .

— What did Julie and Alice – remember them? What did Julie and Alice visit the cinema to see, Begbie? What film did they see?

The laughter building in slow ripples around him. He could feel Renton, only Renton, sharing his anger.

— Can anybody help Francis Begbie?

Can anybody help Francis Begbie?

— Elaine! You never let us down!

Then the sooky voice of Elaine Harkins, entitled, impatient. *Francis Begbie held everybody back again.* — They had decided to see *Gone with the Wind*, starring Clark Gable and Vivien Leigh. Alice went to purchase some ice cream and popcorn from the refreshments stand.

The refreshments stand. Paggers at Tyney.

Frustrated by the local electrical shops, Franco decides that his best bet is to get a UK mobile. He opts to pick up a cheap one on a pay-as-you-go deal, and heads to Tesco's at the Foot of the Walk, which he remembers being a Scotmid. Hopefully, he considers, he won't be needing this device for long. Stepping outside, he tests it by calling Terry. It goes straight to voicemail (— Terry here. If yir a lassie, leave a message n ah'll get back tae ye. If yir a laddie, dinnae bother. Simple as.) but at least he knows it works. Looking across the street to the Marksman Bar, he recalls old associations, then thinks about family.

As he crosses through the Kirkgate Centre, Franco is aware that a gaunt but wiry young man in a red Harrington jacket is staring right at him. It's Michael, the younger of his two sons with June, whom he has heard is gaining a reputation.

As he moves over to the wall by the shuttered store, the boy's slitted eyes widen slightly. — Aw, it *is* you, Michael says, dismissively. — My ma said ye were coming back ower.

Franco wants to retort, *no, it's somebody else.* Instead he manages, — Aye. Want tae get a cup ay tea?

Michael considers this for a second. — Aye. Awright.

As they head down Junction Street, Franco notes two youths, wide and loud, coming down the road towards them. On spotting their approach, the young men fall abruptly silent and avoid eye contact. Franco is accustomed to inducing such a reaction in Leith, and turns to his son in a half-apology before realising that Michael hasn't seen the boys and is striding ahead, lost in thought. Franco examines his profile, can't see anything of himself, or for that matter June. The boy seems like a totally discrete entity.

The Canasta Cafe in Bonnington Road is still hanging in there, albeit as an even more depleted incarnation than when he'd last been in town. They find a booth and settle down and are served the traditional milky coffee, both repulsive and oddly reassuring to him. Franco asks his son, — What's the story wi Sean?

Michael starts talking; grudgingly, sparingly and in terse, economical sentences, as he would do with a cop. Franco learns little new. Michael talks about Sean in a general way, revealing nothing about their closeness or otherwise. They could have been bosom buddies, or had a relationship like him and Joe. Both his sons' backstories, from the meagre info he's garnered, appear to offer few surprises. It seems Sean was prone to mood swings, his life-and-soul-of-the-party flamboyance followed by June's brand of broken resignation, which made him an ideal candidate for junk's levelling ministrations.

Michael, on the other hand, looks like he's picked up some of Franco's own brooding aggression. It's hard for him to work out who landed the worst inheritance. One would be bent out of shape, then crushed by the world, offering no resistance to the heroin- and alcohol-soaked streets. The other would attempt to bend it to his will, then be broken by it. Franco feels disappointed, as part of him had hoped that his own rags-to-relative-riches story might have somehow inspired his sons. He realises how paltry and unrealistic this conceit on his part is.

Michael keeps a searching gaze trained on him, as if demanding some kind of deeper revelation than the superficialities his father is prepared to offer. Franco feels like he knows that look from somewhere, and can't quite place it, but it isn't the shaving mirror. Wherever its origins, it's annoying him. So Frank Begbie shrugs, takes a deep breath. — You know, I never changed his nappy. Nor yours. Not once. Left youse full of shit till your ma came back. There's another couple of kids that are mine, around here somewhere . . . I don't know them, barely knew their mothers.

Michael's intense scrutiny of him never wavers.

— My girls though, my sweet Californian girls, Franco says, almost wistfully, — I changed them without thinking about it. I always thought I wanted boys. 'If it's a lassie, it's gaun back,' I used to say. Now I'm different. I like girls, I don't like laddies.

— Good for you –

— Fuck laddies, Franco cuts him off. — It's youse I never wanted. No really.

At last his son blinks. He takes a cigarette from a packet. A woman behind the counter looks like she is going to say something, but instead turns away.

Franco feels his own mouth tighten in a satisfied smile. — I liked the *idea* ay having sons, but I was never really interested in you or Sean. Never loved youse like I do my girls. My beautiful, rich, spoiled daughters. You boys, he shakes his head, — tae me there was never any real point in you boys.

Michael's tight sneer of a mouth suddenly flaps open. The cigarette between his fingers is directed at Franco, — Is that aw you've got tae say tae me?

— Naw, Franco says, rising to depart. — Whaire's it your ma steys again?

Michael smiles for the first time. Lights up the cigarette. Looks at his father. — Fuck knows.

12

THE EX

Michael's ostentatious non-cooperation is superfluous; the address he is heading to has stuck in Franco's mind, as it's next to the stair where a much-hated rival of his had once lived. Walking from the Foot of the Walk along Duke Street, to Easter Road and up Restalrig Road, he looks at a video clip that has come in, on his almost-dead US phone. Grace and Eve are sitting on the couch, waving to the camera, one with enthusiasm, the other coyly guarded. Melanie's text: *We miss you and we love you!*

Franco feels something stir inside him, but clicks off the phone and fights it down. It is Lochend, and in the drizzle the darkening streets surrounding him conjure up nothing but a steady flow of paggers and vendettas past. This is no place for him to be conflicted. He hunches into a bus shelter and pulls out the Tesco phone, trying to punch in Melanie's cell number through the use of antiquated, multi-function keys. Rage rises in his chest, and he tries to breathe slowly, as with the activity of his big fingers and the jumping display on the liquid crystal, the shifting hieroglyphics slowly take shape as her number. Present with him in the bus shelter: a dead pigeon, a discarded kebab (which looks in better shape than the deceased bird) and two empty tins of Tennent's

Super Lager, one stacked neatly on top of the other. Euphoria rises in Franco as Melanie's full number, with the US +1 dialling code is completed in its entirety.

Then the phone dies. It just switches itself off.

Franco presses the buttons feverishly. Nothing. It has perished. He looks at it in searing fury, thinks about crushing it under his heel. Instead he boots the cans down the pavement and stuffs the phone back into his pocket.

Breathe. One, two, three.

The rain has whipped up and beats on the back of the bus shelter, as Franco briefly succumbs to a phantom memory, warm and good, but never completely dancing out of his mind's shadow to reveal itself fully. A girl's hand touching his, her hair grazing his face, her scent in his nostrils. Did things like that happen to him, before Melanie? Surely yes. But he can't allow it; can't permit this place to be anything other than what he's made it. Then the drumming eases off as the wind drops and the rain peters out, back into a thin drizzle.

The stair is easily found. At one time he'd made fairly advanced plans to fire-bomb the house next door, which was occupied by Cha Morrison, his old nemesis. It astonishes him now to think that he cared enough about this guy to consider doing that. What great crime had Morrison committed against him, or he against Morrison? Nothing whatsoever sprang to mind. It had all been talk, which had then ramped up, becoming a bizarre sequence of threat and counter-threat. Otherwise there was zero basis for their rivalry. They had jointly manufactured this conflict to give their lives drama, imagining it into brutal reality.

68

He goes into the neighbouring stair and realises that of the six flats, he can't recall which one is occupied by June. He has no idea what name she will be using. There is no sign of 'Chisholm', her maiden name, or, to his relief, 'Begbie', which she'd taken to calling herself, and had registered Sean and Michael's births under, although she and Franco had never married. No door suggests great wealth, so he opts for the one that gives the strongest impression of teeming squalor. It is painted black, some of which has spilled onto the frame, and it looks battered, with a Sellotaped, yellowing piece of paper, indicating that a J. McNAUGHTON resides there. He taps on the door and, sure enough, June answers.

Even since he'd last briefly seen her at his mother's funeral, surprisingly obese, June has massively expanded. It's impossible to square this version with the thin, brittle one of his memory. She looks at him, and, for an excruciating second, seems as if she is going to hug him. Her lips quiver, and her eyes implore. But then she turns abruptly, and heads inside. Assailed by the smell of cats and old, congealed deep-fried fat and, most of all, stale tobacco, he follows her into the flat.

Franco finds it hard to believe that he is facing her. She has sat opposite him in a faded floral-pattern armchair, part of a suite that is way too big for the cramped council flat. He can barely fathom how small the homes are. The room seems to conspicuously flaunt poverty.

— The game's no straight, aye, she says, obviously doped up on antidepressants. Her eyes seem dulled and set far back into a now-bulbous head, which was once little more than a skull.

69

— Aye, he agrees, as a wary boy of around fourteen comes in. He fixes June with a sneer of defiant belligerence as he picks up a packet of cigarettes from the coffee table, then swiftly leaves.

— Yours? Franco asks.

— THEY ARE MA FAGS! she shouts after the departing boy, as she sparks up again.

— No the fags, the laddie.

— Aye, that's Gerard. June takes a drag, her cheeks buckling in. — Ah've goat Andrea and Chloe tae. As well as oor Michael and Sean . . . Her eyes glaze over and a tissue, torn from a box on the coffee table, goes right to them. As she coughs raucously, Franco watches June shake: her fat wobbling inside shapeless, washed-out leisurewear garments. Her first pregnancy and Sean's birth had seemed to wreck her body, but rather than bloat, June had shrunk into a Belsen skeleton, and he'd pretty much lost interest in her after that. He had muttered something like 'fuck sake' when she told him she was expecting Michael. There had been the jail, and their domestic life together, in which he recalled her swathed in blue light from the television set, through a fog of cigarette smoke. Although still a specialist in tobacco consumption, June is now obese and looks as grey-skinned as he'd done after his longest prison stretch. She inhales again, her chunky face caving in so radically it is as if her teeth have been extracted. — So you goat married again, ay?

— Aye, official, he announces, looking coolly at her, waving his rings, — no just common law. We had tae, for my immigrant

70

status. Wanted tae as well but, ay. If you feel the love, why no make the statement?

June bristles a little. — Aye, they say it was that American lassie ye met in the jail.

— She was the art therapist, aye. *She expects me to say, Ah ken how it looks. Fuck that.* — She's young, good-looking, intelligent, from a wealthy family. We've got two lovely daughters. So what about you? Any romantic ties?

June looks up at him and coughs, managing to shake her head before being beset with an eye-watering fit.

— That snout'll kill ye, he observes.

June sucks in some air and wheezes, — Ye pack them in, likes?

— Aye. Stopped the peeve n aw. Got bored wi it aw, ay.

— What aboot aw the other stuff? The fightin?

— Aye, got fed up with the jail. This art thing's a good living, and I enjoy it.

June shifts her head, and it seems to sink into her body. Franco can't discern a neck. — You were eywis good at art. Back at the school.

— Right, Franco laughs.

— Angie Knight, when she heard ye were back, she goes tae me, and June's expression takes on a coquettishness he finds grotesque, — 'Tell ye what, June, ah widnae be surprised if you n Franco ended up back the gither.'

— Ah wid, Franco says brutally, thinking: *She's a fucking simpleton. Why didn't I see it before? Probably because I was too.*

June's face suddenly and dramatically flushes red. It is such a violently abrupt transformation that for a second Franco

71

believes that she's having a seizure. Then she starts to cry. — Oor son, Frank, oor Sean, what are you daein aboot it? Somebody killed our laddie and you're daein nowt aboot it!

— See ye, he says, getting up to leave. It was a familiar pattern. They would whisperingly condemn his violence with those sour, baleful expressions, until they wanted some cunt sorting out, then he would suddenly become the big hero. Manipulation. He'd discussed all this with Melanie, with his mentor, John Dick, the prison officer. It had suited them all to keep him as he was. It still suits them. He will leave them back here in Edinburgh. They can either shut the door in his face or seize him in a hypocritical embrace, it won't matter; he will be walking away from them all.

— Find whae did it and hurt them, Frank, yir good at that, she shouts after him.

This stops him in his tracks. He turns to contemplate her. — I mind I battered you bad a couple ay times. Once when you were expecting him, Frank says. — That was just wrong.

— Christ, it's a bit late tae apologise now!

— Who's apologising? It was wrong, he accepts, — but I'm not sorry I hurt *you*. I'm just indifferent. Always was. I had no emotional connection to you whatsoever. So how can I be sorry?

— Ah'm the mother ay oor . . . you . . . June stammers, then explodes, — you've nae emotional connection tae *anybody*!

— Anger is an emotion, Franco says, opening the door and exiting.

He goes downstairs and out into the street, heading to the bus stop. Thinks of the nights in bed with June. She'd had a flush of desirable youth, her body had been lithe and firm, as arousing as the insolent whip of her fringe, and there was that slutty chewing of her gum that excited and irritated him in equal measures. Yet he can't ever remember caressing her. Only fucking her hard.

In his pocket, two phones, the Tesco one, so cold and rough and dead. He pushes it aside and gently squeezes the sleek American iPhone. He thinks of Melanie, spooning with her in the night, the fragrance of her, as her blonde hair tickles his nostrils. The sickle-shaped birthmark on her wrist. The love flowing through the skin on their bodies like blood. How she was his tender underbelly. How if they wanted to plunge him with a knife they would go straight through her into him. Into that part rendered soft by loving.

13

THE DANCE PARTNER 2

I got to see the blonde American lassie they had all been talking about. The news of her had spread through the prison system like a virus. People flocked to take her art classes; looking for a smile, a whiff of perfume. All about the accumulation of wanking material. The violent sexuality of imaginative space, where you went when you were on lock-up in that box. The last freedom.

I just thought, why? Why was she doing this? She came from money. Why work with the scum of the earth? But she surprised me. As well as being a good person, she was strong and righteous. There was nothing wishy-washy about her. Yes, she'd had all the advantages, but she'd chosen to try and make a difference in the lives of some of the most broken, lost men.

I recall in that first class she wore a tight green sweater and black leggings, with a green band in her hair. Afterwards, I thought I'd be pulling the fuckin end off it all night thinking about her. But I didn't wank for a second. I just lay there, remembering her words, her voice, constructing romantic fantasies about her. They made me feel pathetic and weak. But I imagined talking to her, alone. Without the giggles and comments of all the arseholes in the group. How could I talk to her? I didn't try. I worked.

There was the portrait I started, Dance Partner, *of Craig Liddel. Seeker. He was the guy I'd got the big sentence for killing, my second manslaughter conviction, reduced from murder, as the court (correctly) deemed it was self-defence. It was our third confrontation, the first being in jail, when he came off best, the second at an old mill house in Northumberland, where I had the advantage. The decider bout in the car park was conclusive. In the picture Liddel's face, not set in a sneer, or crumpled with cold contempt or murderous rage, as it was when we met, but open and smiling. Around it, a series of ghosts of men, women and children. Then, Melanie Francis, approaching me, intrigued. Asking me about my work. The way she called it that; not my painting, but my work.*

I told her it was the man I'd killed. The people whose lives around him I had changed. His family and friends. There were others; the women he'd never know, the children he'd never have, and the places, the Eiffel Tower, Statue of Liberty, he'd never see.

— Do you aspire to see those places? she asked me.

I looked into her deep blue eyes and realised for the first time, to my shock and horror, that I did. — Yes, I told her.

I was falling for her from day one. It seemed ludicrous. I was daring to dream, to fantasise a future for us together when I'd barely spoken a word to her. I thought of us being together in America, in a big convertible, driving to Big Sur and the Joshua Tree. I could find no weakness in her warm, missionary light, couldn't even determine its source; political, religious, philosophical, or just rebelliousness against her own privileged class? I didn't care. I read as much as I could, fighting through my dyslexia, now I had motivation, till my brain hurt. I was listening to audiobooks, and finally learning to decode all that jumbled nonsense. She was a powerful catalyst, yes, but this change wasn't just about her.

I grew bored with the staple True Crime books I had used to develop my reading skills; most were shabby affairs of self-serving bullshit, ghostwritten by grubby journos to impress kids, and wankers whose balls would never drop. I read more challenging stuff. Philosophy and art history. The biographies of the great painters. To learn, yes, but also to impress her.

But who was she? She was good and strong and I was bad and weak. That's what hit me most of all from being around her. That I was weak. The notion was ridiculous; it went against everything I'd come to believe about my persona and image, against the way I'd consciously forged myself over the years. Yet who else but a weak man would spend half his life letting others lock him up like an animal?

I was one of the weakest people on the planet. I had zero control over my darker impulses. Therefore I was constant jail fodder. Some mouthy cunt got wide; they had to be decimated on the spot, and I was back in prison. Thus such nonentities were in total command of my destiny. That was my first major epiphany: I was weak because I wasn't in control of myself. Melanie was in control of herself. In order to be with somebody like her, to live a free life, not in a tenement or scheme on the breadline, or even a suburb and crippled with a lifetime of debt, I needed a free mind. I had to get control of myself.

I told her this.

14

THE MENTOR

Franco had returned to Elspeth's quite early the previous evening, and called Melanie on the American phone. The battery finally died in mid-conversation. This frustrated him, as he sensed that she was ramping herself up to say something important. The Tesco device seemed to belong to an era from about three prison sentences back. It sat in the palm of his hand like the last of an endangered species. He plugged in the charger and pumped electricity into this corpse, seeing if it might reanimate. He'd put ten pounds on the account, at the sales clerk's advice. — Twenty's too much, she'd told him earnestly. He'd shaken his head in disbelief. Now he saw what she was on about, the thing seemed designed to fall apart as soon as he exited the supermarket. Now he had to remember to get an adaptor for the US charger. Then, suddenly, the jet lag he thought he'd mastered hit him like a sledgehammer, and he retired early, sleeping deeply and restoratively.

Rising into a dull morning, Franco makes his usual breakfast, with provisions he'd picked up in Waitrose, substituting feta for Swiss cheese, and this time is able to tempt his sister into joining them. As they sit around the kitchen table, with the exception of Greg, who has gone to work early, Elspeth asks, — So how is June?

— Same. But fatter, he adds.

George and Thomas smirk, then stop under Elspeth's reprimanding stare.

— Did she tell you about the funeral arrangements?

— Aye, but there's nothing much, other than what we already know: it's on Friday, two o'clock at Warriston, and I'm footing the bill.

— Well, it is your son, Elspeth glared, — and you can afford it and she can't.

— I didn't say I was complaining.

Elspeth looks doubtfully at him, but sees the boys taking an interest, so pulls back. — Greg says he's taking the afternoon off.

— I told him that there's no need.

— We're still family, she states, her gaze challenging him. But there is no response; his eyes are on his plate.

— Wonder what happens when you die, George says.

Fuck all, Franco thinks. You cease to exist, that's it. He is about to say something, but considers it might not be his place.

— Never mind that, Elspeth barks, — finish your breakfast.

— But it's just so strange to think we'll never see Sean again, George says. — Never ever.

— Nobody knows, Franco offers.

— Do you think you go to heaven or hell? Thomas asks him.

— Maybe both, Franco says. — Maybe there's some kind ay transit between the two, when you get bored with one, you can mix it up a bit, and head to the other.

— Like on holiday? Thomas wonders.

— Like a bus between two airport terminals, George volunteers.

— Aye, Franco considers, — why not? If nobody knows, what happens after could be anything we imagine, or maybe nothing at all.

Thomas is still in holiday mode. — Holidays in hell, he says dreamily.

— Been there, done that. Frank Begbie looks at his sister. — Mind the time we went to Butlins at Ayr? He turns to the boys. — Nah, your mum won't, she was just a wee baby.

The boys seem to look at their mother in an almost mystical light, trying to envisage this. — I can't imagine Mum as a baby, George says, half shutting his eyes as if to conjure up the image.

Elspeth turns to her sons. — Right, you two, jildy.

— Ah've no heard that word in years, Franco says.

—What does it mean? George asks.

— It means *hurry up*, Elspeth says briskly, — so less talk, more rock.

As his nephews depart, Franco leans back in his chair. — Who was it that said that? Was it old Grandad Jock?

— Like Butlins at Ayr, that was before my time, Elspeth says snootily. — What have you got on today?

— I'm meeting an old friend.

79

— Another auld lag fae the nick, I expect. Elspeth crunches on a slice of toast.

— Aye, Franco grabs the teapot and tops his mug up, — and he's done even more time than I have.

Elspeth shakes her head in contempt. — You're such a loser, Frank. You just cannae help yirsel –

Franco raises his hand to silence her. — He's a screw. A prison officer. The guy who got me into reading, writing, painting.

— Aw, right . . . Elspeth says, and she looks genuinely ashamed and penitent.

Franco decides to quit while he is ahead, gulping down his tea and going to his room to get ready. The Tesco phone has, to his astonishment, shot into some kind of life. It glows a radioactive lime green. He tries to type in Melanie's number, but the zero key sticks to send 0000000 flying across the screen. — Fuck, he curses, drawing air down deep, filling his lungs.

Of course he'd see John Dick. Before Melanie there was John, the man who believed in him, despite Franco being determined to present all the evidence to the contrary. The radical prison officer, who went against everything established, from the narrow, reductivist government economic and social policy, the institution's petty rules and procedures, to the self-defeating fatalism of the cons themselves. Dick brought in the writers, poets and artists, to see if anything would gel. Saw a spark ignite in a few, Frank Begbie being the most unlikely.

They meet in the Elephant House cafe on George IV Bridge, close to where he'd started out yesterday, at the

Central Library. His impression is that John Dick looks well; longish face, dark-framed glasses, black hair cut short, a permanent five-o'clock shadow, and baggy clothes which conceal a wiry but muscular build. Franco recalls that when they first met, Dick had the relaxed bearing around him that he knew came from possessing a physical confidence. Amid all the other chunky, aggressive screws, John Dick seemed like a prisoner whisperer, his soft voice having the gift of turning down the volume in others. With the exception of Melanie, he probably listened to nobody in his life like he did to this prison officer.

John immediately expresses his regret that he won't be attending Sean's funeral. Franco nods, not needing to ask why. The notion of the screw and con as friends would have had the hysterical and embittered on both sides screaming 'grass' or 'compromised' within seconds.

John Dick elicits a promise from Frank Begbie that he'll return to the city to talk to the prisoners when his exhibition hits Edinburgh. While agreeing, the con-turned-artist insists on no press; he won't be a rehabilitation poster boy. Being feted by the 'isn't he marvellous?' artsy ponces of the left, or sneered at by the bitter 'he'll never change' cynics of the right, holds zero attraction for him. Those are the narratives of pygmies, and they will continue to steadfastly pursue them without his help. He has a life to get on with.

Franco recounts the genesis of his fame. — That actor wanker who came to our art project, the one you and Mel set up, tae get inspiration for this hard-man part he was up for. Said we would be big mates, he winced at his own naivety, —

81

but he never returned my calls when I got out. I had made a bust of him. I mutilated it in rage. Then the others. I exhibited them like that as a joke. That's when it took off. They wrote that review, mind, I keep it here, and Frank Begbie goes into his wallet and pulls out a folded newspaper article. Hands it to John Dick, who opens it up and reads:

The exhibition, featuring the efforts of three inmates from Edinburgh's Saughton Prison, contains some forceful and realised works of art, devised under the tutelage and supervision of art therapist Melanie Francis. The California native has worked with violent prisoners in her own country, and believes that the mission of art in such environments 'is, put simply, about the re-channelling of energy that, in turn, leads to the reassessing of personal behaviours and life objectives. There is so much raw talent here, which has never had the opportunity to shine.'

None more so than repeat offender Francis Begbie. His striking portraits and sculptures of Hollywood and British television stars, complete with vicious mutilations, taps into our subconscious desire as a public to build up and then destroy the celebrity . . . .

— Then his ex-wife, that actress he'd been cheating on, Franco laughs, — she pays way over the odds for the piece. It starts that *Schadenfreude* art movement, he says, a sour contempt creeping into his tone. — Bring me your celebs. I'll hurt them, age them, degrade them, envision their first child being delivered by Fred and Rosemary West. Etch the pain on their pretty faces. Show everybody that they're just like us.

— It doesn't matter where it came from. John Dick hands him back the paper cutting. Franco recognises how John has risen in the prison service, hacking out a space from which to undertake his progressive experiments. His canny, couthie style is a front that conceals a devastatingly sharp mind. People will always underestimate him, then never be quite sure how it is that this self-effacing smiler invariably gets his way. — Art only has the value people are prepared to pay. You tapped into a mood. You have talent.

— My talent was for hurting people. That's what I was venting, the desire to hurt another human being. Frank lifts the coffee to his lips. It is hot and stings him, so he blows on it. — Society is fucked, I just give messed-up people what they want. It doesn't make me a talent, unless it's for spotting the weakness and twisted desires in others.

— We all have these impulses, but only losers and psychos indulge them. John Dick smiles, thin-lipped. — Others sublimate it into art and business. And make loads of money. You just saw sense, learned a bit of self-control and moved into a more profitable club.

— Here's to self-control and profitable clubs. Frank Begbie deftly raises his cup.

John Dick joins the sober toast, then checks his watch. — I should be getting back to work. Can I drop you off somewhere?

— No, I'm going to take a wee walk down by the docks. All that new stuff down there; Ocean Terminal, the casino . . .

— Aye, John Dick nods, — it's certainly all change in that neck of the woods.

THE DELIVERY BOY 3

The fresh fruit and veg were never that fresh, as the orders were usually made up a day in advance. I grabbed a box that said: Forth Ports Authority, Leith Docks, Jock Begbie. The ticket on it looked like 3 November, but for some reason it was a smudged mess, and I wasn't big on reading anyway. It was actually for 4 November, but I mistakenly loaded it onto the delivery bike.

When I got down to the docks, it was 4.20 p.m. on the cheapo digital watch I'd bought from the garage, but dark, drizzly and shite, the way Scotland often is at that time of the year. The orange sodium lamps were already on and splashing their reflections across the wet pavements and streets. The first weird thing was that the security bam, John, wasn't on the gate. I cycled right through, over that jarring strip of cobblestone, then across the iron rails of the cattle grid. I pedalled in the near-dark, heading for that imposing brick bothy. The old dry dock was barely lit by the overhead lamps. As I drew closer I heard voices; urgent, threatening sounds, carrying in the still night. I stopped and carefully climbed off the bike, and pushed it slowly and silently forward, resting it against the back of the bothy. At first it seemed as if the voices were coming from inside, but then I worked out that their source was the front of the howf.

I crept round the building and I could see them, standing over by the edge of the wharf. Handsome Johnnie was a bit away from Grandad Jock and the other two, Carmie and Lozy. An overhead lamplight was bathing them in a meagre glow, their breath dragon-like in the cold air as their shadows spilled over the cobblestones. I could tell Johnnie was scared. His palms were extended in appeal. — C'mon, boys . . . Jock . . . it's me . . .

— If ye jump, and go feet first, you'll brek yir legs, my grandad said, looking down into the dock. — But you've got a chance ay surviving. Well worth a punt!

Carmie had a length of rope in his hands, and moved towards Johnnie. — That wey or oor wey, Johnnie boy!

I crouched down against the side of the bothy. I was shiteing myself. I mind that the left side of my face went into a twitching spasm.

— Wir giein ye that chance, Grandad Jock sneered, his head cocked to one side. — Wi owe ye that, and he turned to Carmie and Lozy. — Ah'd be right in sayin that we owe Johnnie that, ay, boys?

—Ah reckon so, Jock, Lozy said.

— Carmie's no sae sure, but, ay-no, Carmie? my grandad smiled.

Carmie's big heid looked distorted under the bleary light. — Ah'd say that a pilferin, double-crossin grass is entitled tae nowt. A grass whae betrays his ain mates.

— Auld lang syne, but, Carmie, auld lang syne, Jock said sagely. — So what's it tae be, Johnnie?

— But ah cannae . . . boys . . . it's me . . . Johnnie pleaded.

— Aw, we ken it's you awright! We ken that! Carmie chuckled darkly, like Johnnie was a kid who had been rumbled stealing sweeties from the local confectioner's.

— If we tie ye n then fling ye in yir done, Johnnie. Or hing ye ower thaire fae yon crane like Carmie wants. See sense, Grandad Jock implored. — What's it tae be? Thoat ye were a gambling man. Thoat that wis how this mess aw sterted. The gambler's instinct deserted ye? Shame . . .

Johnnie stepped slowly to the edge and looked down. I took a hunkered step back further into the shadows, and felt my heart thrashing in my chest. I still half believed, wanted to believe, that he would be okay, that they were just 'putting the frighteners' on him (a favourite phrase of Jock's) and that they'd all soon be in the Marksman pub, laughing and joking, Johnnie suffering from nothing more than soiled keks. But there was something strange about them; it was their scary stillness.

— If ah wis you ah'd just dae it. Just turn n jump, my grandad Jock said, and he pulled out a long blade. I could see its silvery glint under the overhead light.

Then Johnnie closed his eyes and he just vanished into the darkness. Maybe I shut mine too. It's freakish, the way your memory deceives you, because I know I saw his face with only his lids exposed, but I never witnessed, or had no recollection of, him actually jumping. And there was no sound of his screaming or hitting the bottom. But then I couldnae see him with them any more, on the edge of that dry dock, and there

86

was nowhere else he could have gone. My grandad nodded at Carmie and Lozy and they went to the wharf's edge and looked down. — It's done. Better jildy, he said.

— Is eh away? Lozy asked.

— Eh's potted heid awright. Jildy, Grandad Jock repeated, then turned and walked towards the bothy. If they'd gone to the right, they would have seen me, but they went left, and it gave me time to wheel my bike round to the other side of the brick building.

I heard them laughing in the dark as they walked away. It was like they were finishing a shift or walking home fae the pub or the football.

I went over to the edge of the dry dock and looked down. The light from the lamp above dissipated over the lip of the berth and nothing at the bottom was visible through the pitch black. I could hear no noises from below.

So I climbed down the iron rungs into the dock. I could hear my heart thrashing in my chest. I was shiteing it though at the same time I mind of feeling excited and alive. But I was concerned because it was so dark. I couldn't see the bottom till I felt it under the sole of my trainers. I looked up; I'd come a long way and had a longer way to go back. Then behind me I heard those soft moans, and the sound of somebody whispering words that made no sense.

I saw a dark, crumpled heap, with thin weak breaths coming from it. It looked like a wounded beast waiting to expire. The bizarre monologue continued. Perhaps, I minded thinking, Johnnie was asking all the women he'd wronged to forgive him, to help him, but he was beyond assistance. When I got closer

his glazed eyes looked up at me as he repeated, — Please . . .
Frank . . . please . . .

The rear of his head was smashed in, and thick blood was
oozing from him. I stepped away to avoid getting it on my
trainers. His eyes were wild, but fogging over. I knew that he
was dying.

And I quickly understood what he wanted me to do.

So I did it, then I backed slowly over to the wall of the dock.
I looked up at the rungs leading to the top. I was shaking and
I was exhausted. I knew that there was no way I could manage
that climb, get out of the dock, and that it would be dangerous
to even try.

But I couldnae stay where I was.

16

THE PATRON OF THE ARTS

The limousine purrs slowly along the kerbside, stopping just in front of him. It seems incongruous on Leith Walk at this time; too early to be a wedding or hen party, no hearse in convoy. Franco tries to look in, but the tinted windows reveal nothing. Then the passenger-side one winds down, and a chunky, gold-ring-encrusted hand appears, followed by a big shorn head. — Get in.

Frank Begbie obliges, instantly beset with the impression that Davie 'Tyrone' Power hasn't changed much. He'd always kept his head shaven, so there has been no visibly dramatic balding and greying effect over the years. And still a fat cunt, Begbie thinks, as he lets the comfortable upholstery suck him into its guts. Argent's 'God Gave Rock and Roll to You' plays at low volume on the car radio.

— Heard ye wir back in toon, Tyrone says, without looking at him. — Sorry for your loss. Losing a kid, that's a bad yin.

Frank Begbie remains silent. *One . . . two . . . three . . .* He watches Tyrone's pattern of breathing. You can tell a lot about somebody from the way they breathe. Power inhales his air evenly through his nose, but then suddenly gulps at a big mouthful, like a shark rising to the surface to swallow prey. Some might see only aggression and strength in that motion, but Frank Begbie registers weakness. It is maybe indicative of an anxiety. Or perhaps just too much coke has gone up his hooter.

He looks at a cable snaking out from Tyrone's electronic cigarette lighter. His pulse rises. *Surely not.* — That phone charger, he ventures, pulling out his mobile device, — will it fit ma iPhone here?

— Dinnae see why not . . . Tyrone looks at the connection. — Aye, plug it in.

— Barry, Frank says, instantly aware it has been years since he's used that word, as he snaps the plug into the phone socket with a satisfying click. The device starts to throb, a sliver of red soon visible at the edge of the battery icon.

— So an artist, then, Frank? Tyrone turns to him with a jesting twinkle in his eye. — Ah'm no gaunny bullshit ye wi aw that ah-kent-ye-hud-it-in-ye shite. I'd never have seen that yin coming in a million years!

Frank Begbie responds with a measured smile. — It surprised me tae.

— Heard you moved in wi some American lassie. Art therapist, Tyrone probes.

Franco feels his spine stiffen. He sucks in a steady, slow breath. *Always the way with these cunts. Ferreting for a weakness.* He senses his stomach soft against Melanie's naked back. *One . . . two . . . three . . .* — Still at the same place?

— Naw, new hoose, up the Grange, Tyrone says, cursing a driver in a slow-moving Mini in front of them.

It is to the Grange they head. Tyrone drives with scowling impatience through the traffic, to the south side, and a leafy neighbourhood, where, behind prodigious stone walls, gravel driveways lead to grand villas. He stops at an enormous sandstone house that exudes wealth. Several cars are parked outside a garage, some covered in custom sheeting, indicating all belong to him. Tyrone was always daft about cars, Frank Begbie recalls.

Tyrone cuts the engine and unplugs Franco's phone, which has stopped at 21 per cent charge, the battery icon barely in the green zone. The wallpaper has fired up, showing a picture of a smiling Melanie, with prominent white teeth of the sort almost unknown in Scotland. — Nice, Tyrone smiles, handing the phone back to Franco. — The missus?

— Aye.

— So is she still an art therapist, then?

Melanie is now employed part-time at the university, but mostly works on her own art projects. But this is none of Tyrone's business. — Aye, Frank Begbie says, following him into a grand hallway that is luxuriously furnished, with paintings adorning most of the wall space. Franco doesn't recognise the artwork, but can tell from the quality of the frames that what is inside them will have substantial value.

— You'll appreciate this, being an artist, Frank, Tyrone says, with a self-styled raconteur's delight, as he leads him through to a large drawing room, with a dining area to the rear, and two monumental, ornate chandeliers above. And there are more paintings. — One ay the biggest private collections of Pre-Raphaelite-influenced Scottish art. This one is a David Scott, and these two are by William Dyce. And I've got these original Murdo Mathieson Taits. He sweeps his hand over a wall festooned with several canvases of figures and landscapes. — No bad for a boy fae Niddrie Mains!

— Dinnae really git art, Franco says dismissively.

— But you're an artist, man! Ye make your living by –

— Ever listened tae *Chinese Democracy*, Guns n' Roses?

— What?

— A lot ay people say it's overproduced. That it cannae be spoken aboot in the same breath as the likes ay *Appetite for Destruction*. I think that's shite. Frank Begbie looks challengingly at his old boss. — You have tae use the production values available at the time.

— Dinnae ken that one, Tyrone says irritably.

— Check it oot, Franco smiles. — It comes highly recommended, and he moves over to the dining table, running his hand along the polished sheen of its surface. — Nice. Mahogany?

— Aye, Tyrone nods, gesturing at Frank to sit down, and he accordingly flops back into a well-upholstered couch. Tyrone then lowers his own bulk, with surprising daintiness, into the armchair opposite.

Frank Begbie looks around for traces that might help him ascertain who else lives here. Tyrone had been married, with grown-up children, yet there is no evidence of any cohabitee in this grand room. — So how's things? You still wi what's-her-name? he fishes.

The face on the man across from him barely registers anything, no indication that Franco has spoken, let alone that the subject is off-limits. Then Tyrone's eyes suddenly narrow. — You know that your boy . . . Sean, he says, stretching

92

out the word to make it sound like *yawn*, — Sean was mixed up with that wee cunt Anton Miller?

— No.

— And this bird, Frances, Frances Flanagan, they say that she was there on the night he got done.

This is certainly news. Two new names. *Anton Miller. Frances Flanagan.* The police hadn't confirmed anyone was with Sean, yet this makes sense; somebody had tipped off the ambulance, even if it was too late. Maybe the girl had been there, and had let in the murderer, not knowing what he was going to do, then panicked when he'd killed Sean, and perhaps ran away and called the police. Or maybe she'd set him up. Or even stabbed him herself. Yet Frank Begbie is suspicious. He's heard this type of talk before, and it just isn't in Davie Power's nature to do good turns. — So why ye telling me this?

— It's no just about old times' sake. Tyrone shakes his head slowly, then cracks a smile of genuine delight. — And I won't insult ye by even pretending that's the case. See, I owe several bad turns to that wee Miller cunt. In fact, I wish nothing but a shower of shite to come down on him. You do bad very well, Frank, Tyrone says, trying to gauge Frank Begbie's reaction. — He's a nasty little cunt. Shooters, the lot. Cowardly drive-by gun-downs in the street. That's not on, he says, shaking his head again. — And he's behind your laddie's death, as sure as night follows day. Sean was serving up for him. Drugs. So we have a mutual interest, he contends, rising and heading to an opulent-looking marble cocktail bar built into a corner of the lounge.

— If some wee cunt was bugging you that much, Franco says, watching him pick up a dimpled glass bottle of whisky from a shelf behind the bar, — you'd have done him by now. Aw they wide cunts that came through fae the schemes over the years, Pilton, Sighthill, Niddrie, Gilmerton . . . you've done them all, he says, thinking about an old mate of his, Donny Laing, who had publicly challenged Tyrone and had then vanished. — What's different about this boy?

— Miller is the epitome of cunning. Tyrone's shaven dome bobs. — A whole new breed of schemie, a proper gangster instead of a mindless thug. He gazes at Franco a second too long. — He has brains and knows how tae play politics and build alliances. He's united all the north Edinburgh mobs; Drylaw, Muirhoose, Pilton, Royston, Granton and even the new-build scheme part of Leith, doon by Newhaven, Tyrone explains, lowering the whisky bottle to the marble-topped bar.

Begbie nods. Leith has always been its own entity. The thought of it now being just an outpost, a territory owned by some young ned from a scheme, this dismays him much more than it should do.

— He and his mob have ambition and a certain entre-preneurial zest. Miller commands a strong loyalty among them. If I move on him, they'd all be on me. There would be a war, which would be bad for business, and bad for the toon, Tyrone advances, and Frank Begbie nods in under-standing. Tyrone has always nurtured a perverse sense of civic responsibility. Edinburgh's old gangsters were historically so successful because they were able to evolve from that status, integrating themselves into the respectable business community, and minimising the theatrics of violence. They largely avoided the turf wars, shootings, and True Crime confessional and finger-pointing biographies, replete with *Daily Record* serialisations, that characterised their Glasgow neighbours. They were safe, ordered and long-established. They recruited the brightest talents from the schemes, but crushed the emergence of any genuine mobs from these peripheries, anyone who might have designs on city markets.

Franco can see that a new firm who didn't play by old rules would be a major headache to them.

And there is pressure on Tyrone from another front. — This new Police Scotland bunch are Weedgie-run, it's basically the auld Strathclyde polis, and they are coming down harder on us than Lothian's finest ever did, God rest their souls, he explains, then faces Franco with a conspiratorial stare. — But an outsider . . . which you are now . . . well, I would make it worth your while. You'd be getting revenge for your son, helping me out, getting paid, and ridding your home town of a very malignant force. You sorted out Craig Liddel . . . Seeker . . . Tyrone corrects himself and smiles, — you can do Anton.

— I also did big time for it. I'm done wi that shite.

— Like the polis will give a fuck about anybody taking out Anton, Tyrone scoffs, lifting the whisky bottle.

— I'm a reformed character, Franco says, his face as immobile as a block of stone.

Tyrone, again, seems not to hear him. — This is a twenty-two-year-old malt, he explains, pouring two generous measures of the whisky into thick Edinburgh crystal glasses. At a miniature guillotine on the bar, he decapitates then lights up a couple of Havana cigars. He hands a glass and smoke to Franco, who looks at them, then at Tyrone. — You've still got a taste for violence, I can see it in your eyes. Drink up, Tyrone instructs, toasting him.

Frank Begbie regards him with a cursory smile. — Like I said, reformed character, he repeats, dropping the cigar into the glass, hearing it hiss, and rising out of the couch.

He watches Tyrone stare incredulously, first at the defilement of his hospitality, then right at him.

— Ah kin see masel out, Franco says, lowering the glass to the coffee table, turning and leaving the room, aware that the neck of the man behind him is burning. Not many would turn their back on an angry David 'Tyrone' Power, but Francis Begbie just sucks in some air and smiles to himself as he walks down the hallway and out the front door.

17

THE UNCLE

The rain has stopped and the sun comes blinking out from behind smoky clouds, like an old lag adjusting to freedom. A subsonic starting pistol seems to fire, its invisible pitch opening up new possibilities for Edinburgh's rejuvenated citizenry. But for Frank Begbie, it is about closing old chapters; tomorrow they are to cremate his son. The funeral will be a big day; he senses that in the fractured grief- and alcohol-fuelled narratives that will besiege him, a certain truth and understanding might emerge. After rising early he decides to go for a run, starting off at a slow, ungainly trot, picking up speed, until his tight leg loosens up.

Suddenly, he feels, then sees, the iPhone pop out of the pocket of his tracksuit bottoms, bounce on his thigh, and as he stops and turns, watches it hit the grille of a drain inlet, flip on its side and slide down into it. It seems to sink in slow motion into the filthy black water. Anger rises in Franco, and he grips the bars of the heavy iron drain cover. As it rises, the veins in his arm pop to the surface. But he can't rummage in that filth, can he? *One . . . two . . . three . . . it was fucked anyway . . . get a new one . . .* He lets it fall back in place, shaking his hands to get rid of the muck, and moves forward, heading for a converted factory unit that houses an old friend's boxing club.

97

Inside, the gym buzzes with activity. Fighters go through their rituals under the supervision of coaches, three of the four rings full of sparring trios or duets working on pads. Around a cluster of heavy bags, office workers do boxing circuit training comprising bag work, sparring, and strength and conditioning exercises, to set them up for a desk-bound day.

Franco nods to his old pal Mickey Hopkins, who sits behind the reception desk, talking into a mobile phone. He receives an acknowledging wink in exchange. Then he begins stretching out, before working up a nice, satisfying rhythm on the speedball. *One . . . two . . . three . . . one . . . two . . . three . . .* He feels the righteous eyes of strong men glaring in stoic approval, some of whom he knows have danced with the devil and stepped back from the edge of the cliff. There are such men in gyms all over the world, including his local one in California. He likes being around them; most of them have the sense to know that the wisest of human beings are students, forever learning how to deal with life, continuously readjusting in the face of the shifting opportunities and threats it presents.

Frank Begbie wraps up his hands as Mickey Hopkins finishes his call, picking up some pads as he nods to the ring. The men climb through the ropes. It is all about breathing, and Franco draws in an even pull, expelling as he launches each punch combo, shouted out by Mickey, into the silver dot on the trainer's pads. — Double jab, cross, left hook, double right hook, left uppercut, jab . . .

Franco finds himself in that glorious tempo, which opens up into transcendence, as some onlookers stop their own activity to acknowledge the dance the men are undertaking. After the session he is sweating and blowing hard, and he lets his breathing slow, become regular. Sitting around with some of the boys, he is careful not to ask questions about Anton Miller, content to let people volunteer information. Whether they are Miller's friends or foes, they have to live with him in this town. The overall impression he garners is of a genuine respect for the young man, as well as an obvious fear. These qualities would make him very dangerous to Tyrone.

Mickey and some of the boys take him to lunch, roast chicken at a nearby cafe, and they catch up over old times. It strikes him that the men present around the table have been keeping him at arm's length for years, and are now welcoming him into the 'he used to be a bam but he's alright now' club. He realises that they all discovered how to obtain membership to that fraternity years ago, and, conversely, how long it has taken him. For the first time since he stepped off the plane, he feels at ease back in his home city.

When he returns to Murrayfield later that afternoon, Frank picks up the phone on the sideboard and dials Melanie's number. He longs to be in Santa Barbara with her, dawn sweeping through their bedroom windows, her sleeping naked on her stomach, hair magnesium in the sunlight, the room cooled by Pacific air. He feels a bit self-conscious as Elspeth is sitting on the couch drinking gin and watching daytime TV. It goes to voicemail, and Frank tries to explain the situation with the Tesco phone, before the beep goes, cutting off his message. Elspeth looks sour, and he wonders if he should have asked her first about making a long-distance call. Some folk could be funny about that sort of thing. So Franco sits in the chair opposite her, and they exchange some banalities. Then he looks at a picture of the boys on the sideboard, in their matching maroon Hearts tops. — Good lads, he offers.

— Aye, never had any problems wi them at all . . . Elspeth says, then hesitates. Franco knows that she is thinking of his kids, perhaps realising it might not have been the best thing to say.

He decides to keep it light. — How come ye brought them up tae be Jambos?

Elspeth looks at him in mild dismay. — Greg's dad takes them to Tynecastle.

— Our family was eywis Hibs. Tradition, ay.

Elspeth openly scoffs at him. — You can fuckin sit there wi a straight face and talk about our family? Aboot traditions? You, whae spent maist ay yir life in the jail, then just ran away tae California. She ramps up her anger. He looks at the glass in her hand. Wagers it isn't the first of the day. — Where were *you* to take your nephews, or even your ain sons, where were you to take them *anywhere*? Elspeth's bile spills from her. — Did their *uncle Frank* ever take them to Hibs?

— Fair comment, Franco concedes, picking at a lace on his trainers. — I just thought that with us having a Hibs background you might have dug your heels in a bit, that's aw.

— What? Like ah gie a fuck about any ay that pish. She scowls at him. — I see what you're daein, Frank. I see what you've become. You're the same evil bastard but you've just

100

learned to control your anger. I can see it in your eyes, the same murderous, selfish killer's eyes –

Breathe . . .

Franco finds himself bristling, as a volcanic rage wells up in him. *That same shite Tyrone had come out wi, the nonsense about ma eyes. One . . . two . . . three . . .* — What are you talking about? He shakes his head, lets himself fall back into the chair. — Your eyes are your eyes! *Relax and enjoy the joust. If you lose your cool first, you lose.* — How can I change my eyes? Ye want me to wear zombie contact lenses or something?

— You're worse. Elspeth takes another sip of gin. — You've learned how tae be sneaky and manipulative. At least when you couldnae control that rage ye were honest.

Frank Begbie draws in another deep breath and drops his voice. — So if I freak oot and smash the place up . . . he looks around the comfortable room, — . . . that would be me being *honest*? But if I try and talk things through with people, then I'm a psycho? You're no making any sense, Elspeth, he snorts dismissively, pointing at her drink on the coffee table between them. — That's a big glass ay gin, hen. Maybe you want tae ease up. Your old man's daughter?

Elspeth is stung by the remark. An awareness that you are drinking too much is one thing, but another party openly registering it is a different matter. She thinks about Greg, and wonders how much he has picked up on. Surely not the boys . . .

She raises her head to see her brother looking at her, as if he's read her thoughts. Franco might have been fearsome

101

when he exploded but he was always scariest when he nursed his wrath, keeping his powder dry. That simmering incubation had never lasted long, it had always been beyond him to prevent his molten anger erupting, but now it seems to her that he's mastered that art. In Elspeth's mind this makes him even more dangerous. The air is thick with a veil of threat. She has never felt that directly from Frank before, despite witnessing him administering violence to other family members, notably Joe.

Frank breaks the silence, gets to his feet, standing over her with a strange smile. — But then mibbe if your ain life was a wee bit more fulfilling you might no drink so much. Just putting that out there, he says, dissolving into unself-conscious American, and wandering through to his room.

On the bedside cabinet, the Tesco phone is now displaying 100 per cent charge, but Franco finds that he can't open it. — Unbelievable, he says to himself, drawing in a deep breath, and opting to relax by lying on the bed, reading *A Clockwork Orange* on his Kindle. He recalls seeing the movie of it in his youth. Reading is a struggle, but a rewarding one, as his mind works the pulsing symbols into sounds, then rhythms in his head. *Don't read books, sing them*, was the breakthrough advice he'd been given by the specialist in prison.

There is a knock at the door, and Greg enters. It is obviously time for some reconciliation. — I heard that you and Elspeth . . . ehm, well, I think we're all a bit nervous about the funeral tomorrow . . .

— Aye.

— The boys are at my mum's. Will you come through and join us? We're about to have some roast chicken I've cooked.

— Sound, Franco says, rising. He doesn't particularly want company, and a second helping of roast chicken didn't excite, but he has burned a load of calories today and it would be sensible to eat again.

The atmosphere around the table is tense. Franco looks up at Elspeth, knows she is drunk. A bottle of white wine has been opened. Greg will get one glass out of it, if he's lucky. Suddenly his sister starts snivelling, pushing a hand up to her eyes. — Oh my God . . . she says softly.

— Sweetheart . . . Greg puts his arm around her. — Are you alright?

— No! Ah'm no awright! My nephew's gone, wee Sean, Elspeth groans, sounding wrought with pain. Then she turns to Franco and says sadly, — I mind when I was a young lassie, I was so excited and proud when you and June brought him back to the house.

Franco stays silent. He recalls that time, the irritating fuss Elspeth and his mother had made. *The bairn this, the bairn that.* The bitterly resented implication that his life was now over, that he would live by proxy through this child. And he realised that he'd been manipulated, that the pregnancy and the birth of the kid had represented a (forlorn) hope by June and his mother that he would change. Thinking of the latter, he wishes that he could have taken Val Begbie to Santa Barbara, had her meet his daughters. Shown her how it had worked out fine after all, like he'd always assured her it would, throughout those decades of midnight police raids, calls from the cells, court appearances, and grim, ritual trips to prisons. But all Val – by then in the advanced stages of cancer – got was a brief meeting with Mel, and some pictures of Grace as a newborn.

— But you, you dinnae care, Elspeth is roaring at him. — You never cared!

— Elspeth, this really isn't helping, Greg protests.

— I'm trying to find out what happened to him, Franco says. — If I didn't care, I wouldnae be trying, would I?

— Aye, but you don't care about *him*, Elspeth bubbles. — You didnae know him! He was a lovely laddie, Frank, a great kid, till the drugs got him, she states, almost breathless. — Had a smile for everybody and a great big laugh. I'm fucking sad he's gone! Aren't you, his fucking *faither*, aren't you sad he's gone? she begs. — Tell me! Tell me you're sad!

— What? Are you kidding me? Franco's eyes narrow to creased slits. — We've no seen each other in five years, and you want me tae sit here and talk aboot how ah feel aboot my son being murdered, to you, now, wi the funeral the morn? Never gaunny happen, Franco says emphatically.

— Elspeth, Greg pleads, — it's Frank's son. People process grief differently. Please, try to show a little respect, let's just help each other get through this.

— But he never even tried to help them! Look at him! Just sitting there like nothing's happened!

Franco sets his knife and fork down. — Look, ah made the decision that I had nothing tae offer them –

— Even when you made it as an artist!

— I have my own family . . . my other family, my new family.

— But those boys needed a faither . . . n that other laddie, that River . . .

— And they didnae get one. It's shite, but it happens. Tae me. Tae you. Tae loads ay folks. I failed them, aye, but I couldnae make it right for them, he says firmly, waving his fork in the air. — That ship had long sailed.

— So ye just wash yir hands ay the mess you created! Elspeth snaps. — That River, you've never even met that poor bairn, she bellows in accusation.

Greg scrunches up his face, but Franco remains calm. — All I can do for them is try to live my life in a decent way. Show them the different consequences ay that. Show them that acting like a radge means a twelve-foot concrete box in Saughton, which is not good. But opening yourself up and finding what you're good at and expressing yourself: that means a house by the beach in California, which is pretty damn fine. That's the only lesson I can impart to anybody. I'm not going to preach. He lays down his cutlery and spreads his hands. — It's all there for people to look at, if they would just care to open their fuckin eyes.

Elspeth flinches at that, but continues to glare at her brother.

— People grieve in their own way, Greg repeats, rubbing his wife's arm. — I think Frank's doing very well to hold it all together. It isn't going to do any good for us to start freaking out at this stage. He looks at Franco, who is spooning up

105

some mashed potato. — You don't know what he's going through inside.

— Aye, naebody does, but we can guess! Nowt! Elspeth declares. — There's a beautiful young laddie been stabbed tae death by a maniac, and naebody cares! Naebody!

— I really think you should sack the peeve. It's no helping anybody, Franco says, as he cuts off a piece of chicken breast and starts chewing on it.

Elspeth looks first at him, then Greg, and rises to her feet, storming through to the front room. Greg turns to Franco, and makes to rise to go after her.

— Let her go, Franco suggests. — Perhaps I'm wrong, mibbe a couple ay drinks might be what she needs. As you say, we all deal with things differently, and that's obviously her way. There was a time when I'd be joining her, getting pished up and creating a scene, but that doesn't work for me any more, he shrugs. — Now tell me something that's been bothering me . . .

— What? Greg says, lowering his voice and leaning in towards Franco.

— Am I getting a faint trace of coriander in this sauce? and he half closes his eyes to savour the taste. — It's very good.

106

18

THE FUNERAL

Within five minutes of Juice Terry dropping him, Greg and
Elspeth off in the drizzling rain at Warriston Crematorium,
Franco feels uncomfortably wet. A cold dampness has settled
under the collar of his shirt, seeming to spread between it and
his skin. The Tesco phone appears to have mysteriously unlocked,
and he manages to send Melanie a text, having little confidence
that it will actually reach her. There are groups of people assembling, some who look gravely over at him. Elspeth, thankfully
silent this morning (probably, he considers, due to a hangover),
has started circulating with Greg. However, Franco is disinclined
to make small talk with anyone, and is glad of Terry's company
as a deterrent. The scud-flick cabbie's gaze has shifted to a girl
with brown-blonde hair, who wears a black zip-up top and
smokes an electronic cigarette. — Tried tae git that yin intae
the Roy Hudd, he grins. — A right wee doady-basher. Gied it
the message n even screen-tested it, but she's an awfay pish-
heid, n she's tied in wi that Anton Miller boy. Your auld buddy
Larry Wylie's been there n aw, n thir sayin he's goat the David
Bowie, Terry rolls his eyes in disdain, sweeping the rain out of
his curls, — so it's a 'steer well clear' job.

Franco takes an interest at the unsolicited mention of
Anton Miller. — What's her name?

— Frances Flanagan.

Those new names are once again featuring. Franco watches Frances Flanagan as she looks over at a group of swaggering youths. Wonders if they were friends of Sean's, and if the other name he's been hearing lately, Anton Miller, is in their midst.

— Mo's lassie, Terry notes. — Mind ay Mo Flanagan?

That name rings several bells, and Franco nods, recalling Mo as an old YLT foot soldier back in the day. South Sloan Street suggests itself. Another recollection is that Mo hit the drink badly, and Terry informs Frank that he died several years ago. — Lassie's got the same weakness as her auld man. Shame, cause she's a wee honey n aw, he laments. — That'll no last but, ay.

Franco looks across at Frances Flanagan, now talking to two older women. She did possess a fragile, vicious beauty, her scraped-back hair highlighting lacerating cheekbones. He shivers as the cold, trickling rain seeps further into him. Thinks of California and dispassionately considers how much he hates this place. He checks the Tesco phone for any signs of Melanie, laboriously punching out another text to tell her he's now at the funeral.

There is a fair crowd gathering. From what he's gleaned, Sean seems to have been a bag of drugs, perennially locked in to shady deals, but he was evidently popular enough. Or perhaps the crowd was simply about his youth. You could be a bad bastard, but if you died young, you were sort of forgiven; there was always the possibility of change, however realistically remote. He thinks about the very first funeral he attended here, his old grandad, Jock Begbie, how that one could have been held in a phone box. Very little about the crematorium has changed in those thirty-odd years. The same functional buildings and landscaped gardens, tucked away in this secluded, inhospitable nook of the city. The constant rain.

Then he sees June, kitted out in black clothes. They look quite expensive, like she's really made an effort. Her sister Olivia is alongside her, recognisable by her trademark pensive expression. He recalls fucking her once, when she was babysitting the boys. He and June had returned home, and June, pished, had passed out cold on the settee. Franco had picked her up and deposited her into the bed like a sack of coal. Then he'd gone through to the living roon, nodded to the couch and said to Olivia, — Get them fuckin off, then. Me n you.

She'd protested that they shouldn't, and he'd countered that it was only a bit of fun. Olivia had looked at him strangely, but then started to undress. He was over to her and was guiding her onto the couch, then jumping on her and getting up her quickly, in a silent, aggressive cowp, groping roughly at her breasts as he pumped. It was over swiftly. Afterwards she'd started to cry, and he'd mumbled, — Fuck sake, youse cows ur daein ma fuckin heid in, and retired to bed.

Olivia is now overweight, but not yet at June's level of morbid obesity. The black insect-dead eyes in her suety, pockmarked face gaze at him in much the same expression she'd dispensed back then. A visible shiver racks her plump frame. Franco is considering that the episode perhaps wasn't as sordid as it seemed; what was youth but a violently puckish romp? If there have to be lamentations, he considers, poking somebody isn't one worthy of inclusion on the list, especially as he can feel almost zero connection to that incident.

Increasingly his life seems fractured, as if his past had been lived by somebody else. It isn't just that the place he now resides in and the people around him are poles apart, it's like he himself is an entirely different person. The overriding obsessions and foibles of the man he'd once been now feel utterly ludicrous to the current resident of his mind and body. The only bridge is rage; when angered he can taste his old self. But in California, the way he is currently living his life, few things can vex him to that extent. But that's over there.

June catches his eye and approaches. Franco would have raised a hand to stop her advance, had he anticipated that she would wrap her meaty arms around him. — Our laddie, Frank . . . she wails miserably, — our bonnie wee beautiful laddie . . .

Franco looks over her shoulder, focusing on the stonework outside the Chapel of Rest. The stink of fags from June is so profound that no perfume could even begin to cover it up. If he had still been drinking, the effects of last night's alcohol would quite possibly make him retch. — Aye, it's a sair one, right enough, he says through gritted teeth. — Scuse me a sec, and he pulls her clinging arms from him. Fortunately Michael, wearing a charcoal-grey suit, has appeared and June fastens onto her second son, announcing in a high bleat, — MIGH-EY-KEL . . .

This gives Franco the opportunity to slip back over to Terry. The cab-driving scud-merchant is chatting to a well-dressed woman who raises a flirty eyebrow at him. But as Franco approaches them, he hears a familiar voice rasp in his ear, — Ye should've got in touch!

Larry looks pretty much the same, maybe pared down a little with age. It interests him in a morbid way, how the passing years chunk up some, while reducing others. — Larry, Franco acknowledges.

— Ah kent Sean well, Frank. Larry moves in close and drops his voice. — Tried tae keep a wee eye on him. Steer him right, he mutters, blinking a little under Franco's unwavering gaze. — But eh goat in wi Anton Miller n that crowd. Larry is now whispering, as his eyes swivel round to scan the attendees. — Notice *he's* no here the day tae pey his respects, but, ay.

Franco wouldn't have known Anton Miller from any of the young men present, but it is good to have his absence confirmed. There are certainly enough of them. Some steal reverential glances at him; others offer cocky half-sneers, as if they fancy their chances. A year in London, five more in California, and another world has grown up in his absence. Or perhaps an oddly familiar one, merely staffed by different personnel.

— So while yir here, consider anything ah huv at yir disposal, Larry says, with ponderous formality. — Ye want tae borrow the van, any time, it's yours. Ye need a place tae stey, yir welcome at mine.

— Cheers, Larry, Franco notes, still scanning the crowd, — but ah'm fine at ma sister's.

Michael stands a little apart from the groups, chatting with another young guy, flinty-eyed and with a fistful of sovereign rings. Franco sees them staring at the young woman, Frances Flanagan. But she doesn't notice, as she is gazing at him and Larry. Larry turns and winks at Frances, beckoning her over.

— Frances here kent Sean tae, Larry informs him as she joins them, — ay, doll?

— Aye. Sorry like, she says to Franco. He concedes the girl's beauty. A long, angular jaw gives her a sharpness and intensity perfectly congruent with her piercing eyes and their unusually arresting emerald green.

— Heard ye were there at the time.

Frances looks at him as if he'd just told her that she is standing in a field full of landmines. Frank Begbie can almost see a speeded-up movie playing in those expressive eyes. — Well, ah wis and ah wisnae . . . she says sheepishly.

According to Fat Tyrone, though not known to the police, she had been with Sean when he was in the room, wasted on a cocktail of drugs so formidable it might well have destroyed him had his adversary not got there first. It seemed likely, as she explains to Franco, that she had woken up, after passing out with Sean, to find him dead in a spillage of blood, the door of the flat unlocked. She had understandably got the fuck out, then called the ambulance. — We should talk aboot this later, Frances says, aware of the proximity of Larry's rapacious gaze.

Franco sees the sense in that, but his brain is buzzing. Was her story true? Or did she know the killer and was protecting him, or was scared of him? Was it her? A lovers' tiff over drugs or money? She's slight and slender, but Sean

112

was so wasted, as the cop, Notman, had said, he'd have been easy enough to finish off. — Aye, he agrees, — we should.

— Right, she nods. Franco watches her depart, joining two other young women. She certainly is a good-looking girl. In the USA she would have perhaps taken the Greyhound bus to West Hollywood, done some waitressing jobs while she took acting classes and waited to be discovered or married. He thinks of young women like her whom he's known, and what a strange currency feminine beauty back here could be. Many women were thankful that they had it, but were then determined to spend it as quickly as possible. It was more often treated like any other windfall, something to be pissed away before anybody else got their hands on it. Here, Frances would drink and drug her looks into a haggard mess. Despair seemed to cling to her. Then, he supposed, looking around the crowd, most men did the same with their own pleasing youthful features, and he was beset with a sudden awareness that it was only prison that had stopped him from peeving himself into a jakey mess. People led tough lives; they worked, were tired, often depressed, and didn't have the time or money for spas or gyms or sensible diets. Over her shoulder, he gets a glimpse of Tyrone, with Franco's old friend Nelly. A few feet away he hears a woman say something about the place being full of 'hooks, crooks, hoors and comic singers'. That seemed about right.

June is suddenly back at his side, pointing to the chapel. — We huv tae go in.

The service tells Frank nothing about his dead son. The minister's speech is all bland platitudes. Yet some draw obvious

113

relief and comfort; June's soft wails break out in gentle intervals, through the fug of her medication, flanked as she is by him and Michael. Throughout the proceedings, his second son's lower lip sags, his eyes tarnished in sullen suspicion. Michael never looks at him, and Franco concedes to himself that he can hardly blame him, given how their last meeting had played out. Otherwise, there are plenty of old faces. Some are genuine friends, like Mickey and boys from the boxing club; others, many of whom he's crossed over the years, seem basically along for a thinly disguised gloat.

As well as June and Michael he has Elspeth, Greg and Olivia sharing the front pew with him. Joe sits behind them, looking bedraggled, pished and spoiling for a fight. The only alleviation from the minister's dreary recitations comes from the Tesco phone; it suddenly explodes into a hurdy-gurdy ringtone, compelling Franco to answer it. — Aye?

— Are you paying too much interest on your loans? a robot voice enquires. Franco snaps it off, June looking at him in her old-school wounded way. Then it's time for everybody to leave. He sees Kate, another of his exes, who looks well, with her two sons, Chris, about fourteen, and River, around twelve, who is his own. More than any of Franco's offspring, the kid, whom he's never seen outside some infant pictures she'd sent him in prison, looks disconcertingly like him. He shakes the boy's hand, asks him about school, tells him to work hard at it, and be good to his mum. It's about all he can run to, and he's relieved to be interrupted by his old neighbour, Stevie Duncan, and his wife Julie. He hasn't seen them for years, and is delighted to hear that Stevie's mum, old Mrs Duncan, is still alive and living in the sheltered housing complex at Gordon Court. It is the same one his grandad Jock died in. He recalls that she'd knitted him his first ever green-and-white Hibs scarf. They are good people. — She would have been along, Frank, Stevie tells him, as they file outside into the cold. — It's her legs, she cannae stand about for long.

— That's a shame. Ah'd love tae pop up and see her.

— She'd like that, Frank.

The funeral is followed by a reception in a hotel on Leith Links. People come up to him, many of them barely recognisable as old acquaintances. Gavin Temperley has ballooned. — Pittin oan the Coral, Gav, Franco observes playfully.

— Good livin, Temperley smiles back with a faintly suppressed air of desperation.

Then another voice in his ear, hesitant and cagey. — Awright, Franco . . .

He turns to see a thin and haggard man, with a greasy mop of sandy-grey hair, under which sit two large dark eyes with a dull sheen, set far back into a face of ghostly pallor. — Awright . . . Franco warily responds. — How's it gaun?

— Ye see it aw, Franco.

Spud Murphy looks so old and wizened to him that if he hadn't spoken Franco wouldn't have been able to confirm his identity. — Cannae be as bad as that, surely!

A gallows smile pushes Spud's features into some kind of animation. Then they tumble south again. — Sorry aboot Sean. It's a bad toon, Franco. Aw changed. A bad toon now, likesay, Spud warns.

Franco nods, as that couldn't really be disputed. All towns have their bad sides; this one is no worse or better than any other. In California, they lived only a few miles away from where a film director's privileged son had recently gone on a rampage, shooting people dead because he couldn't get his hole. *Thank fuck they don't have guns here*, he thinks mischievously, looking at poor Spud. Despite its movie representation, militaristic foreign policy and creeping racism, he finds America generally such a mannered place compared to here, but then they let lunatics buy guns, and that could change everything.

Over Spud's shoulder, he can see June, still tearful, being comforted by Olivia, with Michael looking on, seeming almost nonchalant. Franco feels a strange reverberation coming from deep inside him. *Breathe* . . .

One . . . two . . . three . . . who are we . . .

To think that this was once his family, and these were once his bosom buddies. He contemplates Mel and Grace and Eve, trying to isolate details of their faces as they slither through his mind, their friends Ralph and Juan, and even his in-laws and his agent, Martin, back in the sun of California. And they call this grey place Sunny Leith. It was bizarre. Life often seemed like a meaningless joke. You either got the custard pie in the face, or you got to giggle at those who did. — Right enough, Spud, Franco almost bellows, fighting back a gurgling laugh.

As the drinks kick in, so the procession of old lags from all over town sidling up to him, full of conspiratorial talk in jailbird whispers, grows exponentially. The inanities and the exhortations to violence, most regarding vengeance against Anton Miller, are almost overwhelming. He feels the bleakness crawling into his skull. Franco breathes in steadily, trying to tune it all out. That pressure on your brain. Eroding focus. Diverting the flow of thought down old, ruinous neural canals. He is thinking of his heads of actors, and specific mutilations on them. Of his canvases, those attic versions of Dorian Gray, drenched in blood red. He keeps his eye on Frances Flanagan, and is almost pleased when Elspeth and Greg come over to rescue him. — There's a boy from the local paper here, a crime reporter, Elspeth informs him.

— Disgusting that they won't leave a family alone to grieve, Greg muses, looking at the reporter, ruddy of face and grubby of dress, who stands alone in a corner. Then he turns to a group of youths, who have been stealing glances at Franco.

Frank Begbie has registered this too, deciding that at least some of them had to be mobbed up with Anton Miller. He might not be here but he would still see everything that went on. — Aye, he agrees.

— Hmm. Greg takes another glimpse at the young team. — Do you think there's a danger that you might be seen as a hero by some young kids around here?

Franco gives a matter-of-fact shake of his shoulders. — I *am* a hero to some young kids around here, he says, pausing to look at Elspeth. — I was a hero to my son and I was never there for him. Now he's in a grave at twenty-one. And I'll no be here for anybody else's son either.

Greg sees his wife's eyebrows arch towards the ceiling in dismay.

Terry is chatting to some members of the young team. Franco watches as he jokes easily with them, all the time drawing their girlfriends into the conversation, eliciting giggles as he then ignores the boys. The young team are keeping away from Tyrone, who stands at the bar, a brooding vengeful aspect hanging around his big shoulders like a cloak. And he is with Nelly, Franco's old buddy, who studiously avoids him. He is about to go over and say hello, and perhaps offer some kind of apology to Tyrone, when suddenly Larry is back in his face. — So, Franco, what's changed about Scotland, then?

— Cunts still have bad teeth, drink too much, take too many drugs . . . he looks over at Tyrone, — they've got fatter. That's what's changed.

Larry's face creases in a grin. — Like they've no goat fat cunts in the States? It was thaim that started aw this fat-cunt shite!

— Aye, it's a global problem now, Franco smiles, noting that one thing about Larry was that people avoided him. Elspeth and Greg, for example, who have sloped off across the room. He has his uses.

— Too right, Larry argues. — They say three hundred million Chinkies are obese these days. That's nearly mair obese Chinkies than Americans ay aw sizes. That means a lot ay shite grub's gittin scranned. Ye dinnae git that wey on a handfay ay rice!

— Heard *Chinese Democracy*?

— Thaire's nae democracy in China.

— Naw, it's an album, Guns n' Roses.

— Nup.

— Check it oot. Comes highly recommended.

— Right . . . So how's life in California then, Frank?

Frank Begbie looks over at a couple of old adversaries. One is Cha Morrison from Lochend, who originated from the stair next to the one June now lives in. With a fistful of sovies closing round a beer glass, he looks like the cat that got the cream. It is, he reflects, something of a result for Cha; he gets to laugh at Sean's demise while drinking the booze his father, a long-term rival, has paid for. — Been enjoying it, but there's something missing, he considers. — Like a war.

— Funny wee temperature in this room, Larry acknowledges.

Frank Begbie remembers that Larry was once a victim of Cha Morrison's blade; his assailant did time for it. He feels his pulse starting to race. He makes himself breathe slowly and evenly, in through his nose, out through his mouth. *Even. Stay even.* The best time to hit somebody is when they are drawing in a breath.

— Awright, Frank? Larry asks.

There follows an ominous lull in energy, like on the dance floor of a busy nightclub, just before the DJ is about to drop *that track* that will send the floor crazy. And he realises that *he* is the DJ. They are all looking to him to drop the tune. To swing the fist or boot, to throw the glass, to launch the headbutt, or even the blood-curdling scream across the room, that will set the place alight. — They always say 'listen tae your gut reaction', Franco says softly. — If I listened tae my gut reaction, not one cunt in this room would be breathing,

119

he smiles cheerfully. — And that wouldnae be good, he says, looking across at Frances Flanagan.

— It's Miller, that Anton Miller, Frank, Larry declares. Franco scents the fumes of drink on his breath, reckons that he is approaching that jakey loop, where he will make the same point over and over again. — He was in and oot ay that flat. Sean owed him, and he didnae like him hinging aboot wi wee hairy there. He nods over at Frances, who stares at a row of full wine glasses on the table. — Mark ma words, Miller's the one.

— So I keep hearing, Begbie says.

Then Cha Morrison bounds over, a big grin etched across his face. He stinks of drink, obviously from a celebration that pre-dates this one. — Better crematin that rubbish. Soas the disease cannae spread, ay-no.

Franco had thought that he would experience a violent psychonosema at those words, but there is nothing. He is breathing smoothly, and even smiles at Morrison.

Cha Morrison hasn't envisaged this reaction, and seems genuinely upset by it. — Ken whae eh took aw that queer stuff offay? The poofy artist, Cha sneers, bending his wrist and puckering his lips, as bodies start to close in around the two men. — Ye gaunny paint ays a picture then, sweethert? Oooh, ducky, how's the weather treatin ye in California?

— I was a bit fed up wi aw this, Franco laughs, — but you've fair cheered me up, with the drunken jakey act. Ah've kind ay missed aw that. The weather in California is very, very good, n thank you for askin. What are you daein these days? Stacking shelves at Tesco wi bairns fae the school?

— You're a fuckin shiter. Morrison steps forward, only to feel a firm grip on his shoulder, yanking him back. He turns round to see not only Tyrone but Nelly and the boxing club boys. — I suggest you get tae fuck, while ye still can, Tyrone offers. Cha mutters something, but the boxers and Nelly are already ushering him outside, with Franco being led in the opposite direction by Elspeth. He glimpses Michael, who has moved close to the source of the commotion. — Proud ay ye, Frank, his sister is saying, — the wey ye didnae react tae that spiteful drunk. Ah never thought I'd say it, but I am.

— A little self-control goes a long way, he smiles, but never takes his eyes from the door.

He sees Tyrone come back in first, heading to the bar, followed by Nelly, a few steps behind him.

– Lucky ah didnae fuckin well go oot thaire. Joe is at his shoulder, then looking to Elspeth, — Ah'd huv fuckin well kilt the cunt . . .

— Aw aye, by breathin on um? Elspeth challenges, and they start to bicker.

Fortunately, Mickey and some of the boys have come back in, and Franco gratefully heads over to meet them. Mickey tells him what happened, that they just kept the peace. Nelly cracked Cha on the jaw, but then he staggered off down the road, and a brutal stomping was averted. — He was swearing revenge on everybody, but it was aw just drunkard's talk.

— Sound. Thanks, Mickey, he says, almost feeling sorry for Morrison, for so long in the frame to be his defining nemesis, but replaced first by Donnelly, and then Seeker. — I didnae want any scenes here, no today. Franco slaps his back. — I should go and thank Tyrone and Nelly. I was a wee bit out of order with the fat man last time I saw him . . . And he is ready to head over to make his peace at the bar, when he sees Frances Flanagan furtively scanning the room, then slipping out the door. Her behaviour suggests she intends her exit to remain undetected, and is going further than the toilet. She'd said they needed to talk. They would do that. Franco makes some lavatory excuses and heads off, following her outside, relieved to escape them all. He gets into the street and looks down the road.

Frances seems to have vanished in the drizzle, but she's only crossed over to the Links side of the street, and is cutting through the park. He sets off in pursuit and catches up with her, walking behind her. His eyes instinctively go to her arse. The undulating movement of her buttocks beguiles him for a second, then he recalls discussions with Melanie about the objectifying male gaze, and he lifts his eyes to take in all of her frame. He thinks about men looking at his daughters in that way, as they grew up. What would he do? He would kill them. Tear them apart. Toast the memory of their stares with a pint of their still-warm blood.

No. Breathe. One. Two. Three.

By a large oak tree, he pulls up alongside her. — Awright?

She stops and tenses, her startled eyes wide as she looks at him. Then she glances across the near-deserted park. — Aye . . .

— No fancy steyin?

— Nup. No wi that Larry there, she says, scowling. — He ey tries tae go hame wi ays.

— Seems like a few people go hame wi you.

122

She looks him up and down, finding her confidence. — What's that meant tae mean? What's it tae you?

— Like oor Sean?

He can see that hits her like a fist to her stomach. — Nup . . . he wisnae like that. We were mates.

It is now Frank Begbie's turn to feel something strike him forcibly inside. *He wasnae like that.* He'd considered Cha Morrison's taunts to be standard wind-ups, but they now seem to have some basis in fact. What sort of young man would be content with being 'mates' with a girl like this? But it's all too much to think about right now. He sucks in some air and tries to reset himself. — Still surprised ye never steyed for a wee peeve. Ye like a drink, ah hear.

— Ah'm sober for three weeks, n even if ah wis drinkin ah widnae wi that Larry aroond.

— What aboot drinkin wi me? Franco suggests, as a maroon-and-white Lothian Transport bus pulls up in the road adjacent to the park. Up ahead, some gulls sit on the sodden football pitches, as if ground-nesting. — Mibbe having that wee chat we were talking aboot?

Frances wraps her arms around herself. — Ah'm AA, she says, evidently disappointed at her own announcement.

— Me tae, Franco smiles. — Well, no AA cause ah cannae be arsed wi meetings, but ah dinnae drink, ay. Let's get a coffee. You near here?

— Aye, this wey, she says, nodding across the misty Links, and they set off together.

Walking with a young woman, in Leith, takes Franco back to an earlier self still brimming with possibilities, before the ever-tightening vice of violence began to shut down his options. Despite feeling the cold insinuating itself into his chest, he is oddly at peace, as he saunters through the haar like a ghost: a man of this place, yet almost dreamily detached from it. He listens to her talk, enjoying the soothing rhythms of her feminine Edinburgh accent, how she emphasises some words like a question. It is stock AA stuff; her conversation peppered with terms like *journey* and *closure*, but it sounds awkward and performative, like a kid wearing a set of ill-fitting adult clothes. At one point, she arches a brow and asks him, — How do you stey sober when you don't go to meetings?

— Ah dinnae drink.

— But it's a disease, and –

— Is it fuck, he scoffs. — It's called choice. Ah chose tae be a bam. Now ah'm choosin no tae be. Simple as that. Ye go tae these meetings and they're full ay so-called *sober* jakeys, wiring themselves full ay nicotine and caffeine and obsessing aboot peeve.

— But what dae ye dae when ye feel that pull?

— Paint and sculpt. Fling on my tracksuit and go for a run. Glove up and hit a bag.

Frances is silent at that, and for the rest of the way to her Halmyres Street flat. After one cup of coffee, during which she grows more nervous, fidgeting with the cup, Frank Begbie declares, — Ah'm gaunny get us a cairry-oot.

— Ah dinnae . . . she starts.

— It's up tae you whether you have a drink or no, he states, and he heads outside and down to the off-licence, returning a short while later with half a dozen bottles of red wine.

124

— I dinnae . . . Frances protests again, never taking her eyes off the wine.

— You do. You want one, Franco says, sitting at the table, as he opens a bottle with a corkscrew he'd bought in the shop, — ah kin tell, and he pours the wine into two tumblers, as she has no wine glasses. — A nice wee civilised glass of wine, he sings, though he knows that his will only be for show.

She has drunk two glasses and is on her third by the time she realises that he hasn't touched his. — You no drinkin?

— I'm a bit slow, he says.

Frances isn't so slow. She is getting drunk, flushing with a bombastic confidence, but with part of her brain still reserved for sobriety. *This would be the time for her to stop*, Begbie thinks, as he recharges her glass, *but that's never gaunny happen*. — Ah like aulder guys, she ventures flirtatiously. — They treat ye right. Dinnae muck ye aboot as much as younger fellys.

Franco laughs in her face, shaking his head. — Larry, a bag ay disease, wantin ye tae go bareback wi um. Juice Terry, tryin tae get ye tae dae his crappy scud flicks. Aye, they're proper gentlemen! The young team must be bad bastards, right enough!

That hit home. Her eyes fill with a steady anger. — It's . . . it's no fair! They never leave ye alaine. She shakes her head, and knocks back another big swig of claret. — How can they no just let ye be . . .

He recognises her dilemma: how the good-looking girl in their environment could be corralled into a similar pen as the hard man. How they had one resource to fall back on, were put on a pedestal for it, and discouraged from learning anything else, could never get past it, as it steadily entrapped them. But other things could imprison you too. — It's a curse, so it is, the drink, Franco holds up his full glass. He looks at it in contempt; has zero interest in its contents. — Your auld man, Mo, he was rotten wi it. A nice guy, but eh couldnae pass a boozer. The old Irish genes, and reared in Scotland . . . not a great mix, not a recipe for a sober life.

— Did you ken ma dad? Her eyes are big, sad, imploring.

— Aye. Franco picks up the empty bottle by the neck, his eyes flashing with violence. — Good guy; his lassie though, ah'm no that sure aboot her but, ay. The last person tae see Sean alive. Pits you right in the fuckin frame in ma book.

Frances's bottom lip quivers. He raises the wine bottle, and in a sudden violent movement brings it crashing down against the table, shattering it. Glass flies across the room, eliciting a loud gasp from Frances. — Now it's time, he holds the jagged bottle neck up to her face, — that you started gabbin.

Frances gapes at him in abject terror. It's as if she realises that every other nightmare she's experienced in her life has been solely to prepare her for this one. She nods, taking up her drink and throwing it back. Then she starts to talk in such breathless compulsion, it seems like only another threat of violence could get her to stop. — Me n Sean went up tae this flat he was steyin at, and we got wasted. Totally blootered. On everything. He took loads, ah did n aw, but no as much as him. Naebody took as much as him. She screws up her eyes, then opens them wide. — Ah passed oot, n when ah came to, ah found him like that. The door wis open, n ah got the fuck oot. Then ah phoned the ambulance, fae the payphone at the Esso garage.

Franco lowers the broken bottle to the table. — What did ye run away fir? How did ye no phone the polis?

— Ye say ye kent ma dad, Frances says, in reprimanding tones.

Franco doesn't like the taste of that, but is forced to swallow it. — Was the door locked behind youse when you went intae the flat?

— I think so, but ah cannae be sure, she trembles. The way he looks at her, his hand still round the neck of the broken bottle. It's like he's going to rip her face apart. Frances reaches slowly for the intact, open bottle, emptying the last of its contents into her glass.

— So if it was locked, either somebody had a key, or Sean came to, and heard them at the door. He knew who it was and he let them in, Franco speculates.

— As ah said, Sean was even mair wrecked than me. Frances laughs bitterly as she looks him in the eye. It is a look of appeal, and it goes to another drink. He places the broken bottle on the table and picks up the corkscrew, opening another for her. — Ah doubt he'd have been able tae get up off the couch.

— Who else had a key?

— Fallon would have one, she says, lifting her glass to her lips.

— Who?

127

— Fallon. He's the landlord, Frances says off-handedly, feeling a satisfying thump of the wine's anaesthetic, — it wis his flat, and she lifts the bottle he'd opened and starts to pour.

— Where does he stey?

— Ah dinnae ken, Frances knocks back a full glass like a shot, — but I ken where he goes for brunch every morning . . . tae that Valvona and Crolla place at the top ay the Walk, she says and looks at his glass. — Ye no gaunny take that drink?

— Telt ye, ah dinnae drink.

Frances pulls his glass over and starts on it, even though she has an almost-full one alongside it. — You're gaunny tell me that ah shouldnae be daein this, she suddenly giggles.

— Dae what the fuck ye like, he responds, — ah dinnae care.

— Ah ken ye dinnae, she cackles in scorn. — But at least ye dinnae pretend tae. No like the rest ay them. At least you're fuckin honest.

Franco raises his eyebrows. The charge of wine has now put her in a place beyond fear. This girl is doomed. — One other thing. Whae do *you* think came in and chibbed him?

— Ah dinnae ken.

— Anton Miller?

— Nup . . . she says, and he is wrong about the wine's effect, as Frances is incapacitated by terror, even through the emboldening drink, — ah dinnae ken. Honest, ah wis wasted. Ah really dinnae ken, and she starts to cry, her face swelling with drink and tears. — Sean was ma friend, eh wis the best friend that ah ever had!

128

And Frank Begbie leaves Frances Flanagan with her wine, and the sense that everything she has told him is the absolute truth.

19

THE TEXTS

The breeze has stiffened a little and fog has blown down from the north of the state. On the back decking Melanie Francis stretches out, then pumps her arms with the 3lb weights wrapped round her fists in Velcro, completing a burning set of exercises. On finishing her routine, she goes into the kitchen, looking to her phone for signs of incoming calls. One from her mom, but still nothing from Jim. Panic bolts are starting to surge in her chest.

Melanie feels that she let Jim down badly by calling the police. If she had elaborated on how Paula's rape ordeal weighed on her, he would perhaps have understood. But it proved to be an error, and now she has allowed Harry, with his barely suppressed age-old agenda, into their lives. He doesn't belong. Only the girls and Jim do.

Her mind rushes back to the opening night of that show in Edinburgh's Fruitmarket Gallery. They were all euphoric after its success, sipping wine and chatting. Suddenly she realised that Jim, whose work had taken most of the accolades, was nowhere to be seen. For a horrible second, she thought, in spite of the ankle bracelet he wore, that he'd used the show as a front to run away. But then she went out to the fire escape, and he was standing there on the stairs.

When she'd asked what he was doing, alone in that draughty spot in the semi-dark, he'd looked at her, as if to say *I was waiting for you*. But what he said, with hushed conviction, was that this was the very best day of his life. Then his gaze was both searching and acute as he whispered, — It's probably asking too much, but there's only one thing that would make it even better, and he'd closed his eyes.

It was then that Melanie had kissed him on the mouth. It was all she could do. He was all she'd been thinking about. It was the most intimate kiss she'd ever had: simple, delicious and trippy. His eyes remained shut and hers did too. When they heard a noise from the gallery and broke off, he'd smiled and said, — Thank you.

— My pleasure, she'd insisted, and they squeezed hands and headed back into the party.

The Dance Partner, the picture of a serene, Jesus-like Craig Liddel, had been sold. She listened to him talking to the wealthy collectors who paid big money for it. They were a youngish husband-and-wife team. The woman wore a sparkling blue cocktail dress. — This man you killed, how do you know he would have turned into this saintly figure?

— I don't, but it's not about what he might or might not have done. By killing him, I rendered that question a matter of speculation. It's about what *I* do now. In order to take his life, I had to dehumanise him, and myself. In order to save my own, I now have to rehumanise us both. It's not an easy thing to do, he'd said, calm and sincere, — it's a battle I have to fight every day.

Francis James Begbie.

She goes to hunt for Elspeth's number, but there is nothing written down on the pad, he must have punched it straight into his iPhone. Then, just as Melanie is about to lower the cellphone to the coffee table, a series of texts flood onto the display, or rather the same three, on repeat:

This is my new number.

Lost my iPhone.

At funeral – love you – call me when you get this.

Melanie calls the number. He picks up straight away. — Jim . . . I was getting a bit worried . . . These texts all came in at once . . . How did the funeral go?

— So good to hear your voice! This fucking phone! Jim gasps down the line in delight. — Funeral was okay . . . It's just great to get it out the way. I'm not going to stay too long now. Just want to see a few people . . .

Melanie has internally debated whether or not to tell him about Harry, and the washed-up body of Santiago. Jim has a right to know, but it is her mess and her imposition. It is unfair to add to his stress levels right now. As she listens to the regenerated Scottish burr in his voice, she thinks she can hear a knock at the door, then is aware of a rustling noise coming from outside, just as the line goes dead. She calls Jim's new number again, as she heads to the door. This time there is only a loud, continuous beep from the phone as she opens up and looks outside.

Nobody is there.

Then, over by the garage, trying to look in Jim's workshop, is the figure of a man, his back turned to her in the failing light. He first thought: *it's Harry* . . . and her heart sinks.

Then he turns and stares at her.

It isn't Harry, it's Martin, Jim's agent. — Hi, Melanie, he says.

20

THE LANDLORD

Frank Begbie had left Frances Flanagan and walked up to York Place to catch a tram. He had just got on and settled down, when the Tesco mobile went off. It was so good to hear Melanie's voice, but to his rage, it cut off almost immediately. He'd shouted out: — FUCKER, drawing the attention of a sour-looking elderly woman, before he'd sucked in air, and forced a wan smile at her.

He'd started to take the phone apart, realising that the battery must be loose in its mountings. Removing it, he placed the device in his mouth and bit under one of the pins, pulling it out. He felt enamel chip on the underside of his tooth, but when he eased up, the pin was sitting further out, and the reinserted battery seemed held more securely.

When he got to Elspeth's, he opted to go to his room after dinner, and put the phone back on charge. He picked up his Kindle and started to read *A Clockwork Orange*. Sleep quickly took him, and he had the most peaceful and restful night he'd enjoyed since his return to Scotland.

He rises early the next day, blinking into a weak morning light filtering through the thin curtains. The room is cold; the temperature has dropped in the night. The Tesco mobile is charged, flashing at him in a green 'come-hither' wink. He grabs it and calls Melanie, thinking that she'll probably still be up, enjoying some work or relaxation time with the girls asleep. A voice immediately tells him that he needs to top up the phone in order to make a transatlantic call. — Fuck yir transatlantic call, ya cunt, he replies to the unmoved robot voice. However, he has enough credit to phone Larry. — Need tae borrow the van. Like you sais at the funeral.

Larry's silence indicates to Franco that he's trying to conceal his annoyance that he's been taken up on an offer he'd made under alcohol's costly latitude. Eventually he coughs out a reluctant, — Sure . . . come roond, and tells him the address. Franco slings his sports bag over his shoulder, as he hopes to get to the boxing club later, and heads for his friend's place at Marchmont.

The biggest shock is Larry's flat. It is spacious and luxurious. There must have been more money in the Edinburgh drug trade than he thought. Larry is hung-over, but grumblingly hands Franco the keys. — Right . . . look eftir it but . . . nae drivin oan the wrong side ay the road, he says in forced cheer.

It's liberating to have wheels again, and Franco's first port of call is Leith. Driving past Leith Academy, he once again recalls his torturous dyslexic days there. Hetherington soon gave up on him, bar the odd ridiculing disdainful comment such as 'We won't ask Francis to read. After all, we only have two periods, not two days'; the laughter would echo in his ears and he felt the fury rising inside him, while he fought down its eruption. His mind drifts to the time the teacher had asked Mark Renton to do the honours. — No, Renton had said.

— What? What do you mean 'no', Renton?

— I'm no reading it.

— Why not?

— Cannae be bothered, he said, as chuckles broke out in the class.

— Well, I'll give you something to be bothered about. Hetherington's voice went high, and he pulled out the tawse from his top drawer. — Read the passage, Renton, he commanded.

Mark Renton kept his eyes focused on his desk. — Nup.

— Right, come out here!

Renton rose and came forward, extending his hands, one on top of the other, to receive four of the belt. At every lash, Frank Begbie watched, gritting his teeth. Renton wore a half-smile, one which admitted to the intense pain, yet made it clear that he found the whole thing comedic and ludicrous. He sat down on his stinging hands. — Wanker, he whispered, so that only Franco could hear. Frank Begbie knew that Mark Renton's gesture was one of solidarity with him. He loved Renton after that, and would have done anything for him. They were inseparable friends. Yet it had gone so bad between them. Drugs. They got Renton, just like they got Sean.

At Tesco's in Duke Street, he puts thirty pounds on the mobile. The sales assistant, a different one, looks at him as if he is crazy. He dials direct to Melanie, only to have an American voice tell him: — Sorry, it has not been possible to connect you at the moment, please try again later.

— Fuck you, ya cunt! he again spits down the phone, then, looking to the assistant, stops to perform breathing exercises. Life could get at you through a million cuts as well as one manic plunge.

Gordon Court is another trip down memory lane. Agnes Duncan is happy to see him, it has been such a long time. The frail old woman expresses her sorrow at the death of Frank's son, but is delighted when he shows her a photograph of the girls. It's a little scuffed through being in his wallet, but as the ones on his phone are now in the city drainage system, it's the only option, as he explains to her. — Aw aye, mair bad news, she says.

Bad news seems to hunt Ross Fallon down. Several years ago the death of a young man at a party in his house had triggered a tabloid spree, further fuelled by the lurid disclosures of mercenary rent boys. Frank Begbie vaguely remembers reading about it.

This Edinburgh businessman and former prospective Conservative parliamentary candidate (which in Scotland meant little more than no-hoper status) had been further tarnished since then. Not that the corpulent individual tucking into his food in Valvona & Crolla looks uncomfortable, with his gourmet pasta and glass of white wine. Frances Flanagan's information about his brunching modus operandi was spot on.

Frank Begbie positions himself at a nearby table, watching Fallon shovel back his food. He can't believe the aromas and range of produce in this wonderful place, which he has passed a million times and never set foot in. How it was assumed that it wasn't for the likes of him. He speculates as to how different his native city might seem for somebody who habitually shops at Valvona & Crolla, rather than Scotmid.

When the waitress approaches, Franco enquires as to the possibility of an egg-white omelette, and she looks at him as if he has two heads. He settles for a vegetarian verdure breakfast, which he greatly enjoys, dispatching it swiftly as he sits behind the *Scotsman*. He'd heard Greg mention that the paper has decanted from its showcase, custom-built headquarters by the Scottish Parliament to a broom cupboard out at Orchard Brae. Sure enough, it has the shabby, beaten, depressive tone and content of a publication on its last legs. Every article seems either half-hearted and ill-considered or desperately overreaching, as if the journal is drowning in its own pointlessness, occasionally gripped by sudden, panicky bouts of awareness. He goes to the sports pages, but the exploits of Edinburgh's senior clubs fail to excite. Fallon sits for a long time, himself reading a *Financial Times*. *Do those cunts no have anything tae dae?* he wonders, realising that he's badly missing his studio. It dawns on him just how much he likes to get on with stuff.

Finally Fallon shifts his bulk and creakingly rises to settle his bill. Frank Begbie does the same, following him out to his car, then jumping into the van. As he pursues the landlord, it isn't so much the *driving* on the left-hand side of the road that he finds strange, but the act of *sitting* there in the vehicle. Fallon heads out of town, Franco tailing him as far as a large villa, just outside Haddington. Watching him vanish down the driveway, Franco lets him go inside, before striding down the path and knocking at the door. When Fallon answers, Frank Begbie booms, — Fallon, landlord, and pushes past him into the house. — You rented a flat to Sean Begbie, ay?

— Who the fuck, Fallon protests, — you can't come in here –

— I'm in already, so your statement makes nae fuckin sense, Franco says, heading into the front room.

— Get out, or I'll call the police!

— Feel free. Franco picks up a heavy glass ashtray from a coffee table.

He sees Fallon hesitate. His instincts are correct: this guy doesn't want the cops involved in his business. — You no gaunny call the polis then? he taunts.

— Who the fuck are you?

Franco swivels and holds the ashtray up to the light. He seems at pains to see something through the blue glass. — The weight in these things. His eyes swivel round at Fallon.

Fallon gasps, looking at the ashtray, then into Frank Begbie's 200-yard stare. — Please . . . I don't want any trouble . . . what do you want . . . ?

— You rented a flat to Sean Begbie, Franco repeats, slapping the ashtray against his open palm.

— No . . . no . . . I rented to Arbie . . . I didn't know he sublet to Sean or anybody else!

Another name. *Arbie*. — So you knew Sean?

— Vaguely . . . through Arbie and a few others . . . they hung around together.

Franco's eyes blaze, but to Ross Fallon they seem set deep in cavernous slits. It's like two oncoming trains in adjacent railway tunnels. Then Begbie's voice drops, almost to a whisper. — Were ye shaggin him?

Fallon looks scandalised. — No, he yelps, then slips into a confessional tone. — I've had boys here, for parties. Mostly it was harmless, but they took the piss, stealing and stuff. I was stupid . . . I was lonely –

— Ah couldnae gie a fuck how lonely ye wir!

— Sean and I never – honestly!

Franco considers this. There is probably no real reason for him to lie. — Frances Flanagan, she was here, aye?

— Yes.

— Anton Miller?

Fallon visibly trembles at the mention of that name.

— Okay, I'll take that as a yes, Franco spits, — What about this Arbie gadge, where does he live?

— Gorgie. He just got out of prison.

— Give me his address. Dinnae even think aboot tippin him off or I'll be back here. Franco lowers the ashtray onto the table. He looks out the window, then rubs the curtains between thumb and finger, talking in detached, matter-of-fact tones, as if he's addressing the material in his hand. — They *will* be able to put your face back together again after I'm done, he suddenly whips his neck round, his cold eyes evaluating the landlord, — but it'll be a long and painful process and it'll never look quite the same again, and his brows raise skyward, as if actually estimating the extent of the task the surgeon will have.

Fallon's trembling hand picks up a pen and scratches out the address in capital letters on a notepad. He tears off the page and hands it to Frank Begbie. The address seems familiar.

It takes Franco over an hour to get to Gorgie, through the heavy traffic. Then he is astonished to find himself knocking on the door of a second-floor flat off Gorgie Road, in the same street and the next stair to the one where Sean met his end. Fallon had been easy to intimidate. He'd thought this would be the case as soon as he'd seen the obese, watery-eyed man. He isn't sure that the same tactics will yield such impressive results with this Arbie guy, whoever he is.

A second heavy knock, and a white-haired man with a beard answers the door. With his porridge-coloured, fibrous skin, he looks like a prison fixture. Franco can't place the name or the face, but Arbie looks like he has some recognition of him. — Aye?

— Hi, Arbie.

— Dae I know you? Arbie's face contorts in a threatening sneer.

Franco's own features remain glacial. — Do you know who your family are?

— Aye . . . Arbie says hesitantly.

A familiar scenario unfolds for Frank Begbie. It's the type of dominance he has always found seductive; the way he feels himself drawing the power and certainty out of other hard men. Something in his core blazes in affirmation. But it's important not to succumb to this emotion. Not to raise your voice. Psychotherapists had trained him, not to eliminate this mindset – as he'd led many of them to believe – but simply to channel it. *One . . . two . . . three . . .* He breathes in steadily through his nose. — Do you know who your good mates are?

— Aye . . . bit . . .

— Well, you'll ken I'm no one, so if you do know me, we're no gaunny be close, Franco says, watching the man's resistance crumble. — I want tae know about Sean Begbie.

Arbie looks over his shoulder into the stair. — You'd best come in then.

Unless he was in a blind rage, Frank Begbie usually picked on bullies. Not because he was some kind of protector or avenger. In fact he hated the sappy cunts who never stood up to them more than he hated the oppressors themselves. He recalls one occasion, when after battering a tormentor, the excitement of the victim indicated he believed that Begbie's violence was undertaken on his behalf, or for some abstract notion of justice. So Begbie then rammed the nut on the biscuit-erse, in order to ensure he knew that the brutality had been purely for his own satisfaction. That he just preferred to ferociously assault tyrants because *it changed them more*. In his eyes, the sap was already defeated by terror, so there was no real buzz in smashing them. But seeing the bully's confidence and power evaporate, and bearing witness to that change: that was unfailingly enjoyable.

He is feeling this now with Arbie.

Agnes Duncan has a decent hand in her game of trumps with Rita Reilly and Mary Henderson, but she throws it in, having grown bored and exasperated with the activity. This

142

is a condition repeated card games tend to induce in her. Instead, Agnes opts to resume her knitting. She is sure she had left six needles out, but there are only five. Your memory did that when you got older, it played those annoying pranks on you.

21

THE OLD ACCOMPLICE

Franco had a fruitful conversation with Arbie, and then headed to the boxing club. He completed a series of lunges, squats, burpees and push-ups, staple fare from the days in his cell, then undertook some punishing routines on the medicine ball which he knew he would feel tomorrow. Then he climbed into the ring for three rounds on the pads with Mickey. After that, he pummelled the bags for another six cathartic rounds.

Some of the boys said people were looking for him. *People* being Anton Miller. So he was going to let himself be found. He'd heard enough about Miller, the guns, the drive-by shootings, to believe that if the young gangster really wanted him dead, he would probably already have joined his firstborn. It was time to meet Anton.

He walks into a watering hole in Canonmills, well known to a certain crowd, but usually avoided by the general public. It is an understated pub, hidden down a cobbled side street, and one which several generations of Edinburgh villains have drifted in and out of over the years. It is still early afternoon and the place is deserted, save for two older men playing dominoes for coins, and a barmaid in her early twenties. She gives him a soda water and lime, refusing to charge for it, but he leaves a pound on the bar anyway.

The pub TV features the bland, posh, public-relations man, who has been re-elected. He talks in a conciliatory manner, of one nation, while planning massive cuts in public services for the poor, repealing the Human Rights Act, and bringing back fox hunting for the rich. People were deferential to power. You just had to make the right noises.

He nods to the older guys. They have the tight, studiously neutral, seen-it-all faces of retired cons, and Franco definitely knows one, but can only place the eyes in his generic aged countenance. He winks and gives them the thumbs-up, receiving a similar response back.

Sure enough, a familiar figure with an almost bow-legged gait struts into the bar. Nelly hadn't even spoken to him at the funeral, but he'd intervened to eject Cha Morrison. Now he is sitting next to Franco on the neighbouring bar stool. He is bigger and heavier than before, Frank Begbie can see that in the mirror, as his old friend removes his leather jacket. A steroid-munching, iron-pumping pit-bull terrier of a man. — Franco.

— Thanks for coming tae the funeral. Frank Begbie turns to face his seasoned comrade. — Sorry I had tae abscond early before we had a chance to chat. And thanks for getting rid of Morrison. Water off a duck's back tae me, but it upset some ay the family.

— He's aw mooth. Eywis wis.

Franco isn't interested in discussing Cha Morrison, or much else with Nelly. It's Anton he wants to meet. — Listen, mate, it's good tae see ye n aw that, but ah'm no really in the mood tae socialise.

— Neither am ah, Nelly grimly replies. — Tyrone wants tae see ye, Frank.

— Aw aye?

— We kin dae this the easy wey or the hard wey. Nelly stands up, rippling with muscle, as the barmaid takes a couple of discreet steps back towards the till.

— Tell ye what, Frank Begbie says, raising his hands in a surrender gesture, — lit's dae it the easy wey, ah'm way past the cowboy stuff these days. Besides, he laughs, squeezing Nelly's biceps, — ah dinnae really fancy ma chances. Lookin good, buddy boy!

— Top man, Nelly grins. — Aye, ah've been takin care ay masel. He flushes with pride. — You n aw, he says with an appreciative once-over at Franco. — Nae hurry though, and he looks at the barmaid and orders a pint of lager. – You no drinkin?

— Sacked the peeve a while back. Helps ye tae see things a bit mair clearly, Franco smiles, then nods in the direction of the toilets. — Back in a minute, got tae get a pish.

— Nae sneakin away, Nelly chides.

— Ye'd only find me, Franco chuckles, pointing at him.

— Count on it.

Franco heads off to the toilet. He drains his bladder and thinks about the old days with Nelly. They'd always had a rivalry, sometimes friendly, sometimes not so, since they were boys back in Leith. Then, after that, even working together as enforcers for Tyrone hadn't quelled the competitiveness between them. Well, he was now out of that scene. That field was all Nelly's.

At the bar Nelly is settling into his pint of Stella, enjoying the first couple of cold swallows. Something stings his back, like an insect bite. It burns deeper and then he can see the terror in the eyes of the barmaid in front of him. He tries to rise, but an arm has locked round his neck, and the pain grows more intense, ripping into the core of him. As the grip relaxes, Nelly's head swims and he crashes to the floor, his blood oozing onto the tiles.

Frank Begbie pulls out the bloodied knitting needle, with its sharpened point. — Changed my mind, he sneers at the prostrate, bleeding figure. — Let's dae it the hard wey.

He looks to the terrified girl behind the bar. — Phone the ambulance, no the polis. Hurry, cause ah spiked his liver, he says, thinking about how easy precision made things. It astonishes him just how much of an amateur (albeit a highly enthusiastic one) he'd been in his previous life, getting through on sheer aggression rather than calculated design.

Then Frank Begbie waves a fifty-pound note in front of the two old guys and winks, placing it in the pocket of the more familiar of them. — Right, Franco, the old villain says cheerfully, as if he'd just purchased a few sweep tickets.

Yes, he wanted to be found, but not by Tyrone, and he glances at Nelly, now semi-conscious and groaning at his feet. — *Adios, amigo*, he says, then quickly steals out the door and heads down the cold, grey street.

22

THE SELF-CONTROL

After dropping off Melanie, Grace and Eve that morning, Jim had driven straight back to the beach. He had Guns n' Roses *Appetite for Destruction* on the car stereo, preferring it to Mahler. Their truck was parked in the same spot, and he pulled up about twenty yards to the rear of it. It was unoccupied. Then, scanning down the shoreline from behind the stone-built observation deck, he spied them, down on the still-deserted beach. They were heading away from him, towards the rocky promontory of Goleta Point. Instead of immediately following them, he headed back to their beat-up Silverado pickup truck. He took the Alaskan Alpha Wolf hunting knife from his denim jacket, stuck it in his belt, then removed the garment and rolled it round his hand, smashing through the truck's side window.

As the glass shattered, he looked over at the cluster of buildings, only about fifty yards away. Melanie had told him that they housed the university's marine biology facility. But it was Independence Day weekend and they were empty, with no vehicles parked outside. He let himself into the truck. It was full of junk; old wrappings, empty cans of beer and soda. But in the glove compartment there was a handgun. Jim thought that he knew little about firearms, had only once held one in his hand, but realised from his prison training in the library's True Crime section that it was a Glock semi-automatic. It was lighter than he thought. He pulled out the magazine. It was loaded with eight bullets. He pointed it at the dashboard, pulled back the safety catch. Then he placed the gun in his jacket pocket, also putting the knife back in with it.

The leg, that wrecked limb that hadn't healed right, not since the accident when he'd been hit by the car, storming after Mark Renton, held him up as he stole along the clifftop towards the rocks at Goleta Point. By approaching them from above and behind, he'd be able to ensure that the coast was clear of both beachcombers and solitary student stragglers before he engaged. Timing was all. They had turned the corner around the stony headland, and the tide was coming in quickly. Jim walked faster; it seemed that the fleeter he got, the less he noticed the leg. From his vantage point on the cliff above he tracked them moving between two of the bigger rocks at the end of the jagged peninsula, which reached out to the Pacific Ocean like a small, broken quay. It provided perfect cover, shielding them from any eyes above, as the sea swirled in.

He hurried down the beach and along the top of the rocks, until he was standing over them. Jim quickly glanced back above him to the cliffs, then down the beach towards Devereux Slough; all clear, and then his attention was fully on the men, as he stepped forward into their view. They were preoccupied as the blond one had a crab on his knife; he had stabbed it through the shell and it wriggled in its death throes. It looked like a red rock crab, with its brick-coloured top and rusty blotchings on the white underside. He'd taken to identifying the different types of marine life on these trips with the kids. — Think it knows it's going to die? He pointed at the crab.

The two men looked up as one, saw him standing over them on the large rock. Took a step back as Jim jumped down, landing in front of them on the soft sand.

— What the fuck? said the smaller, blond man, Damien Coover. — Look, we don't want no trouble . . .

Jim Francis pulled out the gun. — Too fucking late for that, and he lurched forward and squeezed the trigger. A shot rang out, then a crack, the gulls taking to squawking flight, as Coover toppled over, tumbling to the rocks and sand. He screamed out in agony, against the sound of the sea, the waves dashing on the rocks. Jim gazed out across the ocean; no boats, just Holly, the oil platform, way out on the horizon to his right. The other man, Marcello Santiago, was moving back against the huge black rock face, as the tide swarmed around his shins. — C'mon, man . . . look . . .

Jim ignored him, glancing briefly behind him, still all clear, then back to the men. Coover was moaning softly, clutching his leg. Jim saw he had managed to shoot him above the kneecap. Blood seeped through denim, onto rock and into sand and salt water.

— Never shot anybody before, Jim Francis said. — It's as I thought it would be. No pleasure in it. A fucking shiteing cunt's weapon. He shook his head, looking at Coover in abject disappointment.

— My fuckin leg . . . Coover groaned at Santiago, who kept his eyes on Jim.

Jim pulled the knife out of the crab. Placed the creature on a flat rock, and crushed it under the heel of his boot. Santiago continued to look at him in confusion, trying to evaluate how this might play out.

— Sport, Jim said, reading his thoughts. He placed the gun on top of the rock, by the wreckage of the crab. He looked at the smooth long blade of the knife. — Nice, he said, then took his own weapon from his pocket. — Mine is an Alaskan Alpha Wolf. No quite as long a blade as your boy, but it's got a great grip on the handle, and that convex edge reduces drag. Let's do this, and he threw Santiago's knife onto the sand in front of him, compelling him to move forward.

— No, man, wait –

But Jim was bearing down towards him. Santiago fought through his fear and grabbed the weapon, lifting his head as Jim swept upwards in a blow, opening up his face at the jawline, skin flapping on bone. Santiago swiped at him, but unbalanced himself and Jim barged into him, knocking him over, jumping on him, sinking the blade into his thigh and his teeth into his adversary's wrist, as blood spurted from two limbs and Santiago dropped his knife. With the Alpha Wolf stuck in the man's thigh bone, Jim seized the free weapon and smashed it into his combatant's throat. More blood shot into the air, then Jim's second stab thrust the blade through the man's skull. He had to stand on Santiago's head to try and retrieve the knife for a planned third strike. Again, it wouldn't come, and he turned to see Coover hopping across

151

the rocks, making towards the gun, and he was over in pursuit. — Gimpy's comin . . . he leered, as he gained on his prey. Crouching, without breaking his stride, he picked up a rock and smashed it over the back of Coover's head.

Damien Coover fell prone onto the flat stones, dazed, but managing to roll around, holding up his hands as Jim straddled him, the rock raised.

— Please don't . . . he begged, eyes half shut, waiting for the next blow.

— When you hurt some cunt, Jim said, his face set in a grave scowl, nodding at the still figure of Santiago, who was bleeding into the sand, — it's your duty to enjoy it. Otherwise, you've done it for fuck all. It means nothing.

— Please . . .

The rock came crashing down onto the bridge of Coover's nose, shattering it in a crack of bone and an explosion of blood. Coover let out a high-pitched yelp, followed by a long, sad whine.

— Would you have enjoyed hurting my wife and kids? Jim asked, looking above him, up to the top of the small cliff, then glancing to his left, down the beach. — What would you have done tae them? Tell me!

— No, we were . . . we were . . .

— You were nothing, Jim said coldly, bringing the rock down on Coover's head with another crack. — WHAT DAE YE FUCKIN SAY, YA BAM?!

— No . . . Coover groaned.

— WHAT DAE YE FUCKIN SAY?!

— Please, no . . .

He whispered in Coover's ear: — Begbie's my name, then he sat up, and roared out to Coover, but above his head, as if addressing the ocean, those crashing waves: — FRANK BEGBIE!! He looked back at Coover. — SAY MA FUCKIN NAME! FRANK BEGBIE!!!

— Frank . . . Frank . . .

— FUCKIN SAY IT RIGHT! FRANK BEGBIE!

— Frank Begbie . . .

He knew it was stupid and could prove costly, but he let himself get lost. It took many blows before he was convinced the man was gone, mashing the bones in his face, obliterating him. It felt so different to when he was fourteen, the very first time, when that one effort had been so decisive. But back then there had been no pleasure in that act, no release, only fear and a sense of mercy which was presently beyond him.

He stood over the pulped face, let his breathing normalise. The rage had been a beautiful treat, but it was self-indulgent, and no good at all to him now. He glanced down the beach, then out to sea. Nothing, bar Holly, looking like a black armchair out where the squally grey-blue sky met the choppy brine. Not even a distant boat. Then a solitary plane thundered above on its descent, heading for the nearby local airport, which lay on the other side of the university. The irony was that if he were to be discovered now, it would most likely be by a lone student, somebody who had stayed behind from the Fourth of July Independence Day celebrations, and who would have possibly ended up raped or murdered, if he hadn't removed the threats. But there was no one. If he believed in all that shit, he reflected, he would have suspected a higher power was working with him. But the only power guiding him, Jim realised, was Frank Begbie. And now he had to get rid of him.

Jim felt moved to address the pulped head of the corpse. — Ken what I thought, he said, looking down the empty beach. — You know what I thought, he corrected himself. — It would be great if some other cunt had been with youse. Two wisnae enough.

Begbie was proving hard to shrug off.

Then Jim stood up and stripped down to his underpants, laying his garments in a neat pile. He hauled first Coover, then Santiago, out by the edge of the jagged rock formation. Almost instantly, he got the knife out of Santiago's skull by twisting it, but it took an agonising thirty seconds or so before he was was able to rip the Alpha Wolf free from the man's thigh. Then he removed both men's clothes, stacking them in a separate pile to his own. The inlet between the two big rocks would provide decisive cover, though what he was about to do next was the riskiest part. Jim climbed back up onto the flat rocks and looked down over the sandy beach, first left, then right. Still eerily deserted, not even a solitary beach-comber. He could see beyond it, to the edge of the town. Jim turned out to sea. Way, way out on the horizon, there was a boat, but he was lucky. It was heading in the other direction, and he watched it melt into the reverberating cloud and shimmering sea.

Jim took the heavier man, Santiago, out to sea first, dragging him, relieved when the incoming tide took him up with its buoyancy, almost grabbing the body like a helping pair of hands. The water was cold, and he felt the air being squeezed from his lungs. He remembered the breathing. *Steady.* By breathing properly you couldn't conquer any adversary, but you bought time. You gave yourself a better chance. He swam, pulling Santiago, for what felt like a long distance, but in reality couldn't have been more than twenty yards out before letting him go. He watched the body float off.

When he returned to do the same for Coover, he was tired and the current was stronger, with the waves hitting his face in provocative slaps, so he dared not go so far out. To his surprise, he heard a faint moaning from the man in his arms; Coover was still alive. This wouldn't be the case for long. — Shh . . . he said, as tenderly as a mother would to an infant, holding him under the water, watching bubbles from his crushed nose and mouth rise to the surface. After letting Coover go, he swam back and put his clothes on over his wet body, then bundled up the dead men's apparel. The beach was still deserted. In the distance, towards Santa Barbara, he could see a group of people, probably young, by the way they moved, heading down the sands. He ducked into a winding trail, onto the clifftop, where he gathered his breath and looked out to sea. The tide would have carried the bodies away.

Jim rummaged through the bundle of clothes in his lap, pulled out two wallets, one a decent leather accessory, the other a cheap affair. That was the one with the cash, around three hundred dollars, which he pocketed, along with a novelty cigarette lighter emblazoned with L FUCKING A. He examined the ID, thinking of the movie *The Exorcist* as he

155

read the name DAMIEN COOVER, waiting till he heard the group of youths pass, three boys, three girls, before scrambling down through shrub and walking along by the side of the lagoon.

When he got to the vehicles, he placed the clothes in the Silverado, soaking them and it with gasoline from the spare can in the trunk of his Grand Cherokee, before chucking in the lighter.

He got into his truck, pulled off, and was almost on the road that headed to the freeway before he heard the petrol tank of the other vehicle explode, in a strangely hollow, petulant gasp. It would probably register more dramatically with the students on the beach, but by the time they scrambled up to investigate, he would be well gone.

23

THE AGENT

Leaving the Canonmills pub, and his old friend and colleague bleeding heavily on its floor, Franco jumps on a passing number 8 bus. At the east end of Princes Street, he alights and switches to a tram, heading west to Murrayfield.

Sinking into the padded seat, he appreciates the sleek vehicle's smooth glide along the track. Franco rests his head against the window and concentrates on his breathing. Soon he is in a semi-daydream, thinking again about his schooldays. He remembers saying to Renton, as they sat on the wall by the steps outside Leith Town Hall, that he wasn't taking it. His friend obviously thought he meant the belt, but his concern was more general. He recalls Bobby Halcrow, another troubled dyslexic reader, and a victim of the bullies; a nervous, shambling, fearful figure in the corner of the playground, too scared to make eye contact with anybody. Bobby took it from them all: the laughter, the scorn, the abuse, the humiliation. In his mind's eye, Frank Begbie sees Phillip McDougal, a persistent tormentor, with his gang surrounding Bobby in the playground. — What's yir name? Say yir name.

Gentle Bobby Halcrow, blinking fearfully, his Adam's apple bobbing up and down. — Baw-baw-baw . . .

— That's yir baws, McDougal said, raising his knee sharply into Halcrow's groin. As the terrified boy jackknifed to sycophantic guffaws, McDougal turned to see Francis Begbie staring at him.

— Whae are you fuckin lookin at, daftie? Phillip McDougal shouted, as his cohorts snickered. — You want yir erse kicked tae?

Franco remained silent, but maintained his stare. The voice came from another quarter. — Fuckin beat it, ya mongol, Mark Renton said. Renton was one of those kids who wasn't known as hard, but he had an older brother who was, a factor he ruthlessly milked.

— And you're gaunny make ays, like, Renton? McDougal challenged.

— Mibbe, Renton said, with less confidence.

McDougal moved forward, obviously ready to punch the skinny Renton out and take his chances with the big brother, when Francis Begbie said to him, — A square go. You're gaunny die.

McDougal looked incredulously at Begbie. Before, Frank Begbie might have lowered his gaze to his feet. Now he was holding an even stare. In his mind's eye: a vision of a house brick smashing repeatedly over McDougal's head. Then the bell was ringing. — Eftir school, McDougal hissed. — We'll see whae's fuckin deid then, and he headed off, laughing with his mates, making wanker signs at Begbie and Renton.

— Ye really gaunny fight um? Renton asked, in the excited awe of somebody who realises they'd just got a massive reprieve.

Frank Begbie shook his head. — Nup. Ah'm gaunny fuckin kill um.

Renton would normally have laughed at this, but the other week he had seen the state of Joe Begbie's face. Nobody knew what had happened, although rumours abounded. However, he perceived that something was going on with Joe's younger brother. There had been a distracted air about his friend Francis Begbie, and a brooding silence had settled on him.

In the Begbie household, Franco had once again been getting it from Joe. After a while, he realised, pain was nothing. It was just there. He'd actually begun to enjoy it, simply through savouring the moment he would stop it. Then he did, for good, with one violent action.

Later that day, Franco saw McDougal again, in the corridor, between classes, and the brawny boy ran a finger down his cheek in a slash simulation, pointing at him, just in case there was any ambiguity.

The hostilities were scheduled to take place after school on the Links, in the section of the park down towards the allotments, which was sheltered by trees. Franco remembers walking across the grass with Renton, and a couple of others, dwarfed by McDougal's entourage, and the onlookers who expected a one-sided annihilation. The fight commenced with Francis Begbie springing at Phillip McDougal, shocking everyone with his ferocity. They exchanged punches and boots. McDougal was bigger and stronger and vicious, but Begbie kept on coming. Then they were in a grip and McDougal had him down and was on top of him, battering him senseless. — Had enough? McDougal screamed into his bloodied face, as

159

the oohs and aws of the crowd indicated the extent of Begbie's beating.

By way of reply, some bloody gob flew into McDougal's face from Francis Begbie's burst mouth. McDougal resumed the brutal pounding until police sirens and cries of 'shoatie' filled the air, as a panda squad car pulled up on the road, and the kids quickly started to disperse.

McDougal arose, hailed as victor, but through his triumph there was a disquiet, as he looked back and saw Mark Renton help the battered but unbowed Begbie to his feet. — He's a fuckin dirty animal, McDougal protested to a cohort, as he used the sleeve of his Fair Isle sweater to wipe the bloody saliva from his face.

Frank Begbie didn't show up at school the following day, and there was talk that McDougal had hospitalised him. Feeling pleased with himself as he headed home, Phillip McDougal suddenly felt somebody jump on his back. He saw the horror on the faces of his two friends. Frank Begbie was on top of him, battering him with a half-brick. A dazed McDougal threw Begbie off, and quickly overpowered his adversary, beating him senseless again. He said to the battered, exhausted boy on the ground, — That's enough, ah'm fuckin warnin ye, but there was a fear and uncertainty in his voice that he couldn't hide.

The next day Frank Begbie, two black eyes, one barely open, marched up to McDougal in the playground at the lunchtime break. He smashed his brow into a static McDougal's nose, shattering it, the school bully's blood dripping onto the tarmac. To the shock of almost everybody present, McDougal lay down and took the humiliating, savage kicking, which he knew, even

160

at those tender years, possibly saved his life. When he was done, Begbie turned to McDougal's silent cohorts. — WHAE'S FUCKIN NEXT? he roared. None of them could look him in those slits in the bulbous purple that were his eyes, and his reading skills would never be publicly mocked again.

The tram stops to the pnuematic hiss of the doors, jolting Frank Begbie out of his daydream. When he gets to Elspeth's he calls Melanie, but it goes straight to her voicemail. He does it a second time, just so that he can hear her answering-phone voice. So tranquil and non-abrasive, so different to many of the tones he knew over here.

Elspeth had been at the shops, and returned wearing what he'd come to think of as her spoiling-for-a-fight expression. This involved her scraping her top teeth against her bottom lip, and narrowing her eyes. She'd done that since she was a child; a domineering, self-centred force that neither he nor Joe had been quite able to work out how to deal with, when, as young boys, she'd come into their lives. Franco is thus relieved when a call with a USA number manifests on his Tesco phone. Reasoning that it could be something to do with Melanie or the kids, he picks up.

— Jim, it's Martin. Mel gave me this number.

Franco feels a crashing despondency on hearing his agent's voice. — Right. Hi, he says, heading through to his room, looking out the window.

— Couldn't get you on the other line. Haven't been enjoying a whole heap of luck with this one. Mel said there's been problems with it.

— Aye, Franco concedes, — it's not the best of phones.

161

— How are things in Edinboro?

— Good, he says, instantly feeling an ironic smile twist on his lips. — Got a new tram system, what we'd call light rail in America. Very impressive, he declares, as, from behind the net curtains, he watches his nephews enter the house.

— Great . . . Look, I'm sorry to harass you, but I need to know when you're due back.

— Soon.

Martin lets out a sigh of exasperation at the meagre information proferred by his client. — We've still got a couple of loose ends to tie up. I really need you back here by next week at the latest.

— Just tying up some loose ends myself, Franco says, switching to a transatlantic accent, as he looks outside, to see Greg, who greets him with a wave, coming down the path. — How are things going your end?

— Rod Stewart can't make it, unfortunately. I think he's on tour.

— Too bad, Franco muses, thinking about the Rod Stewart song 'Young Turks' and how it brings Anton Miller to mind, as he leaves the bedroom and starts to move back into the lounge. He has a vision of Miller as a squat, chunky, wise-cracking wee guy, perhaps with a bow-legged gunfighter walk like Nelly's.

— But Nicole wants a bust of Tom, with a very specific mutilation, strictly confidential. Martin sounds breezy. — And Aniston's people want to know when the Angelina will be ready.

— No word from the Axl Rose boy out of Guns n' Roses? Franco asks, as he gets into the front room. He tips George

162

a wink, which Elpseth registers with as much dismay as her son's reciprocal glee.

— Haven't heard from Axl's people . . . I'll chase them up.

— Sound. I can't see myself being here much longer, a few days at the most, he says, looking at Elspeth's tightening face. Maybe it was time to fuck off to a hotel. To tell Elspeth: good luck to you if you've found a nice wee shelter to hide from the chaos and pain the world dishes out. Just don't pretend that it isn't happening to others. And don't kid yourself on that it won't happen to you. But now is not the time. The boys are sitting in front of the TV. Greg has settled down on the settee with a book he's reading about women who had been kidnapped by the Mexican drug cartels. Martin's soft voice on the phone, trying to pin down exactly what a *few* days means. — It means a few days, he says emphatically. — I'll get back to you if that changes.

— Right. Martin's tones dip in weary concession. — Much obliged, Jim.

— Great, cheers, Martin.

Franco clicks the phone off and is preparing for his sister to unload, glad that Greg and the boys are present. This means that any attack will be limited to barbed asides. Then there is a shattering explosion, as the front window caves in, glass flying all over the room. A shard flies into George's arm, drawing blood which spills onto the shagpile. Greg drops his book as Elspeth screams.

It is all but drowned out by a roar from outside. — YOU'RE FUCKIN DEID, BEGBIE!!

163

Franco runs straight for the door, aware of the leg holding him back, like it was stuck in treacle. Once he gets going, he can't feel it, but it has cut his acceleration. *Fuckin Renton. Fuckin radge.*

He gets out into the small front garden, to see three youths in the street. One he vaguely recognises from the funeral. Leaping over the small wall and striding towards them, he knows by their stock 'come on' gesticulations that they don't intend to engage with him. This is another set-up, and the play soon comes into his peripheral vision on the right-hand side, in the form of two guys who get out of a car.

They aren't the youthful men he expects: probably mid-thirties, seasoned bouncer types. Ignoring the younger lads, he walks slowly towards them. One of them, heavily muscled in a blue T-shirt, but with thin legs, shouts, — Miller wants tae see ye!

There is plenty about this that isn't sitting right with Frank Begbie. It is important to breathe steadily, even as he coldly visualises deep lacerations on the faces of the men. — Aye? Miller? Franco laughs. — Ye mean Tyrone!

The two men look at each other. They haven't anticipated this.

— Is that the best Tyrone can dae these days? He looks them up and down in disdain, envisioning the stomping, raking heel that will destroy the thin-legged man's kneecap, leaving him sprawled helpless on the pavement. — Two muppets whae probably work the door at Baby Busters? Cannae git staff, right enough, he bellows.

— We dinnae ken any Tyrone, Thin Legs feebly protests.

— So youse boys are gaunny take ays tae Miller then?

The two bouncers look at each other, as if in realisation that this is no longer such a good idea. Thin Legs is particularly nervous, one eye visibly twitching. — Aye . . . you've to come wi us . . .

Frank Begbie cracks a smile. — What happens if ah dinnae come?

— Wir giein ye a message that if ye dinnae come thaire's gaunny be trouble . . .

— Well, here's a wee message fae me tae yir boss: he's a fat, baldy cunt. Does that sound like Anton Miller? Franco steps forward, as sirens rip through the air. — Saved by the bell. Youse, obviously, he scoffs as the two men back away and climb into the car, hastily driving off.

Franco looks around for the three younger guys. That they'd fled does not surprise him.

The main cop, a veteran whom Franco recognises as a career cunt who would never get out of uniform and would probably never fully understand why, takes statements from Elspeth and Greg. Then he interviews Franco, who tells him nothing, other than he was on the phone when a brick came through the window, and went out to investigate.

When he's done, the old cop fixes him a chopsy smile. — I know what you're really like, you might be able to fool them . . .

Franco dismissively waves him away with a backward sweep of the hand, imitating the cop's own expression and tone. — Aw, is that so? You know, everybody gies me the same speech: cops, family, friends, reporters, villains. And the weird

165

thing is that they aw think they're blessed wi this unique insight in making that very same observation. He watches the cop's features slacken. — That can mean two things: either they're probably right, or they're fuckin simpletons.

The veteran cop's face reignites in a defiant sneer. — Aw aye, is that so? What do you think it is?

— I think one doesn't have tae exclude the other.

The cop looks disparagingly at him. Franco can tell that he feels short-changed. They'd dashed out to Murrayfield, expecting to protect suburbanites, only to be cheated by stumbling on a nest of Begbies infesting the place. They don't stick around for long.

Elspeth calling them was understandable in the circumstances. However, as she is a Begbie from Leith, Franco is wrong-footed by the deep sense of betrayal he feels burn him. You'd think that George had been decapitated from the fuss they're making. He looks across at his pouting, bandaged nephew with a smile. — Cut masel shavin worse, he states, instantly realising, from Elspeth's expression, that it is the wrong gambit.

— WE'VE BEEN ATTACKED, VIOLATED IN OUR AIN HOUSE, BECAUSE AY YOU, AND YOU'VE GOT THE NERVE TO COME OUT WI FLIPPANT REMARKS!

— They were just kids. If they'd wanted to send heavies doon –

— No, *these* are just kids, and she points to Thomas and George. — Get out! GET THE FUCK OUT OF OUR HOME!

— I was going tae suggest ah left, Franco agrees. — I don't want you getting caught up in this.

166

— A bit bloody late for that!

— Sweetheart . . . Greg coos, placing an arm around his wife's shoulders.

Franco retrieves the Tesco phone from his pocket and dials Larry. — I'll sort something oot now, he nods to them, as he walks outside through the French windows into the garden. Larry won't be pleased, as with the van, but he extended the invite, and he has a spare room.

After a few rings, Larry picks up. — Of course, Franco, anything for an auld mucker, he sings down the line. — You git packin n ah'll swing by n pick ye up pronto.

Franco feels the overwhelming whiff of performance, yet expresses gratitude and moves back inside. — Sorted, he says. — Larry's comin tae pick ays up.

— Sorry it's come to this, Frank, Greg mutters sadly. — Enjoyed having you around. But the kids . . .

— Totally understand, Franco replies. It feels inadequate, but it's all he can stretch to. He goes to his room and gathers up his belongings. He calls Melanie on the Tesco mobile. Nothing at all. Maybe he needs to put even more credit on it. He doesn't want to ask Elspeth if he can use her phone. He'll wait till he gets to Larry's.

Larry is as good as his word, arriving within the half-hour. The shifty-eyed, jittery-looking emergency glazier is already replacing the window, his presence enforcing a strained civility.

Elspeth, who had studiously avoided him at the funeral, blushes a little at Larry's presence, as she follows Frank outside. In her teens she had nursed a devastating crush on

167

her brother's friend, and had once made a drunken pass at him. Larry shoots her a crocodile grin, indicating that he remembers the occasion only too well. — Elspeth . . . been a long time, doll, he says, as Franco puts his red case into the back of the white van. — Nice house. He surveys the home, hands on hips. — Very you.

Gazing from him to the van, Elspeth retorts, — Nice van. Very you.

Larry bursts out his most appreciative touché smile.

Greg has joined them outside, and is still half-apologising to Franco. — Really sorry we have to part this way. Good luck.

What the fuck does this cunt want fae me? Franco gives him a stony nod of acknowledgement. Yet when he turns to his baleful-looking sister, an uncharacteristic word slips from him. — Sorry . . .

The uniqueness, to say nothing of the obvious heartfelt nature of the apology, seems to shake them both. They look at each other in blank stasis.

— Right! Fit for action? Larry grins, breaking the silence.

Franco is relieved to climb into Larry's van, and doesn't look back as it tears down the street.

They aren't gone long when DI Ally Notman arrives at Elspeth's to investigate. It is immediately clear to her that he isn't concerned with the window, obviously tipped off by colleagues that Frank was staying in the house. — He's not here any longer, Elspeth informs him. She's done with cops, and isn't for asking him in.

Notman stands on the front step, regarding the formidable cross-armed force in the doorway. — You say your brother went away with Larry Wylie?

— It's Frank who was attacked! Elspeth's loyalty both shocks and confuses her.

— You know, I can believe it, Notman says. —When the old neighbourhood psychopath is the good guy, then the city really does have problems.

— I'm sorry, Elspeth retorts in pompous authority, now embracing the role she's been strangely cast in, — but you *do not know* my brother. He's worked hard to turn his life around and make a go of things, but some people won't let him be!

Greg can scarcely believe what he's hearing.

— Your brother, Notman begins, — has been a running sore on this city –

— Get away fae here! Elspeth cuts him off, her face contorted in rage, to the extent that Notman stands back off the doorstep. — My nephew was murdered, and what have youse done about it? Nowt! Just go. She points to his car, parked in the street.

— Look, Notman adopts a reasoned tone, — I don't want to –

— You've got aw that DNA stuff, Elspeth hisses, looking him up and down in contempt, — you must have a forensic team tae gather the information and match it against your records!

— That's right, Greg, who has materialised at his wife's shoulder, sings, — we're not asking for the world, officer.

— When I hear a member of the public use the term 'DNA' I squirm inside. Notman shakes his head contemptuously at them. — Everybody that's watched a *CSI: Miami* is now an expert in polis work. It isnae like that –

— What's it like then? Elspeth's chin juts out, as Bill and Stella Maitland, the next-door neighbours, appear, lingering in support. — What you're saying is you're no going to tell us who was there by the physical evidence, or who you've hauled in for questioning, if anybody, or if ye found the knife or murder weapon. That you're gaunny dae nowt! Well, our Frank'll find oot whae did this!

— That would be a big mistake on his part, Notman says, turning and heading to his car.

Greg swallows hard, and says to his wife, — Frank would be proud of you.

It's the wrong thing to say. As it sinks home, Elpseth bursts into angry, frustrated tears, to be comforted by the advancing Stella, who leads her into the house.

24

THE DANCE PARTNER 3

Melanie was surprised to see Martin, Jim's agent, who had driven up yesterday evening from LA. He was desperate to get in touch with her incommunicado husband. She issued him with the UK number, with a warning about inherent transmission difficulties, citing her own fruitless attempts to contact Jim. — Sometimes it works, she told him over coffee.

— There's another reason I came, Martin confessed. — I had a visit from a cop, a detective in the Santa Barbara PD, name of Harry Pallister, he said, not stalling on her reaction. — He told me he was investigating a complaint you made about a couple of guys harassing you on the beach. He asked about Jim. I didn't like his tone, so I challenged him, and asked him if Jim was a suspect in anything. He said no. Then he was on his way. Something about all this just didn't quite sit right, so I thought you should know.

Melanie expressed her gratitude to Martin, telling him as much as she felt able, which was just about everything she knew. He appreciated her candour, offering any assistance he could, and then left to head back to Los Angeles.

She is therefore expecting another visit from Harry, yet when it comes, it still causes real discomfort. She has only just got Grace and Eve strapped into the car, when he arrives. Melanie knows that her skittish, distracted behaviour has been noticed by her daughters. It has taken them much longer to get ready than usual. The girls have been acting up, and Eve has bitten Grace's finger. It isn't acceptable, but her older daughter is determined to make an issue of it. They have just settled down, when Harry pulls up, with that suffering expression on his face. He is out the car and asking her, — Mel . . . sorry to trouble you, just wondered if anything else had popped into your head about those guys?

So Melanie moves out of the kids' earshot, away from the driveway, up onto the stoop, compelling him to follow. — Nothing that I haven't already mentioned, she says stiffly. Martin's news from last night has put her on edge. She hasn't talked to Frank properly for a couple of days; the time differences and this awful phone he bought have made it awkward. Now Harry's limpet-like presence, with the same insinuating tones, going over old ground. Here, on her front porch, and so early in the morning.

— When you came back, you're sure Jim was with you?

— Where else would he be? Melanie says brusquely. Harry looks heavy-eyed, still focused, but as if at the cost of great mental effort. There is a whiff on his breath. Alcohol. For a second she considers confronting him about his visit to Jim's agent in LA, but decides against this. It's preferable that he remains unaware of her knowledge of this line of enquiry. She recalls Jim's – or Frank's – mantra regarding the cops: *tell them fuck all*.

Harry nods slowly, cagily taking a step back, as if under-standing that he's overstepped the mark. He is a policeman first and foremost, and he hasn't mentioned the burnt-out car. Jim was right; a cop couldn't be trusted socially with people, in the same way an alcoholic couldn't be around a cabinet full of liquor. He would always have to open it up, to see what was inside. Now it seems like he already has. What sort of cop stank of alcohol at this hour of the morning? And on some deep psychological level (which is now starting to openly manifest) Melanie knows that Harry wants to replace Jim, which first means having Jim out of the way. Melanie realises she has made a decision there and then: Harry cannot be allowed to break up this family.

The cop has embarked on a game of silence, which she is in no mood to play.

— I really have to get the girls off, she states. Melanie now knows that she isn't taking them to the school and kindergarten, but she's not going to tell Harry that.

— Of course . . . but, Melanie, you know you can talk to me, Harry says earnestly. His words are slurring a little and she can see, in the sunlight, the puffiness around his eyes and cheeks. — Off the record. As a friend.

— Right, she nods.

— You do have friends, Melanie. People who care about you . . . remember that, Harry says, leaking desperation.

— I appreciate your concern, Harry, she says blithely, almost laughing in nervous tension. The incongruity of it burns her, and she knows he isn't fooled for a second. Melanie isn't sticking around though; she heads to the car and climbs

173

in. He will need to do the same, or block her in her driveway. Whatever Jim has done, it has been for her and the girls. He'd always said that their protection was the only thing he believed in. But it went further than that. She knows that he also, on a very deep level, believes in vengeance.

Melanie is relieved to see Harry, after taking a lingering look at the car, turn away and get into his own vehicle. — What did the man want, Mommy? Grace asks.

— Nothing, honey, Melanie says, delighted to hear the sound of Harry's engine starting up, and to watch his car pull away. — Now, I got a big surprise, she announces in the same fake upbeat tone she'd used on Harry. — You guys are gonna stay at Grandma's for a few days!

The kids see through it in much the same way the sauced-up cop had. — Why? Grace asks.

— I need to go to Scotland to see Daddy. He's quite sad because his friend is very sick, she explains, starting up the car and edging into the street.

— Daddy! Will you bring him back? Eve asks.

— Of course I will! Daddy said that he had too many presents from Scotland for two special little girls. He needs me to help him carry them.

Grace is unconvinced. — Is Daddy okay?

— Of course he is.

— Are people nice to him in Scotland? Eve asks, with a frown.

— Yes, they are!

Melanie watches Eve scowl in the mirror. Her face, so like her father's, says: *they'd better be nice to my daddy, or else.*

174

She calls Jim again, but can still get nothing. Follows it with an imploring text. When she gets the girls down to her mother's, Melanie tells Jane Francis that she needs her to look after her granddaughters for a few days. She explains she really has to go to the funeral (even though it has passed) in order to support Jim. Jane loves the girls, and is delighted to do this, offering only a half-hearted interrogation in response. Then Melanie heads for LAX to get a flight to London.

When she learns she's been allocated one of the stand-by seats, Melanie relaxes, feeling in control. However, this soon turns to helpless despair as she sits in a cramped economy class, a fat man almost shoehorned in on her left, a wan, tense-faced woman on her right, and a screaming and sobbing pair of very small children in front of her. Melanie will have eleven hours of this till London. She closes her eyes, tries to blot it all out. Thinks about meeting Jim for the first time, back in the prison. That picture he had painted, *The Dance Partner*. How far they have come since then, and how it had been his idea that they joined the salsa club together.

25

THE FLAT

Unlike Elspeth's view of the van, Franco considers, the flat in Marchmont certainly isn't very Larry. This time he pauses to really take in the large, bright, bay-windowed, second-storey affair; its wooden sealed-and-sanded floors and tasteful furnishings suggest that his old friend hadn't been involved in the decoration project. — Nice gaff, Franco observes, looking at several framed pictures that give it a homely touch. They are all portraits of the same boy, ranging from a baby to around seven years old. The boy has Larry's mischievous smile, without the undercurrent of malevolence that Franco assumes might develop with age. Or perhaps not. It's obvious that there has been some judicious editing, removing all traces of the mother from the shots. That relationship hadn't ended well, he evaluates.

— Aye, it's awright, Larry agrees, picking up a computer game console, and switching on the large flat-screen TV it's hooked up to.

— Business must be good, Franco says.

Larry turns to face him, briefly looks as if he's thinking of lying, then seems to decide that the truth is more fun. — I won a million and a half quid on the lottery, he grins and, for the first time, Franco realises from his electric smile that

Larry's teeth are capped. — Never thought I'd tell any cunt, but there's a few ay them that ken. Thought you'd appreciate it. A lot ay them say 'why you?', and they go on aboot aw the things ah'm meant tae huv done.

Franco responds with a nonchalant shrug. — Ye get what ye get, no what ye deserve.

— Thoat you'd see it that wey, and Larry flashes those big, white teeth, incongrous in his weak, skinny frame. — Ah'm on borrowed time wi the cowie, but ah've pit maist ay it intae a trust for the wee man. He glances to the pictures on the sideboard and the wall.

— Sound, Franco says. — Ye still see the laddie's ma?

Larry swivels round to face him. — That fuckin hoor? She wanted ays back when she heard aboot the Lotto win. Telt her tae fuckin bolt! Said she shouldnae listen tae fuckin gossip aboot me huvin money, n any thit ah did huv, the wee man would get the lot when he was aulder. She'll see fuck all, he scoffs, his smile widening. — Telt her if she made any bother, she'd get fuckin plenty ay it back. Explained tae her that thaire wis younger birds in the picture, and he points to the storage system under the TV, which is full of DVD cases, a solitary female name on each spine. — Make ma ain scud vids, he beams, — like that Juice Terry cunt!

— Terry's a proper star these days, Franco says, — but this looks a wee bit dodgy.

— Aye, Larry agrees, but he's swiftly re-engrossed in his game, only interrupting it when his phone rings in his jacket pocket. He extracts it and heads into the kitchen. — Hi . . . Right . . .

177

Franco can barely hear Larry's low voice as he watches the images on the television. He can never see the attraction in those games. He recalls an echo of violence past, pasting a guy's face against the glass of an Asteroids machine in a Rose Street pub. That was a while back. He tries to recall why he'd done this, but nothing comes to mind. He picks up the console, as the scene changes to HIGHEST SCORES.

SFB	1338
LARRY	685
FF	593

Despite Larry's labours in working to get the highest score, he is some way behind the top shooter. SFB had to be Sean Francis Begbie.

Franco rises to the cabinet under the TV, regards the series of home-made DVDs. Scanning the girls' names on the spines, he picks up the one marked 'Frances', extracting the disc and pushing it into the hydraulic slit on the player. The image of the game is replaced by more human action.

It is badly filmed, one camera position, showing two bodies in wide shot, an unedited continuous one of Larry fucking Frances Flanagan. As he winds the action forward at speed, Franco realises that Frances seems to be drugged. He discerns this from the way she is compliantly pulled into different positions by Larry, and fastened up in bondage and a ball gag, before having certain implements inserted into her. Again, he winds on, stopping it when he sees Larry crouched behind her, the lesions visible on his chest. Franco finds it hard to be blasé about the heinous nature of this; he can't help thinking of his own daughters. Was there a possibility that they could turn out like Frances, becoming victims of men like Larry? He swallows down the bile, and switches off, removing the disc and replacing it back in the case. He wouldn't have bothered had Larry come in and found him watching this, but it's probably better that he doesn't know.

Then Larry returns to the room, only briefly registering Franco's presence at the TV, as both men sit back on the couch. Larry picks up the console again. — The auld girl, he says.

— How's she daein? Franco enquires, knowing that he's lying.

— Still nippin ma heid, so same auld, Larry says, getting back into the game. — You'll git that Anton cunt, Franco, he announces, as he shoots at an oncoming robot. — A leper never changes his spots. He's your man.

Franco isn't thinking of Anton, but his own mother, Val, or rather her funeral, which was the last occasion he was home. She was a good woman, he reflects, but her sons and husband were all Begbies, who brought her nothing but different versions of hell. He recalls how when Elspeth had phoned to inform him of her death, he'd wanted to cry, but couldn't, and how that desire had strangely been more for the benefit of Melanie, who had squeezed his hand throughout the call. Sometimes it's hard to fit in with people, he considers, looking at Larry. — Ah'm gaun oot.

Larry glances at him, then points at the DVDs. — That's some ay the birds ah've been ridin. That wee Frances n aw. Set ye up wi any ay them, if ye like.

179

— Ah'm married, Franco says.

— Nivir stoaped ye before!

— Wisnae married before.

— As good as!

— That was before, ay, and he leaves the flat, Larry's sly smile buried into his psyche.

Outside, Franco walks the grey streets, sees people heading home from their offices, or on to pubs, theatres and cinemas. The wind starts to bite and clouds loom ominously. He feels isolated, shut out by the city, and is soon bored. Where can you go in Scotland in the evening if you don't want to have a drink? He's averse to owning up, but he already misses chatting to his nephews and Greg, and, yes, even Elspeth.

He calls Melanie from the Tesco phone and it goes through, but straight to her voicemail. He should send a text, or an email, but he hates that method of communication more than any other. His dyslexia means that even now it's a laboured process, bundled with inherent frustrations. And he feels the relentless magnetism of the pub and alcohol, tugging at him like it never did when he was back in the USA. Who can he call when he experiences this pull?

26

THE DANCE PARTNER 4

The Santa Barbara Dance Center was downtown, on the corner of De La Vina and West Canon Perdido. Jim and Melanie Francis had enrolled to come along for an introductory salsa session. To their surprise, the woman they met there was familiar. She'd been with the dancing couple at the club that memorable evening; they would soon agree that Sula Romario was the sexiest person they had ever met in their lives. The athletic Ecuadorian woman, with the luxuriant tumble of dark curls, had a low, husky voice that stripped layers from your skin, while her luminous ebony eyes burrowed into your soul. Sula had looked them both over, walking around them in that small ballroom, before her pouting, dark-red lips declared, — It's good. Now we dance, and she taught first Jim, then Melanie, the basic steps on a count of eight; left foot forward, right foot back. Then she let them try it out together.

Jim had never been a dancer, but the steps were not unlike boxing ones, and he took to it quickly. Melanie loved to dance, and soon they were increasing the tempo and moving smoothly across the studio's polished wooden floor, to Sula Romario's approval. They mastered the right turn and cross-body lead so slickly that Sula decided to put them immediately into the class. — You dance well, she said to Melanie, and then turned to Jim, — but you . . . you have the fire in your soul!

— Aye, is that right? Jim smiled.

Then the lights flicker on, but Melanie keeps her eyes shut, trying to force herself back into the satisfying stew of memory and dream. It isn't working; Jim's face fades under the glow burning through her lids and she blinks awake to note that, thankfully, she's missed breakfast. The remains of a croissant are visible down the front of the fat man.

Disembarking at Terminal 5 in Heathrow, she heads to the Plane Food restaurant, orders some eggs and checks her phone. There is a call from a Santa Barbara number she doesn't recognise, and a message on her voicemail. She plays it and her blood runs cold.

— I've been drinking. I may even have a *problem*. Harry's voice is sullied by bitterness. — So now maybe I'll be *interesting* enough for you to acknowledge that *I fucking exist*. Wouldn't that be something? People like you . . . *women* like you . . . you know *nothing*. Nothing!

Melanie can feel the noise of the fork in her hand rattling involuntarily against the plate. She wants to erase the message, obliterate those dumb, sneering tones. But she doesn't, she plays it again, empowered by the fact that he has compromised himself. She calls Jim, but there's still nothing except a strange tone that's meaningless to her. Boarding the connecting flight to Edinburgh, Melanie has only a vague idea as to where Elspeth's place is, having been there with Jim several years ago, before Grace was born.

Landing at her destination, her neck and spine sore after all the flying, she finds herself almost hallucinating from the combination of jet lag, exhaustion and the curious exhilaration of being back. She had never planned to go to Edinburgh to work, it had been an exchange programme for a year between the Scottish prison service and the California correctional system. But Melanie had taken to it. Yes, the city is as cold and grey as she remembers, but it is also breathtakingly beautiful. Sitting in the taxi, listening to the driver's banter, she recalls why she loved the place; the majestic vistas, the fresh air, but most of all the militant, almost paradoxically dramatic, unpretentiousness of the locals.

She has to find Frank, and curses herself for not getting the number for Elspeth, or even his exes. The mothers of his sons. It still astonishes Melanie, given the strong, warm, gentle and *exclusive* way he is with her and the girls, that there are other women with whom he had children. That he'd previously led a different, more desperate life was something she had known from them meeting in prison; this had been intellectually and emotionally absorbed. But the hardest bit is acknowledging the existence of, and dealing with, those who had shared that life.

Checking in to the familiar small hotel on Dalkeith Road, Melanie hasn't asked specifically for room 8, but that's the one she's allocated. Lying down on the bed, she recognises that this was the scene of their first time together as lovers, and memories come flooding back. This was where she and Jim went every Monday, when he was given day release from prison on the Training for Freedom project. — I could fuck you senseless, he said. — But I'd really like you to show me how to make love.

— I'm happy to do that, Melanie replied, — provided you agree that we fuck each other senseless after.

The deal was struck, and had to be honoured. It was so straightforward, because Jim couldn't have fucked her senseless. He was lost, rendered impotent in all but mind, useless among real people, like so many men who had undergone long-term prison sentences or were compulsive viewers of pornography. Melanie was patient, and in her hands his sexuality was carefully restored. It seemed to her that he was keen, even relieved, to be able to start from scratch.

But now she is here, alone. Where would she find him? It has to be Leith. The old bars. Tracers blazing behind her retina, she resolves: *I'm not going back without him.*

But she can't do anything without proper sleep.

27

THE COUPLE

The pub is in a narrow south-side backstreet, close to Holyrood Park. It has avoided the slow gentrification of the neighbourhood, still managing to feel smoky, even though no cigarettes have been burned in there since the ban many years back. Franco instantly thinks of June's lungs as he heads to the battered wooden bar and orders a drink.

Turning to scan the hostelry, he spies John Dick sat in the corner, waiting for him. Dick has a pint of Guinness in front of him, but notes with approval the glass of orange juice Franco brings to the table. — Still off the sauce, I see.

— Choose life, Franco says, sinking into the padded seating next to the prison service man.

— You've made a pretty decent yin for yourself!

A couple sitting across from them, by the dartboard and a jukebox with an OUT OF ORDER sign, are having a heated quarrel. — You ken how! the woman, squat frame, dark curly hair and pinched face, challenges.

— Thanks to you, Franco says to John, glancing over at the couple.

— Thanks to *you*, John points at him, — having the intelligence and the courage to see that the other one was going nowhere and rebuilding it. He takes a sip of his pint. Then his voice goes low in reprisal. — Now you're going to throw it all away, and for rubbish that's jail-bound anyway.

— Think so? Franco says, hearing the defiance flood into his voice, knowing that his prison mentor will perceive it as empty as he does.

— Frank, I thought that making bad decisions in life was a habit you'd got out off. John's tongue darts out to remove the foam from his top lip. — Now you're getting back in the gutter with a wee creep like Anton Miller.

Feeling himself regressing to a sullen teenager, Franco decides that it's time to get a grip. — I've never seen the boy, he explains patiently. — Wouldnae ken him if he walked in here right now.

— But you've been asking around for him. And I hear he wants to see you, John fixes him in that owl-like stare. — Why are you doing this?

— Daein what?

— Sticking around. Sean's gone, John says coolly, — There's nothing for you here. Nothing but Miller and other trouble. He looks over at the screeching couple. Knows they are on Frank Begbie's radar. — Go back home to Melanie and the kids, Frank. That's your life now.

Franco draws in a deep breath, and looks intently at John. — I dunno who you've been talking to, he calmly protests, — But the fact is that I've not asked *one single thing* about Miller. It's other people that's been dropping his name here, there and everywhere, saying that he was involved with Sean.

They are disturbed by a roar from across the bar. — CAUSE YIR FUCKIN STUPIT! YOU'VE EY BEEN FUCKIN

STUPIT! the man shouts at the woman, who seems to shrink into herself, then seethe in a silent rage.

— Whether he was or wasn't, it's not your battle. John Dick shakes Frank Begbie's wrist gently, to get his attention back from the couple. — He'll exterminate you, Frank. You're just an obstacle. He's cold-blooded, there's no ego at work there, just superpowered insect brain. It'll be a bullet in the head from a drive-by, you won't even see it.

— Cheer me up some more, Franco says, looking at his orange juice on the table. He has no intention of drinking that shite, any more than he has of taking alcohol. *Scotland? They've never fuckin seen real orange juice.*

— CHEAT!!!

They are again diverted by the warring couple. The woman has got to her feet. — YIR A FUCKIN CHEAT, JIM MULGREW! A FUCKIN TWO-FACED LIAR! She turns and appeals to the rest of the bar, including Franco and John.

The man, Jim Mulgrew, waves her away with the back of his hand. — Aye, so you say!

Frank Begbie looks away. He knows the type. Wankers, who want to suck the world into their pathetic and tedious orbit. Jakeys are always fucking drama queens. *Look at me. I'm hurting. Feel my pain.*

Naw. Fuck off.

And now John Dick, a person whom he greatly respects (and such individuals are thin on the ground), is reading him the riot act. — The only person you're damaging now is yourself. And Melanie and the kids, they're the real ones you're waging war on.

— Who said anything about a war? Franco asks, then realises that *he* did, back at the funeral. — I just want to know what happened to my son.

— War is what Anton Miller does, Frank. John lets out a long sigh. — Keep out his road.

— Sound advice.

— But?

— There is no but. It's sound advice, end of, Franco states emphatically. — John, every cunt has been nipping my heid, giving it Anton this, Anton that. He did your laddie, aw that shite. I'm no interested. He shakes his head and he looks over at the feuding couple. The woman has turned pointedly away from the man, but is still sat at the same table. He finds himself willing her: *just fuckin go*.

— Mind the boy that stole that money from you, down in London? That old pal you used to tell me about? John Dick asks. — That you were so mad when you saw him years later, you charged across the road, so consumed with rage, you never even noticed this oncoming car that smashed ye tae pieces?

Renton.

— Mark Renton. How can I forget? The guy I killed, Craig Liddel, Seeker they called him, we had a long vendetta, and it was one that I started. I got obsessed with the boy, just because he was a mate of Renton's. I thought he knew where Renton was, Franco laughs sourly, — that they would both be laughing at ays. In reality, Renton would have fuck all to do with the likes of Seeker, he'd only met him in rehab, then sometimes scored drugs offay him. I only got involved with Seeker cause of my obsession with getting Renton. It

188

was pointless. Now he's deid and I lost eight years of my life. Over nothing, he laments.

— What do you think of that Renton guy now?

Frank Begbie seems to consider this, rolls his bottom lip over his top one. — I can see it from his point of view. See that he had to get the fuck out, he acknowledges, his brow furrowed. — It's funny, but he was probably the only real mate I ever had.

John Dick runs his finger over the rim of his glass. — Do you see what your obession with getting even with him has cost ye? Something that now means nothing to you? Your obsession with *all* those people?

Now Franco is getting irritated with John's badgering. The way he challenges him constantly, like he did in prison, talking to him like nobody else ever had. *Because I see what you are,* John had once said to him. This had enraged, challenged and then ultimately helped Frank Begbie so much. Because he knew that John saw past what he had been prepared to show to the world. But then again, things change. Now maybe John Dick has become just another person in this town he needs to get away from. — Of course I do, Franco states. — If you get obsessed with losers and associate with them, ye become one ay them. That's been the point of *everything*, recognising that. My life wasted on these useless vendettas; Cha Morrison, the Sutherlands, Donnelly, Seeker . . . I'm no adding this Anton boy tae the list.

John seems satisfied with this response, and his mood becomes more playful. — So what would you dae if he walked in here right now, Renton, this old mate who ripped you off?

— Fuck knows, probably buy him a drink and tell him he owes me a few grand with twenty years' interest on it, he laughs.

John now chuckles along with him. — I watched you reprogramme yourself painstakingly, through those books you read. And I know how much of a struggle that was, with the dyslexia, and his mentor is looking at him in unbridled admiration. This always used to make Franco feel like a kid, eager to do better. He hadn't felt that way since his old Grandad Jock had taken that interest in him. It would have been good to have had somebody like John back then, instead of Jock and his mates. He might have had different options. — Don't throw all that away. Don't go back down into the black hole, Frank.

Frank Begbie considers this. — Sometimes I wonder if I've ever really left it, John.

John Dick is about to protest, when the man named Jim Mulgrew rises and punches his female associate in the face. She lets out a yelp and sits with her head in her hands. This draws gasps and cries of derision from the other drinkers. Frank Begbie remains still, looking over at Jim Mulgrew who bristles indignantly in his chair. The barman approaches the assailant. — Right, you, get the fuck ootay here!

— Ah'm gaun, Mulgrew says, rising to exit the bar.

The woman is rubbing her jaw. It hadn't been such a hard punch but there will be some swelling. There is something horrible in her eyes, alongside the fear and pain, a kind of satisfied vindication. — He'll be back, she addresses the assembled drinkers.

— No in here he'll no, and neither will you, the barman announces. — Gie him a few minutes tae git doon the road, then you're ootay here n aw.

— Ah never did nowt, what did ah dae?

— On that, time to depart, Frank Begbie says to John Dick, realising that, before, he would have got involved in this incident, to everyone's detriment. He recalls one such time when an aggressive domestic argument was taking place in a bar in Leith. He'd gone over and wrapped an arm around the shoulder of each party, pulling them towards him in a gesture of conciliation. Then he'd rammed the nut on the both of them, one after the other.

— Okay, Frank, sorry to get on your case. John Dick stretches out his hand. — I know you're going through a rough time.

Frank Begbie grabs it and shakes it. — If ye didnae gie a fuck, ye wouldnae have said anything. But don't worry, John, I'm in a good place, and he taps his head and winks at his mentor. It is important to say the right things, express the correct sentiment. A prime minister could quietly protect rich paedophiles using the Official Secrets Act provided he publicly proclaimed that he would leave no stone unturned to bring such people to justice. It was the expression of the contrary action that gave you the licence. People generally wanted to believe that you meant well; the consequences of thinking otherwise were too grim to contemplate.

— A better place than those wastes ay space. John nods over to the woman and Jim Mulgrew's empty chair.

Franco looks across at her, now muttering perceived injustices under her breath. — They should learn the salsa,

191

he ventures to John, — that whole lifestyle, it would stop them from gettin at each other's throats.

And Frank Begbie feels deeply pleased with himself as he bids John Dick farewell, almost skipping out of the bar to the van. Then, as he opens it up, he feels something hard pressing hard against his temple. Knows it to be the barrel of a gun. — Don't fucking move or I'll blow yir heid off, a voice calmly says. Then a hand reaches into his jacket pocket, removing the Tesco phone, and at the same time a hood is placed over his head. As this act shuts out the world's light, he takes a deep breath, filling his lungs like a reverse sigh.

He can see nothing, except some feet and grey flagstones, as he is pushed into the back of a vehicle. From the step and size of it, he envisions some kind of large SUV. Then he feels his seatbelt being snugly fastened across him, like he would do with Grace and Eve. Not a single glimpse of the faces of any of the men who have taken him, just the awareness that there is one on each side of him in the back seat, as the vehicle accelerates away.

28

THE DELIVERY BOY 4

It was the day after the incident with Johnnie when I next saw them. I was walking home from school and I looked in the windae of the Marksman Bar in Duke Street. There they were, through a fug of blue cigarette smoke, sitting drinking, full of cheer. It was that euphoria that always came from gloating at the suffering brought down on some rival. I sensed it in others as I grew to feel it in myself: that arrogant, showboating impulse, where you feel invincible and revel in your own power.

Grandad Jock saw me as he looked up from his pint, his snidey eyes locking onto mine. I could tell that he caught something in them. He smiled, and I was scared.

Johnnie's body was found two days later. A security guard had seen an unusually big flock of seagulls around the dry dock, fighting, squawking, attracted by the corpse. The rats had also been busy, so the identification took a while or so some locals said. A lot of cunts would probably have been delighted to envision Johnnie's handsome face eaten off by scavengers. That grinning face that would have hovered over many of their wives and girlfriends, as they moaned in pleasure beneath him.

It was in the Evening News and on Scotland Today. When Grandad Jock came round with Carmie and Lozy for the card school, I asked them about it. Jock tippled that I knew more *than I was letting on. — Good riddance tae bad rubbish, he said softly, not looking up from his hand of cards.*

— I thought Johnnie wis yir pal!

There was a silence around the table. Then my dad looked at ays with a drunkard's mean scowl. — Keep your neb oot, son. Ah'm telling ye . . . he slurred, — keep it oot ay things you ken nowt aboot!

But he was the cunt that kent nowt. My grandad raised his head and winked at me. —Naw . . . it's okay, he said to my dad, and he rose, gesturing me to follow him oot intae the hall. We went through the kitchen oot to the wee paved backcourt where the bins were. It was cold. He seemed not to feel it. He lit up a fag, gave me one.

— Mind that dug yir faither came hame wi, ages ago?

Ah minded ay Viking, the German shepherd dug ma dad brought hame one time fae the pound when he was pished. A barry dug, but he bit everybody n we hud tae get him destroyed. — Aye.

— Ye loved that dug, mind? But it bit ye. Dug couldnae help it. Eh loved ye, but eh still betrayed ye.

I nodded. Viking sank his teeth into my ankle for no reason. We'd been running in Pilrig Park and he just turned oan ays and bit me. Probably got too excited and couldnae control himself.

— Wisnae really the dug's fault. He took a big drag, blew the smoke oot into the cauld air. — Wis jist his nature. People are like that tae, boy. Thir yir friends . . . then he bared his teeth at me, — till thir no. Ye understand that, pal?

— Aye, I told him.

194

— Good. Let's get back intae the warm, and we stubbed oot our fags and returned tae the front room, him tae his game ay cairds.

But that night I did something ah'd never done before, and would vow never tae do again. I went doon tae the phone box and called the bizzies.

29

THE YOUNG WARLORD

In some ways the silence on the drive suits him. In others it's worrying, indicating that he's subject to a chilling restraint and professionalism. Power's wankers wouldn't have the discipline to maintain such a hushed silence. At the very least, they would have been compelled to scoff at his Tesco mobile phone. He estimates three men, one driving, two in the back with him. But instead of trying to work out where he's going, he focuses on his breathing, slowly, through the hood, warm on his face, and he lets his thoughts drift off, away from the unwelcome interventions of his grandad, to his wife and daughters. If he was finished, he was going to bow out thinking about them.

Under that dark hood, he is lifting Eve high over the sand dunes, then holding up an aggressive, pinching rock crab for Grace's attentions. She is laughing, dancing in front of it with delight. Then Melanie is in his arms, as they salsa across the floor, to the girls' enchantment. He wants to show his daughters that this is what real men do with their sweethearts – that this rapture, beauty and fun is what they are entitled to expect of love. He is breathing evenly, he is at peace. The constant stopping at the lights tells him he's still in the city, but they might be taking him anywhere. Then, suddenly, he feels familiar cobblestoned bumps under the SUV, knows the sequence of them. This is followed by the rumbling of a grid.

They are at Leith Docks.

They stop the car and help him out. They handle him firmly, but not over-aggressively. As the hood is pulled from him and he blinks into a fading light, a dark, short-haired, flinty-eyed man in his early twenties comes into focus, facing him. The man is well dressed, not in casual or gangster fashions, but like a young professional. His face is fresh and unblemished, apart from a thin scar above his top lip. Franco thinks of the person who gave him that scar. Was he gone for good, or perhaps strutting around a different town with impunity? — You must be Anton.

The young man nods. There are two other men with Anton, almost flanking him, maybe a step behind. In clothing and bearing they look like cheaper, inferior versions. Frank Begbie is instantly less impressed. He now reads their silence as deference to a disciplined leader, rather than inherent competence.

— A wee bit ay advice, Franco says nonchalantly, — get yourself checked oot. The STD clinic.

Anton Miller's face is still impassive, though one eyebrow slightly raises. His henchmen bristle, the chunkier one stepping forward. — What was that? he says, his fists balling.

— The lassie Flanagan, Frank Begbie says, completely ignoring the other man, never taking his eyes off Anton Miller. — Decent pussy, but pits it aboot too much. Larry's been thaire, n he wis ey a bareback man. Doubt that's changed.

Anton Miller nods slowly, in mild appreciation. It's as if Frank Begbie has passed a test, or maybe two: of insight and bottle. — I've no brought ye doon here tae discuss my health. Ah wanted tae look you in the eye and tell ye something straight.

— Ah think ah ken what it is, Franco says, — that ye had nowt tae dae wi Sean's death. Well, ah'd figured that oot for masel.

Anton lets both his brows rise. — Aw aye, n how did ye come tae that conclusion?

— Too many bams aw singin fae the same song sheet. Orchestrated by a cunt who ey does that sort ay thing. Whae's been daein it since the year dot.

— Power, Anton scoffs.

He notes the stockier henchman, the one who'd come forward, exchange a look with the other guy; thinner, hook-nosed. — Golden rule: that fat cunt says *sugar*, I think *shite*, Franco half smirks. — Never had that many rules that stood me in good stead. Wish ah'd remembered that yin mair.

Anton smiles, allowing Franco to feel the younger man's cool charisma. What sort of education he's received is neither here nor there: his intelligence is obviously formidable. Then a focused gleam comes into his eyes. — You dinnae seem tae be that upset for a man who's just lost his son.

— Ah was never close tae him, Franco shrugs. — Nae sense in lyin aboot it, or playin oot some fucked-up drama tae suit other people. Of course ah want tae know what happened, but that's aboot it. He looks around, taking in the overhanging cranes, glancing across to the factory units, over the top of the new-build casino. — I've nae emotional invest-ment in this place. Besides, times change. Franco nods at

Anton and his associates with a half-grin. — I'm oot ay my depth here.

— Franco Begbie, ootay his depth. Anton seems to toy with this idea. — You had some rep in this toon.

— Mibbee once. But you type ay guys were always better than me; the likes ay you and Power. Ah wis never in that league. Ah wis jist a thug. A good thug, but that was it, and he thinks about Davie 'Tyrone' Power's statement. — I never hud you boys' entrepreneurial zest.

A slight smile that might have been a reaction to flattery plays across Anton's lips, but his tombstone-grey eyes stay glacial. — Heard you've done awright for yourself. An artist, oot in California.

— No bad, Franco concedes, — but that's aw hype and fashion. They buy ma stuff cause it's in vogue, so ah make tons ay it and flog it while ah can. Some day soon, they'll lose interest. Till then, make hay while the sun shines.

— You're a smart man.

Frank Begbie shakes his head. — Spent too much time in jail tae ever be called that.

Anton looks to his associates, then back to Begbie. — Let's go for a wee walk, just the two ay us.

Franco nods, thinking that whatever is going to happen, one versus one is better odds than one versus three. They stroll together along the edge of the old dock, heading out to the jetty and the breakwater. The wind is cold and biting as they stop, leaning on a railing, looking out to the dank, dull waters of the Forth Estuary. Frank Begbie thinks of the Pacific Ocean by his home, all those hues of blue. What is

199

he doing here, with all those shades of grey? Does Anton want a square go, or is he planning to shoot him and push his body into the sea?

Or maybe he just wants to talk. Certain types of success can be isolating, and make people lonely. — Ah've made money. But it's aw overseas. In banks. Anton is staring out to the horizon, but with intent, as if he sees something out there.

— So ah've heard, Franco says. — And I won't kid on that ah'm no impressed. Even the likes ay Power, it took him twenty-odd years tae get the sense you've got now.

Anton turns to face him, with an impatient, almost mocking leer. — Do you ken how easy it is tae go tae Switzerland and open a business account in a bank? Or even the Cayman Islands? Ye jump on a fuckin plane, n walk intae a bank wi your passport and a bag full ay cash. Tell them you want to open a business account. That's it. Tougher tae open one wi the RBS or Clydesdale.

Begbie remains impassive.

— The point ah'm makin is that schemies have an aversion tae walkin ontae a fuckin plane that isnae gaun tae Amsterdam, or Ibiza or Thailand or some fitba game. Somewhere they're *told* they can go. They'd rather stuff their money under a mattress.

— I trust my bank in California, Frank Begbie states. — Of course, they're ripping me off, but the money isnae gaun anywhere.

Anton suddenly looks at Franco in a different way, as if he considers he might be being played. — You wake up in the sun every morning, nice wife, kids, looking oot tae the ocean. Not a worry or a care. That's gaunny be me a couple ay years fae now.

Franco tries to hold his poker face but he can feel doubt creeping into his expression.

This isn't lost on Anton, who responds with a grin that briefly makes him look boyish, but somehow more dangerous. — Aw aye, you're right tae be cynical. Talk's cheap, every bam says that, but ah've gied masel a target. The amount's written doon in black and white. Ah'm almost there. Then ah go. Dunno where, but somewhere warm and sunny.

Franco thinks of himself at that age, a mere primitive in comparison. It's so strange for such a young man to be able to converse like this. But how much has he really considered? — What will ye dae when ye get there? he asks.

Franco can see by the slight narrowing of his eyes that this question has cut Anton. — That's the part ah still need tae figure oot, he concedes, turning back to the sea. — But ah ken what ah'm *no* gaunny dae. Ma auld man worked hard aw his life. He was a welder tae trade. Then that dried up, the yards shut. So he worked abroad for a bit. Then he came back, and took a job on the TV detector vans. See, he was a straightpeg, did fuck all wrong his whole life. Anton turns back to Frank Begbie. — Fuckin mug.

— Don't think I know the boy, Franco responds, deadpan.

— Take it fae me, Anton jeers. — You've got tae set the world on fire, and his eyes suddenly blaze, as if in illustration. — And see your Sean, ah always liked that boy. He was awright, a good laugh. And whatever cunts are puttin aboot, he never, ever ripped me off.

201

— That's good, Franco says, — you have tae be able tae trust people.

— But eh wis a waster. Anton shakes his head. — Drugs got him. Drugs ah sold, drugs he sold. Ah used tae tell him: Sell drugs, get rich. Take drugs, fuck yirsel. Tae me that's always the ultimate no-brainer. Sean should have got that. He wisnae a daftie. Till he was wasted.

— Ah never knew him that well. Ah was either in jail, or kipped up wi some other bird when he was growing up. Heard he was a drug addict, though. That's disappointing tae me. Franco arches his brow. — These people always disappoint.

Frank Begbie's voice has dropped ominously, but Anton now seems lost in his own dark thoughts. — Ma auld man; ah bought him n ma auld girl a hoose on a nice estate at Barnton, oot ay the scheme. Took them roond there in the car. A big surprise. Drove them ootside this nice walled-and-gated development, landscaped gairdins, the lot, and handed them the keys. He telt me tae stuff it; refused tae even get oot the motor. My ma greetin her eyes oot, her dream hoose, and this prick wouldnae even get oot the fuckin car tae have a look at it. And he wouldnae let her get oot either. Said he didnae want anything that was peyed for by *misery money*. That was what he says: *misery money*. Can ye fuckin believe that?

Franco is silent, looking out to sea. The light is fading. It's getting really cold. — People are hard tae figure oot sometimes, he states, then looks at Anton. — Who do *you* think murdered Sean?

Anton stares him coldly in the eye. — The easiest thing tae say would be Power, or one ay his mob. But that would be a lie. The truth is, ah've no got a clue. But if you find oot, let me know. As I say: he had his faults, but I liked Sean.

— No enough tae go tae his funeral.

— There isnae much ye can dae for somebody when thir deid, Anton shrugs mildly. — You think half the bams who were there, those fuckin ghouls, really wanted tae pey respects tae Sean? If ah'd turned up, there would've been an atmosphere, wi Power and a few others. Ah showed *ma* respect by stayin away.

Franco thinks about this, and his confrontation with Cha Morrison. — Fair enough.

— You know . . . we've got something in common, Anton ventures, a slight wistfulness creeping into his tone. — Sean wisnae the son you wanted. Ma auld man wisnae the faither ah wanted.

— We're baith too auld tae bother aboot adoption papers now.

Anton laughs loudly at that. — You know, it's nice tae meet somebody who isnae scared ay me.

— How d'ye ken ah'm no just frontin it?

— Ah ken, Anton says. — N ah also know that you've got nothing against me.

Franco smiles at that. — And if ah did have?

— Oh, you'd be deid by now, Anton tells him, — and your wife and bairns, and he holds up the Tesco phone. There is a text from Melanie displayed on the luminous yellow-green screen.

Call me as soon as you get this. It's urgent. Love you. X

— You should, Anton Miller says impassively, and hands over the phone. As he takes it, Franco Begbie tries to see whether the younger man is breathing in. He can discern nothing.

30

THE DANCE PARTNER 5

The salsa class at the Santa Barbara Dance Center was busy, and all the participants were couples. Melanie had seen the two gay men in the group, and registered Jim looking intently at the very flamboyant pair. Then he'd studied the other couples, and noting everybody was unconcerned, seemed to lose interest in them. At the end of the session, Melanie got chatting with the men, Ralph and Juan, discovering both also worked at the University of Santa Barbara. The quartet decided to go for a drink together in the wine bar across the street.

This became a habit, often with Sula and other class members joining them. Jim was one of the few present who never drank alcohol. The evenings weren't riotous affairs; there was probably only one occasion when they all got really drunk and Jim had watched them in semi-detached amusement.

Melanie had woken up twice, first just before 2 a.m., then again just after five, but both times she'd managed to bury herself back in the domain of sleep. When she next bats into consciousness, she is horrified that it's almost ten and she feels more exhausted than ever. Nonetheless, she forces herself up and into the shower, getting dressed as some strange British television show plays in the background. For breakfast she locates a cafe on South Clerk Street, relieved to find its offerings more than acceptable to her Californian palate. Two espressos help her into the day.

There is another message from Harry, now sober and penitent. — Melanie, it's Harry, Harry Pallister. I see from my caller ID that I called you yesterday. I can only vaguely remember. I was very drunk, and I apologise. I've been having issues with depression and I've taken sick leave to get treatment, and I've joined AA. Please forgive me. It's Harry Pallister, he repeats. — Bye for now.

— Fuck you and your bullshit, Melanie says out loud to her phone.

As the data-roving facility on her cell will prove disastrously expensive, she locates an Internet cafe, where she finds Elspeth's address from an old email. It dates back to the funeral of Jim's mother, which she hadn't been able to attend as Grace had only been weeks old. She traces the address on Google Maps and sets off for the west side of the city. Edinburgh has suddenly, unpredictably, gotten very warm, and she quickly feels overdressed in her tracksuit top, tying it around her waist.

Mindful of her only previous visit to her sister-in-law's, Melanie anticipates a hostile reception. It had been a Christmas affair, ending in calamity, during which both Elspeth and Jim's . . . no, Frank's brother Joe had gotten drunk and made a terrible scene. This weighs heavily on her mind, as she disembarks from the tram and comes upon the house.

In the event, she is surprised to be treated with great warmth. Elspeth is tearful, explaining that the house had been attacked by thugs looking for Frank, with George suffering a cut on his hand. Melanie fights down her mounting panic as her sister-in-law tells her the story. Elspeth concludes by saying they all agreed that it would be best if Frank moved out, and he went to stay with an old friend, Larry.

Melanie can't recall hearing of Larry before, perhaps in passing, but Frank is generally reticent in talking about old associates. Unlike a lot of dangerous men she's met, he's disinclined to talk about his past. She had taken this as a sign that he'd put it behind him. Now she feels a darker undertow.

Elspeth doesn't know Larry's address, and they try Frank's UK phone again, but it goes straight to voicemail. — It does that aw the time.

The family attempt to get Melanie to stay with them at Murrayfield, but she refuses. Elspeth insists that she at least has a meal with them. Melanie is happy to do so, and to chat to the boys. George and Thomas are both fascinated by her, beset with hopeless crushes for the exotic American aunt they remember meeting a few years back.

— You had the baby, and another one, Thomas says.

— I did!

— When I get older I'm going to get on the plane and visit you and Uncle Frank and meet the girls, George advances.

— That would be so cool. How's your hand?

He shakes a bandaged mitt. — I got a fright, but I think that was just with the window being smashed in and all the flying glass. I've cut myself worse shaving.

As Melanie laughs, Elspeth draws in a breath of dismay, and looks to Greg.

Later, when Melanie rises and announces her intention of going out to find Frank, Elspeth takes her aside. Melanie believes that her sister-in-law is going to try and talk her out of this course of action, but instead she entreats: — Take him back home tae California when ye find him. He doesnae belong here any more. Whatever I think of him, it's obvious that he does a lot better with you over there than he's ever done with us over here. I can see that now.

Melanie recalls Harry's grim conversations and prays that Elspeth is correct. She leaves, unaware that she is being instantly followed down the street by a man who has been keeping Elspeth's home under survelliance, in the hope that somebody else might return there.

Taking a cab down to Leith Walk, Melanie gets out at Pilrig, into a cooling drizzle. The weather has changed again. Her plan involves doing a dry pub crawl, the picture of Frank on her phone to be shown to the inhabitants of every bar until she finds him. And she prays that when she does he will be fine, perhaps a little drunk, having fallen off the wagon, on the tear with some old friends.

In the event, she only gets to do one fruitless hostelry, when, heading down the Walk, she turns to see a limousine pulling up by the kerb alongside her.

31

THE MATE

Once again, the sun has come up in Edinburgh. *Open sesame*. The city changes, instantly bright with optimism. Mischief is in the air. Boys swagger and girls strut, underdressed and exchanging devilish half-smiles. Franco is happy that he opted not to bring a jacket, and sports a vintage grey T-shirt with a prowling bear and CALIFORNIA REPUBLIC emblazoned under it. And now he and Larry are driving through town, talking about old faces and old times. Franco has the bag on his lap, containing items he's borrowed from his friend, which the driver's eye is straying to. — Ah thought ye were a married man, above aw that, he chides, with a salacious cackle.

— Ah wonder how much we really change, Franco drily retorts. He's recalling how Anton and his friends left him at the docks yesterday evening. When they'd departed, anger had got the better of him, and he'd cathartically crushed that source of his misery, the Tesco mobile, under his heel, kicking its ruins into the River Forth. Now he wants to ask Larry to borrow his phone, in order to call Melanie.

But not yet.

— Well, you've no anywey. Larry nods at the bag, the edges of his eyes crinkling. — So whae ye giein the message tae, ya dirty bastard?

— Ye cannae kiss and tell.

— It'll be that Frances! A fuckin rampant wee pump . . . pack a few voddies intae her n it's fill-hoose time! Bet ye hud a sly look at ma tape, Larry ventures, glancing from the road to Franco.

— Ye inspired ays, Larry, Franco smiles, — but it's no her, ah'm huntin bigger game.

Larry laughs, delighted that he's properly bonding with his old pal again. Franco had been out all day yesterday, and hadn't got back till late. Larry had tried to pry as to his whereabouts, but as usual no information was forthcoming. So he contents himself with platitudes. — Aye, the auld days . . . good times, Franco.

But Franco is shaking his head. No, he doesn't want to use Larry's phone to call Melanie, as even this far away he doesn't like the idea of her digits being stored in it. — Were they really, but, Larry? Ah'm just no feelin it, he says, recalling slivers of alcohol-fuelled violence, bonhomie and shagging. Then the long periods in between, of being stuck in a cell. Coming out. A fresh start. A new bird. Big plans. Resolutions made.

Then another wide cunt. Another incident.

The same depressing pattern that had eaten away his youth. All the smells and sneers and hollow laughter of other men like him, veterans in the prison system. Often defiant but essentially beaten; besieged by the horrible truth that they'd never figured out how to stay away from those dreary, spirit-crushing places.

Then the mentor. The dyslexia treatment. The lifeline. The books; those windows on alternative worlds.

210

And finally, the physical embodiment of those worlds. The art therapist.

The *real* Dancing Partner.

— Mibbe we should take a wee trip doon tae Leith, Franco says. — Auld times' sake.

Larry's face cracks open in a grin. — Set controls for the Port ay Leith it is, he sings, pulling off a slick lane change in Waterloo Place, cutting ahead of an SUV, to set them hurtling down Leith Walk.

— Go straight doon Constitution Street, Franco suggests. — Let's take a wee hurl doon tae the docks.

— Huvnae been there in donks, Larry says, but a short time later he is pulling up outside the dockyard gates.

— Just drive through, urges Franco, — it'll probably pish doon in a bit.

— It looks awright tae me, blue skies, ay, Larry says doubtfully, then points to a sign: NO UNAUTHORISED VEHICLES PERMITTED.

Franco's eyes narrow. His voice drops, almost to the point where it approximates that intense but chilling burr Larry knows so well: recognisable, now, following its absence. — Since when did we need authorisation fae any cunt tae go anywhere in Leith?

Larry smirks in complicity, gratified to see Franco getting back to being his old self. He drives the van across the cobblestones and the grid, and under Franco's instructions, they park by an old brick outbuilding. It's deserted: no security around. Franco looks about; how strange it feels to see it properly in the cold light of day. They get out of the van, walking to the edge of the dry dock. Franco looks over. — Did ah ever tell ye the story aboot ma auld Grandad Jock and Handsome Johnnie Tweed?

— Nup.

Franco is still looking down. It's a long way to the bottom, not the pit of hell it seemed to him as a kid, but far enough. The subsidence in the crumbling walls has gathered pace; more boulders lie strewn over the bottom of the dock, despite some angled wooden buttresses on the far side trying to shore it up. His head starts to spin a little. He steps back and turns to his friend. — We were big mates, ay, Larry.

— Aye, still are, but, Franco, ay, Larry says slyly, but with wary concern.

— Big mates, but no mates, Franco considers in a cold monotone. — Mates ay a kind, but at heart despising each other.

Larry regards him in flinty-eyed aggression, briefly taken aback. He seems about to protest, but something reconfigures internally, and instead he breaks into a smile. — So it's aw comin oot now, then, ay?

— You ey kent how tae play me, Franco continues, looking across to the cranes, as seagulls flap and squawk in the distance, probably at the rubbish in the tip beyond the corrugated-iron walls to the east of the yards. To his left, the sun is going down across the silver-grey river, a flaming red, as if poised to burn Fife off the map. — Kent how tae instigate trouble. Makin the snowballs for me tae fling. Probably did a lot ay jail time cause ay you, he declares, without animosity. — My real mates, the likes ay Rents, Tommy, Sick Boy, Spud n that, they were ey wide for ye.

— They fuckin junkies! What aboot me? Larry sneers, pointing to a scar above his eye and a burn mark on the side of his face. — Who gied ays them? Whae bullied me, and every other cunt, and made our lives fuckin hell? Saint Francis James Begbie! Aye, yir mates, Renton, Sick Boy, Spud n that, whaire the fuck are they now?

Franco's lips tighten, and his brows rise. It was a good question.

But Larry is on a roll. It is indeed all coming out now. — Well, thir no wi you! No wi the fuckin bully!

— Takes one tae ken one, Larry. Look at you, since way back at school –

— Nivir in your league, pal, Larry snaps. — Even yir ain mates wirnae safe! Every cunt gied ye a wide berth, and Larry taps his own skull, — cause ye wir a fuckin psycho, he grins, stepping closer to Frank Begbie, pushing his face out, as if inviting a blow. — Now look at ye! A fuckin pussy! Ye willnae even go eftir that wee cunt Miller!

Breathe slowly . . . in through the nose, out through the mouth . . . — Ah ken you've been in wi Tyrone, you n Nelly, the auld Leith boys, tryin tae set ays up, ay, Franco says, in relaxed tones. — Tryin tae blame it aw oan that Anton Miller boy.

— Aye, Larry spits, his stare blazing defiantly at Franco, his eyes seeming to be framing something in a corner of his mind. — N it disnae matter now cause ah've no goat that long, wi the cowie n that. But thaire's one thing ah want ye tae ken!

— Aye? What's that?

— Ah fuckin topped your Sean! Larry rocks back on his heels, almost intoxicated by his statement, and deeply savouring it, as his gaze devours Frank Begbie for a reaction.

Franco merely nods, as if Larry has confessed to getting a parking ticket.

Larry looks at him aghast, his expression tumbling in crushing disappointment. — Did ye hear me? Ah killed that poofy wee cunt, and ken how? Because he beat me at that fuckin poxy computer game! No just cause ay that, but because he couldnae shut his fuckin mooth aboot it! Couldnae stop playin the wide erse. The smart cunt. But he wisnae you, Franco. He wis jist a smart-ersed wee poofter n a junky. Aye, ah went back that night tae that flat n fuckin pummelled the cunt. That Frances wis thaire, but she wis oot ay it n aw. But ye ken the real reason ah wasted um? Tae git back at you! Fir aw the shite ah took offay ye aw they years!

Franco seems to consider this. — Suppose that's just the way it goes, but, ay.

— Is that aw ye can say?! Larry's mouth puckers in sweetie-wife disgust. — So yir no even gaunny dae nowt? You've loast it, awright! Ye widnae take on that wee Anton cunt, try as ah might tae steer ye tae him –

— You always were a snidey bastard, Frank Begbie acknowledges. — Frances talked, put ays in touch wi Arbie. He telt me how ye were playin Sean and Anton for mugs.

Ah know Sean was shiftin loads for him. You were n aw. Ye tax it?

— Too fuckin right! That wee skank Frances'll dae anything ah say. Larry throws back his head, exposing the brilliantly capped teeth. — Another thing that mug Anton cannae control, the big superstar gangster! A dozy bit ay fanny! Ken how? Tiny wee fuckin welt oan um, she sais! Aye, that wee cunt is next on ma list, he declares, thrashing a fist against his own chest. — Think ah'm feart ay you or him now? Larry rolls up his jumper exposing the lesions on his torso. — You gaunny dae something tae me? Go ahead, ah dinnae gie a fuck! Tae the people ah love? Ah think you're a wee bit too warm-blooded tae hurt bairns, Larry declares, turning in a flourish, as if addressing an invisible but appreciative audience.

Franco bobs his head slowly. — You're right about that. Problem is, though, it's no really me ye need tae worry aboot. He looks to the howf.

The heavy wooden door swings open with a creaking sound, as Anton Miller steps out. — Hiya, Larry.

Larry rubbernecks to Franco in desperation. — Dinnae leave me wi him! He'll kill the bairn!

— That's already done and dusted, Anton says.

— Naw, you're fuckin lying . . . Larry gasps.

— The thing is, you'll never ken for sure one way or the other. Anton pulls out a chef's knife. His other hand is bolstered by a knuckleduster. He removes his green leather bomber jacket, slinging it over the bonnet of Larry's white van. Then Anton stretches out, flexing his muscles, solid in

215

a black T-shirt, as if he is getting ready for a workout. — Ah'm giein ye the heads-up n tellin ye here.

— Naw . . . Larry gasps.

— Looks like a tool for carvin, rather than plungin, Franco observes, regarding the knife. — This might take some time.

— Count on it, Anton says, again to Franco's eye, still breathing easily. — They are gaunny find this stirrin cunt in really, really small pieces. He glowers at Larry. — And I think Frances was just tryin tae make ye feel a wee bit better about yourself. But whoever's got the bigger cock now, I guarantee it'll be me by the time we've finished, and he brandishes the knife.

Larry pants, his wild eyes swivelling around, scanning for a way out or a potential weapon. Within two heartbeats, something dies in them, and he leans back against the brick wall of the howf, as if letting it support him. Anton puts the knife into his belt, then springs forward, unloading an impressive volley of punches and kicks at Larry's defenceless figure. To Franco's eye they are delivered with the velocity and precision of somebody who has trained as a fighter: perhaps he'd boxed at amateur level or taken several karate belts. Larry stumbles back, and slumps to the ground. Then, as Anton withdraws the knife and prepares to commence carving up the cowed figure, Franco steps forward and says, — As keen as ah am tae see ye in action against this clown, you'd best take him back in there. He points to the old brick howf. — Security still do the odd run through here.

— Good thinkin . . . Anton seizes the broken, whimpering figure of Larry by the hair and yanks him to his feet, marching him into the howf. There is a cruel focus in the young man's eyes, movements stiffly executed, but replete with an air of ceremony. Franco can see Anton ten years from now as a family man, living in a smart suburb, wearing the same expression, as he carves up the family Christmas turkey.

Franco shuts the big wooden door behind them, so that Larry's screams might be muffled in the highly unlikely event of anybody coming by.

32

THE DELIVERY BOY 5

Things turned bad for my grandfaither and his mates, as the investigation into Johnnie's death gained momentum. They were surprised at how relentless the cops were; it was as if they had inside information. It seemed tae take forever but eventually they all went to jail for Johnnie's death. Under pressure, they blamed each other. A flare-up took place, no in the Marksman, but in the Bowler's Rest pub, a quiet shop tucked away oot ay sight doon Mitchell Street. They probably went there to get their stories straight for the bizzies, but they argued and it got physical. Carmie battered Lozy quite badly that day, and I think Jock took advantage of their fallout, he and Lozy deciding the big man would take the rap for stoving in Johnnie's heid with the rock.

Carmie and Lozy would sit at opposite ends of the Marksman Bar. After the dispute they reputedly never spoke another word to each other or Grandad Jock again, though that might be bullshit. People need myths; they desperately embrace them tae gie their empty lives significance. But what nae cunt could dispute was that the close friendship between them was over under the strain of the persistent polis hassle. The Marksman is a very small bar and there were plenty of other pubs a stone's throw away that they could've drunk in. I suppose neither wanted tae back down.

Pride.

So when the charges were brought, only Carmie was to be done for Johnnie's murder. I don't remember the details of the case but they accused each other in court of accidentally pushing Johnnie into the dock after a drunken argument over cards money. Jock and Lozy were done for reckless behaviour and failing to report the crime or to assist Johnnie. The court proceedings were wild, dissolving into a shouting match. It was back in the time when the Scotsman Publications would cover working-class violence in the city with glee, through their court columns. Now they have a policy of ignoring it, in case it frightens suburbanites or tourists. But the trial was messy. They were all given prison sentences. Not long ones in the case of Jock and Lozy, but they were still very old men to go to the jail. In some ways this was worse for the two of them, as on release they were ostracised as scum: failing to report a friend dying, and probably grassing up another mate, those things could never be forgiven.

Old Jock suffered a stroke in jail, and he was set free early. But his younger second wife, a dirty big hoor we were asked to call 'Aunt Maureen' rather than 'Gran' or 'Nan', had left him for a younger guy. Lozy did his stretch, but Carmie, doing the real time, would eventually die in prison.

I went to see Jock a couple of times, in the sheltered housing complex at Gordon Court, where he lived his last years. His face was twisted in the same lopsided grin, which, thanks to the stroke, was now a permanent fixture – with spazziness and drooling thrown in for good measure. There were no friends left. It was as if now that he was vulnerable, people could openly acknowledge what a cunt he was. Lozy and him, despite, or possibly because of, their scheming treachery to Carmie, they never talked to each other.

The last time I visited him at Gordon Court, I knew he was on his way out. Notwithstanding the attentions of the care staff, the place was minging. He smelt of pish and disgusted me. It was then I decided to tell the cunt the whole story. — Mind when you heard that Johnnie had got his heid mashed in? You aw blamed it on each other; you, Carmie and Lozy. But youse always wondered, who was it that really finished him, that smashed his heid in?

There was a stunned reaction. Jock couldn't speak but it seemed like he was on the verge of another massive stroke. His face flushed crimson as he wheezily struggled to suck in air.

— It was me, ah telt him, as ah stood ower him. Ah wis about eighteen then, and ah couldnae believe that I'd ever been scared ay that auld vegetable. — Aye, ah finished him off. Dropped a big boulder on his heid. Of course, that was a warning sign for the bizzies. They tagged it as a murder rather than the suicide ay another docker peyed off and pit on the scrapheap. So they investigated. Of course, ah called them masel, telt them it was youse, ah explained, as Grandad Jock went aw spazzy on me. The fear and hate in his cunty auld eyes! — Aye, it fair landed yis right in it! That wis when yis aw turned on each other; it wis barry tae watch, ah laughed in his wheezing puss. — So it wis me. Ah fucked yis up, ah goat yis aw pit away!

Why? I could see him ask with his eyes, with every fibre of his being.

— Johnnie asked ays, I telt him, — and I'd always really liked Johnnie. Aw that work ah did for youse, it wis Johnnie that ey saw ays awright, oan the QT like. Nae other cunt gied a fuck. That wis one reason. The other yin wis that it was a barry laugh!

Eh pilled ehsel tae ehs climbin frame n yanked ehsel up. Tried tae come at ays! It wis ridic! Ah booted it oot fae under him and watched him crash tae the flair. — Beat it, ya fuckin auld muppet, ah laughed at um. For some reason ah mind ay gaun tae Methuen's chippy in Junction Street eftir, for a mince-pie supper.

A couple ay weeks later eh was deid. Ah went tae the funeral. Never planned tae go, cause ah ended up in the cells eftir a pagger up the toon the night before. By the time ah got back hame, ah jist wanted tae get some proper kip in. But the auld man and muh ma, n even Joe, they aw sterted tae make a fuss, so ah went along. Nae Lozy present, hardly any other cunt thaire. A waste ay fuckin time. The thing is, he was fuckin well hated aw along.

33

THE HOWF

As he takes Anton's green jacket from the bonnet of the van, and hangs it on the handle of the howf door, Franco can hear Larry's screams tearing out, caterwauling inside his brick prison. Anton is silent, but his blade is certainly doing the talking. Franco is tempted to open the heavy wooden door, to better appreciate the younger man's style. However, Larry's wails mean Anton can't hear Frank Begbie getting into the van and reversing it up against the door, leaving a gap of about five inches.

Immersed in his barbaric duties, Anton only registers something untoward happening when he hears a splashing sound on the concrete floor. He turns to see the nozzle of a petrol can poking through the gap, spilling its contents into the howf. It is soaking his trainers and has got as far as the jeans of the wretched, blood-saturated figure slumped in the corner, only vaguely recognisable as Lawrence Thomas Wylie.

— What the fuck – Frank Begbie hears Anton suddenly shout from inside the howf, as he slams the door repeatedly against the back of the van. — FRANCO! WHAT THE FUCK! So you . . . you're gaunny call the polis, catch ays here – Anton gasps, almost hopefully. In his panic he pushes an arm and part of his face through the gap in the door, which only gives Franco the opportunity to douse him with petrol. He steps back into the howf, spitting and pleading, — WHAT?! WHAT'S AW THIS ABOOT?!

— Dae ah look like a cunt that calls the polis? Frank Begbie says, grimacing at a memory, as he opens the front door of the van, reaching in the back, sticking the empty petrol can there and picking up a full one. He hears the heavy door banging against the vehicle in a rhythm that reminds him of sex. Climbing out, he states, — Now yuv went n hurt ma feelins, as he splashes more petrol inside the howf.

Anton, now again at the door space, doesn't even move back, he just lets the petrol soak him. — What is this . . . ? Ah thoat we wir . . . ah thoat we . . . ah telt ye ah nivir touched Sean!

— N ah awready telt ye, ah ken that ye hud nowt tae dae wi Sean's death, Franco says. He can hear soft mutterings and gasps, coming from inside. Some kind of penitent recitation; it has to be Larry. — And ah do appreciate ye hurtin that cunt, so thanks for that.

— This isnae thanks, Anton chokes. — But how? What fir? he pleads, trying to bolt down the panic in his voice.

— Well, ye mentioned the death ay the missus n the bairns, Franco takes a step back from the door, — tae whom I've become a wee bitty attached. That was an awfay daft thing tae say. Ah wis disappointed; thought ye would have picked up by now that ye dinnae threaten some people, it's just counterproductive. That wis the first reason –

Anton's face crushes forward into the space at the slightly ajar door. — AH DIDNAE MEAN IT!!!

— C'mon, mate. Franco sounds mildly dismayed. — Keep the dignity.

— Listen, Anton Miller's features contort in a sneer, — ma boys'll hunt ye doon, you and your family! They ken ah wis meetin you!

— No massively impressed by these fellies, mate; a cut above Power's mugs, but ah dinnae think they could cross the road withoot you. Ah'll take ma chances there. He waves Anton's mobile phone in his face.

— Look –

— The second reason, Franco looks at the calls list on Anton's mobile, — is they aw think that you did Sean. Ye kin see how bad that looks for me. He shrugs at the soaked, miserable face in the gap. — So littin you live jist isnae a fuckin option, ay-no. Worked hard for this rep, mate. It's a poisoned chalice, but it's cost ays a lot, Franco explains in almost gloomy resignation, hearing Larry's high groans whistling from the howf.

— AH NIVIR . . . AH NIVIR . . . FRANCO . . . Anton looks like a young boy now, his hair plastered to his scalp by the petrol. Fear has stripped the knowingness from his face.

— N thaire's another reason, which, fair enough, is a pretty pathetic yin, but here goes: it's barry fuckin sport, he grins, feeling Anton's phone purring inside his pocket. The henchmen might be here soon. — Never burned nae cunt tae death before. You pit ays in mind ay it yirsel when ye said that thing aboot settin the world on fire, Franco explains, getting back to work, splashing more petrol in.

Anton steps away, then springs forward into the aperture again, pressing his face out. His breathing ragged. — AH'VE

GOAT MONEY!! AH'LL SEE YE AWRIGHT!! AH SWEAR TAE GOD!!

Frank Begbie cocks his fist and pivots a straight right cross into the framed, squealing, petrol-soaked face.

Anton's head snaps back into the howf. It briefly reappears, nose bloodied, as he screams again: — ANYTHING! WHAT DAE YE WANT?!

— I've goat what ah want right here, mate. For you tae burn, Franco reveals, deadpan, lighting a book of matches and tossing it inside. Almost instantly, he can hear a *whoosh*, the spreading fire sucking out the air in the cramped howf, and then there's a big flash and a sheet of flame blazes out the gap of the door, forcing him to hastily jump back. Franco imagines he can still hear Larry's soft whimpers, but if that's so, they are soon drowned out by Anton's urgent shrieks. With a heavy heart, he pushes the young gangster's green leather bomber jacket in through the gap. It was a nice garment and might have fitted him.

Franco looks at Anton's mobile. A couple of missed calls and texts, the most prominent being RYAN. He assesses this to be the stockier, more assertive associate. He examines the texts, at which Anton is quite prolific, trying to decipher the minimal, coded instructions they are full of. He struggles with the keys and fonts, the fading screams of the young man in his head, but manages to type to Ryan: *All good. See you back at mine in 30 mins.*

Then he drives the van forward and gets out, opening the door of the howf. To his astonishment, the flaming figure of Anton comes charging out, a burning ball, running straight at him. Franco wagers that, by this time, the young man can sense nothing, and this suspicion is confirmed as he simply steps aside to let the blazing figure stagger towards the edge of the dry dock and fall in.

Realising that dusk is coming, Franco looks down, and watches the black, twisted shape of Anton. It is not moving but still burning. Suddenly thinking of the Warner Brothers' Road Runner–Coyote cartoons, he feels a shivering mirth snake through him. Then he heads back to the howf, opening the wooden door which is charred on the inside. The smell is almost unbearable; thick, congealed grease hangs in the air, a porcine odour, with a whiff of sulphur. The brick outbuilding's internal walls are sooted, its contents reduced to ruins and ash. The fire has sucked all the oxygen through the air bricks, facilitating an explosion. Then he sees the remains of Larry, his face lacerated and bloody, though otherwise strangely intact, resting on what seems to be a pile of blackened clothing. He looks at his old friend's vacant eyes, staring out at nothing, though those redone teeth still gleam white, and he mouths, *fuckin wanker*, heading outside, grateful for the air.

As the sun slides behind the warehouse buildings to the far side of the wharf, heralding a chill in the air, Franco takes the keys from the van. He gingerly begins to climb down the embedded rungs into the dock. Each step of the slow descent delivers a jabbing pain to his bad leg. On feeling the foot on his good one hit the bottom, he walks across the rubble-strewn deck to what had been Anton, and places the keys in the still-intact jeans pocket of the sooted and tarnished body. He takes the phone and slowly and laboriously texts:

226

You are going to die for fucking with me, you fat arse bandit.

And he sends it to a number he remembers by heart, before placing it in the pocket with the keys.

Then Frank Begbie turns away and looks up in the fading light at those intimidating bars of iron cut into the stone walls of the dry dock, some of them filigreed by corrosive rust, illuminated by the dull lamp shining from above. His leg aches badly, and the climb looms; this isn't going to be easy.

Placing his good leg on the first rung, he sets off. His hands feel slimy and slidy with sweat, and his leg shot with pain, ascending as darkness insinuates its regime, making for the sickly light of the reflected street lamp, not daring to look down, only glancing at the top, which never seems to get closer. Mostly, he concentrates on the bars. At one stage he imagines that his shoe sole will slip. Or perhaps he will snap a worn, corroded bar, his weight wrenching his weak grip from them, sending him crashing to the floor of the dry dock, broken and trapped. Down there, he'd just wait for death or prison, with a burnt body for company, and another one up in the howf.

Then, at last, he finally grasps the top rung. As he draws breath, he suddenly feels a crushing pain in his outstretched hand. Looking up, he sees a boot, grinding on it. Then a pressured jet of liquid blasts steadily in his face. Its pungent aroma fills his nostrils. Frank Begbie looks up at the figure pishing down on him, and knows that his time is up.

34

THE DANCE PARTNER 6

It was a clammy summer's night. The wind had changed direction, the welcoming Pacific breeze replaced by the hot desert air tumbling over the Sierra Nevada. The yard was uplit by floodlights and Melanie docked her iPhone into the system they'd had installed when they'd gotten the place wired for sound. A salsa beat swept out from the exterior speaker, above where Jim reclined on the comfortable all-weather furniture at the large wooden decking to the rear of their house, overlooking the back garden. Melanie was urging him to get up and dance with her, as Juan and Ralph were moving smoothly to the rhythm.

Jim was reluctant at first, protesting that he hadn't had a drink, looking to the empty bottles of wine on the table. Alcohol had been easier to give up than he'd thought. A couple of drinks were useless to him; he got a mild buzz, then just felt a bit shabby and tired. He always said that you needed loads of drinks, and when you had loads, you lost control, and his loss of control was negatively consequential to him and others, so why bother? But looking at the three of them, cheerfully lit up, playful, he got a little melancholy, lamenting how some people had mastered the art of knowing when to stop. Melanie sensed his envy of them; both recognising a skill he would never acquire.

Finally succumbing to his wife's insistent tugging on his arm, Jim rose just as Ralph was starting to fall, his eyes popping, as he clutched at his arm, unable to break his tumble to the decking. It was like some pantomime, and Melanie couldn't work it out, but Juan's expression of horror was clear enough to dispel any notions of the extreme pranking Ralph was occasionally prone to. As Ralph lay on the deck twitching, his husband was screaming, neither he nor Melanie knowing what to do. Then Jim pulled out his cellphone and thrust it at his wife. — Call 911, request an ambulance straight away, tell them it's a heart attack, give them the address, he said, crouching down by Ralph's side.

Ralph had now sunk into unconsciousness and didn't appear to be breathing. As she spoke to the operator Melanie could hear Juan's anguished cries: a mixture of English and a Spanish she'd rarely heard coming from his mouth. She was astonished that her husband seemed to know exactly what he was doing.

Jim had decided that Ralph was likely to be in cardiac arrest so there was no sense in wasting valuable time looking for a pulse. Instead he immediately started cardiopulmonary resuscitation, placing the palm of his hand flat on Ralph's chest just over the lower part of the breastbone and starting to pump by applying pressure using his other hand.

— He's dying, Juan screamed.

— No fuckin way: cunt dies when ah fuckin well say eh dies, Jim snapped, so violently that Melanie and Juan looked at each other, briefly astonished. He now had his elbows locked into his side and was slamming his bodyweight down on Ralph's chest. — One, two, three . . .

After thirty thumps, he opened Ralph's mouth, tilting his head back, lifting his chin and shouting to Melanie, — Pinch his nostrils shut!

Melanie fell down by his side and complied. Jim took a deep breath and sealed his own mouth over Ralph's.

As he breathed into Ralph, his stricken friend's chest rose. He started another round of thumps on his sternum, — One, two, three . . . c'mon, Ralphie son, moan tae fuck!

— Oh my God, Juan shrieked, — where are they! Melanie squeezed his hand with her free one.

Then Jim was back on Ralph, back on the mouth of a man who had, in his own words, 'blown a thousand cocks', and Melanie recalled this drunken, scandalous statement, as she looked into the eyes of, not Jim, but Frank Begbie, the thug, who seemed to be asking himself: What am I doing, why am I here . . . ?

Then there was a convulsion, almost like a mini-internal explosion, as Ralph started breathing again, hollow at first, then more regular. Melanie could feel the pulse in his neck. — He's back! He's back!

Juan crossed himself, and kept muttering, — Thank you, thank you . . . oh, thank you . . .

Ralph was still unconscious, so Jim rolled him gently onto his side into the recovery position. Mucus and vomit trickled out of his mouth onto the deck. Jim asked Melanie to get a blanket, and she returned with one and draped it over their afflicted guest. Grace had woken up with the shouting and, alarmed by all the commotion, had come through, and Jim calmly explained to his daughter that Uncle Ralph had been taken ill, but was going to be fine, leading her back to bed.

When Jim returned, Ralph had regained consciousness but was bewildered. Melanie was telling him that he'd had a turn, but Juan was here and an ambulance was on its way. When it arrived, Jim said he'd stay with the kids, if Melanie wanted to go in the ambulance and look after Juan, who was also obviously in shock.

Ralph was taken immediately to the Heart and Vascular Center at the nearby Cottage Hospital. He was breathing comfortably when Melanie and Juan went up to see him, some forty minutes later.

The next day, she and Jim went to the hospital to visit him. Ralph smiled at her husband. — Hey, Jim, Juan and Mel both tell me that you're one hell of a kisser. I'm sorry I missed it.

— You're lucky the kissing worked, Jim said, deadpan. — You don't know what I was going to do next.

Then he and Melanie drove down to Goleta Point, looking out to the sea, where he explained about the Telford College first-aid course they'd sent him on years ago. It was related to a job that his probation officer had set up, working in a box-manufacturing factory. It was a shit gig and he'd only taken the course as it meant eight Mondays at college instead of the monotony of the assembly line. — Thank fuck for the Scottish penal system, he laughed.

Ralph had suffered a serious heart attack, due to an undetected congenital defect, but this could be corrected by a procedure. Jim had certainly saved his life, and his long-term

231

prognosis following the surgery was good. — He'll soon be able to salsa again, Melanie smiled.

— Good on him, Jim said, picking up a large rock crab that was stranded in a pool. He placed it on the sand, watching it scuttle sideways towards the sea.

— What were you thinking when you were doing that first aid on Ralph, saving his life? Melanie asked.

— I was thinking, Jim went, — with a Leith voice in my head: *so this is what the fuckin salsa leads tae!*

Their laughter echoed out down the beach and up to the clifftops.

The music being pumped into the limo isn't salsa, but bland, easy-listening rock. It's a cheesy ballad called 'I'd Love You to Want Me' and Melanie can't recall who the artist is. The large man sitting next to her, driving the car, seems to know the words, mouthing them softly under his breath. David 'Tyrone' Power had introduced himself as a friend of her husband. He'd told Melanie that he'd been concerned about Frank, and had a mutual acquaintance call by at Elspeth's. They had just missed Melanie, but heard that she was planning to head down to Leith and look for him, just as he himself had decided to do. — I've been working my way up the Walk and Junction Street.

Power explains that he has the boys out searching, and invites her to come round to his place. He tells her there is a good chance that Frank will be heading there, as he had given him a set of keys. Melanie agrees, as she knows Power by reputation, and that he and Frank go way back. In the absence of anyone else, who is there to rely on?

The ballad eases into another, 'When You're in Love with a Beautiful Woman'. Again, the performer's name escapes her, though David Power is once more lip-syncing enthusiastically. Melanie asks him if he knows where Larry Wylie lives. — Unfortunately no. But that's a gey colourful pairing . . . Tyrone grins. — . . . that's an old Scots word, *gey*, means 'very'. Has Frank ever used that word with you? — No.

Tyrone seems disappointed, but fights through it. — Well, my point is, if they've gone out together drinking, we can't rule out the possibility that they might get into a little mischief.

Melanie clenches her teeth, shaking her head vigorously. — Frank stopped drinking alcohol years ago.

— And good on him. But he's under a lot of stress, and getting together with some of the old team . . . well, you never know. He bumped into Nelly the other day, an old friend, who assured me, David Power grins at her, — that Frank's patter is still as sharp as ever.

Melanie thinks about this all the way back to Power's house, that big red sandstone villa that really has to be classed as a mansion. If she found it impressive from the outside, when she goes indoors to her eye it is all wealth, with a complete absence of taste. It brings to her mind a Vegas hotel; it is as if Power has gone once to Paris and Venice, and then said to a designer: make it like that. He seemed to merely desire the most expensive of everything, with little thought as to how it would hang together stylistically.

Now he is trying to show Melanie the paintings that festoon the walls. — Are you interested in the Pre-Raphaelites?

— All I'm interested in at present, Mr Power, is Frank.

— Of course, of course, Power stresses. — And it's David. I've been trying to help him, Melanie – is it okay to call you Melanie?

— Yes, of course it is, she nods. — Where do you think he could be?

— Probably one of his old stomping grounds, Power declares, ushering Melanie to sit down on the couch, as he collapses into the armchair opposite. — Basically where we were; Leith Walk, Junction Street, Duke Street, Easter Road, perhaps Abbeyhill. But my people are out there looking for him, and we'll find him, Power boldly exclaims. — Hopefully he'll be on his way here. His phone is going to voicemail, but he's not great at having it switched on.

Melanie nods in acquiescence. He does know Frank well.

— I've been trying to help him, Melanie. Power suddenly spreads his big hands in appeal. — This city has changed a lot since his day, and there are some dodgy characters around now.

— I think perhaps there always were, Melanie replies, her eye contact steady and her voice low and firm.

— Good point, Tyrone smiles. — But you can't just keep barking up the wrong trees and not expect to elicit a reaction, and Frank, well, don't get me wrong, he's a salt-of-the-earth guy, and we go back a long way, but he can be a wee bitty single-minded.

Melanie can say little to dispute this contention. — You mentioned dodgy characters . . . this Larry . . .

— Oh, Larry Wylie was a nasty piece of work back in the day, but he's harmless now. Quite sickly, I hear. But I'm thinking specifically about a young guy called Anton Miller. I can't prove it *yet*, Tyrone slams his fist into his palm, — but I'm almost certain that young Sean was skimming from him . . . drug money . . . so Miller made an example of him. Sean had that 'I'm Frank Begbie's boy so I'm untouchable' thing going on . . . an unfortunate conceit of youth . . . so I believe that Anton Miller wanted to make a statement.

— And Frank . . .

— Well, quite understandably, Tyrone further volunteers, — I think it's more than likely that Frank's gone after Miller looking for some answers.

— Frank's changed . . . Melanie says, feeling the conviction ebb from her voice. — He wouldn't do anything that would . . .

Tyrone fixes her in a gaze of intent. — However much he loves you and your daughters, his son has been murdered. He tilts his head slowly. — That could send anybody crazy, and he ogles the tight swell of panic in her eyes as she starts to take this in. — I know they werenae close, but it's still his firstborn child.

— Oh my God, we need to call the p— As the word *police* forms on her lips, Melanie thinks of Harry, and immediately halts.

— I don't think the police are going to be much help, Tyrone shrugs. — They don't . . . well, let's just say that we have a bit of a reputation in this town, Frank and I, and they've never been particularly well disposed towards us.

Melanie frowns, grinding her teeth together. — I just want to find him and get him home.

— Of course you do. And as I've said, we're out looking for him. We'll find him, unless . . . Tyrone's tone is deep and grave, — well, we have to acknowledge the possibility that Miller could get there first.

— I can't sit here. Melanie patently exhales. — I'm sick with worry.

— Well, go back to your hotel if you wish, and I'll call you as soon as I get any news. I guarantee that I will be the very first to hear, he says, his tone smug and assured, — and you'll be the next, seconds after.

— In that case, I'd like to stay a while longer.

— Certainly. A text buzzes through on Tyrone's phone. — Excuse me. He rises, pacing across the room, obviously not recognising the number. She watches as the back of his neck glows red.

— Was that Frank?

— No, just family stuff, Tyrone says, turning and putting the phone into his pocket. He heads across to the marble bar and fills a glass with red wine, offering one to Melanie, who, although tempted, declines. — You know, I thought that Frank had done well for himself in the art world, but I can see that he's really hit the jackpot by having such an amazingly smart and beautiful young woman in his corner.

His grin makes her wish she'd gone to the hotel.

35

THE PISH

His son Michael is standing over him, penis out, pishing in his face. And Franco is exhausted, ready to let go of the rungs and fall in beside the still-smouldering body of Anton. He can barely move his head; feels the stagnant jet bouncing off his skull as the urine seems to cloak his neck and shoulders. It's as if a warm shower could be a creeping gateway to hell. — Michael . . . what the fuck –

— Shut it, ya mingin auld cunt, Michael sneers, as he slowly shakes out his cock and replaces it in his pants. Franco then realises where he has seen that lopsided, sly grin before. His son's youth had obscured the fact that the boy is a double for Grandad Jock. At that moment, Franco is utterly convinced it's over, but Michael bends forward and extends his arm. — Gies yir fuckin hand, then.

All Frank Begbie can do is raise his arm up. His life is literally in Michael's hands, and he's surprised when his son grasps his mitt, helping to haul him up onto firm terrain. He stands, bent over, hands on his hips, struggling to get air into his lungs. The bad leg is so sore, it feels fractured. — Why . . . what did ye pish on ays fir . . . then save ays?

— Ah pished on ye cause yir a fuckin wide auld cunt. Saved ye cause yir ma fuckin faither, Michael says, — . . .

and . . . cause ye took they cunts oot. He points back to the bothy, then behind Franco to the dock.

— Well, thanks for the second yin, Frank Begbie says, gathering his breath. He tries to stretch out his sore leg, as he looks at the T-shirt, dark with piss, the Californian bear on his chest saturated.

— So you'll be off then, ay. Michael intones it as a statement. — Ah'm happy tae take credit for Anton n Larry. Mibbe ye owe ays that.

Franco's dispassionate gaze seems to permit this. Michael can insinuate what he likes. It would only help take any heat off him. — At least ah found oot whae did Sean, that was aw ah wanted. He points to the howf.

Michael laughs loudly, shaking his head. — Larry tell ye it wis him? Ye didnae believe that shite, did ye?

Franco realises right there and then that he didn't. He shivers. The sun has gone down and the wet urine is chilling on his body.

His second son looks at Frank Begbie as if he is a fool. And why not, Franco thinks, he is the one exhausted, with a gimpy leg and reeking of pish. — He wis jist trying tae get at ye. Kent eh wis on the wey oot, wanted tae mess wi yir heid, Michael scowls. Then his features expand in a cold grin. — Naw, ah topped the fuckin annoyin poofy bastard masel.

Franco feels a force of rage surge through him, but then it seems to exit his body, shooting up into space, leaving him hollow, almost formless. He looks at Michael, realises that words are failing him. Tries to force out the sentence. — What . . . ye what . . . yir ain fuckin brar?

238

Michael's pernicious laughter rings in his ears. — Do you ken how fuckin embarrassin it was tae huv that cunt mincin aroond wi fuckin bufties aw the time? he challenges. — Ay?

Franco stays silent. He can feel the burning extent of his son's rancour, but this time he can't match it. He is spent. Done. He concentrates on his breathing.

— Eh used tae hing oot wi that ride, that Frances. Seen ye talking tae her at the funeral, Michael half accuses. — Aye, she follayed him aboot like a wee puppy. Slag gied it tae that filthy auld cunt Larry, n Anton wis bangin her n aw. Everybody but me, Michael moans, making no attempt to disguise his self-pitying jealousy. — Ah'd huv fuckin looked eftir her! Kept her away fae aw they druggie cunts, aw they auld pervs whae treated her like shite, hud pictures ay her oan their phones blawin them for fuckin drugs!

Franco remains focused on his breathing. In through the nose, where with every breath he smells his son's piss on his T-shirt and in his hair, out through the mouth. His calves and arms still burn from the climb, but his leg is settling a little.

— When he was gaunny move intae that place in Gorgie, ah got asked by Arbie tae take the keys doon tae him. So ah thoat, the poofy cunt'll huv Miller's gear and cash in thaire, so ah makes masel a spare copy ay the key at that place in St James's Centre, ay. When ah got doon tae his auld gaff in Trafalgar Street, that Frances was thaire. Widnae even gie ays a good look, but she wis ey aw ower a poof that widnae even fuckin ride her. What's that aw aboot? Michael challenges his father.

Franco is silent.

— So aboot a week later, ah thoat ah'd go roond tae the Gorgie flat n see if thaire wis anything worth chorin. Maybe some collies or dosh, seeken that poof's faggot puss by droapin um in the shit wi Anton. Michael's smile flashes in noxious delight. — Ah bangs oan the door, thoat the place wis empty, ay, but whin ah lit masel in, he wis passed oot in a chair. That Frances wis thaire wi him, baith ay them wasted. Ah tries tae wake her up, but she's fucked, ay. That cunt ay a brother ay mine, that fuckin poof ay a son ay yours, Michael asserts, — he sortay comes to but. Starts goadin ays, takin the pish wi that smart fuckin gob ay his, like eh ey did, wi that queer, cock-suckin mooth, that nivir shut the fuck up. Eh looks at Frances, aw passed oot, n goes, now's yir chance, n laughs at ays! In ma face! That fuckin sick queer!

Franco feels flimsy and evanescent. It is like everything has been ripped out of him bar a pervasive nausea, spreading through him like hemlock. — It wis how eh wis . . .

Michael screams in his face, — DINNAE GIES THAT SHITE! YOU TAUGHT AYS THAT! YOU! You said that they wir aw sick, diseased perverts!

And Franco recalls taking the boys out one warm summer's day. They had gone for a walk up to the multiplex cinema, and saw two young men holding hands at a table outside one of the bars at the Top of the Walk. It had disgusted him then: men doing that, in full view of his young sons. Hatred seared him. He had been sent packages of explicit gay pornography by an anonymous tormenting rival during his prison stretches. This had sparked innuendo that had to be dealt with. He'd considered homosexuals to be perverts and paedophiles, and yelled at them, spilling his roaring, demented bile in the street's full daylight. The terrifed men quickly sought refuge in the bar. He remembers that the boys were scared too, or rather Michael was.

Why? Why had he done that? Why had he been so twisted with poison? Why was it what strangers did *mattered* so much to him? Now in California, he and Melanie have gay colleagues and neighbours, and there's Ralph and Juan, who have become close friends. They come to dinner, they joke, chat, dance, play with the kids, engage in jocular flirtation with both him and Melanie; it just isn't an issue at all. It was ludicrous. It was madness, the way he'd needed that sort of stuff back then, nonsense that now means nothing, just in order to rage against *something* that was in some way different. — Well, that wisnae right . . . Franco can feel his words flop lamely out of his mouth. He is aware that he is soaked, stinking of piss, and that he needs to be home. *California. Melanie.*

— Ah loat ay things you did wirnae fuckin right! Michael snarls, his eyes suddenly widening as another recollection pops into his mind. — Mind what else ye sais tae me? When the bastard cut ays wi that wire, acroass ma chin?

Franco once again sees his grandfather in his son's face, fees the macabre, spectral revenge of the old man, here in the docks. Indeed, under the thin light from above, Michael looks an incorporeal force, and Frank Begbie is stunned into silence.

— Ye telt me tae smash the bullyin cunt, wi a brick ower his heid, like you did wi auld jakey Uncle Joe. Ah didnae though, Michael laughs, savouring his father's passive distress, — ah baseball-batted the cunt. Leathered his puss in wi it. That goat um oot ay ma face, right enough, he cackles with a dry, humourless laugh.

Franco recalls that time, the discussion with the frightened boy. Yes, it had been Michael who was originally the sweet wee lad, while Sean was the terror. Sean had bullied his younger sibling in much the same way Joe had with him, and Franco had been moved to dispense the traditional Begbie advice. But now Michael has taken this retribution to a new level. Francis Begbie pulls air into his lungs, regards his creation. — So where does that leave us?

— Well, you git back tae whaire ye fuckin well came fae, Michael growls. — If ah see ye here again, yir fuckin deid. Stepmammy as well. Would've cut your throat n rammed yir fuckin missus eftir the funeral if ye hudnae taken oot they two cunts, especially Anton. Makes life easier for me, but, ay. So go. Michael thumbs over his shoulder. — If ah ever fuckin see ye back here, he repeats.

— Suits me, Franco says, realising that the worst thing he can do to Michael is simply leave him with the burden of being his unreconstructed himself. He'll cause misery, then he'll either die or spend most of his life in jail. A real chip off the old block, and it is, he concedes, largely his father's fault. It would be nice, though, if he brought this torment to the right people. Or person.

He goes to Larry's van. Michael looks at him in raw aggression, takes a step forward, but sees that Franco is only retrieving a bag.

— Okay. Ah'm off. Francis Begbie nods at his son. Then he stops and says, — Ah ken ah huvnae been much ay a faither tae ye . . . but ah couldnae let Morrison say those things.

Michael's jaw drops. — What are ye talkin aboot? What did that jakey cunt say tae ye at the funeral?

— It was aboot Sean mainly. How he was an arse bandit . . . and how you were the same.

— What?!

— What we say aboot each other is neither here nor there. But ah couldnae have him sayin those things about you. Franco shakes his head. — That's what family is. You might have nowt tae dae with each other, you might even hate each other, but naebody else gets tae say things against ye.

— AH'M NO A FUCKIN QUEER! Michael roars, then gasps, — That fuckin jakey Morrison . . . eh said *what*?

— That you were a bentshot like Sean, a *cock-sucking arse bandit* wir his exact words, Franco calmly says to his incandescent son. — That you'd git the same treatment he did, and he stares at Michael, who seems to be almost imploding with rage. — But leave him tae me. This is aw aboot him and me. Always was. Ah'll get him sorted.

— WILL YOU FUCK! Michael howls, then lowers his voice to a snake-like hiss. — He's mine! Ah'm tellin ye! N if you git in the wey, you'll fuckin well git it n aw, he rasps. — NOW FUCK OFF OOTAY MA FACE!

So Franco, carrying his bag, nods, turns and limps away from the dry dock, the howf and Larry's van. At the gates he stops and looks round to see the silhouette of his second son, standing, hands by his sides, under the lamp.

It really is time to leave, perhaps just one thing to take care of, he considers, as he walks out through the dockyard gates, his leg again strengthening with the blood flow that movement engenders. He heads along the Shore by the Water of Leith to Constitution Street, and up Leith Walk. The familiar gradient is beginning to assert itself, when Franco is aware that a car is tailing him. He turns to see a black limo. It moves slowly up to the kerb ahead of him. Stops. It has to be Tyrone. He prepares himself for violence, and it will probably be his last stand, here in Leith. The breathing won't help him now. Jim Francis won't help him now. Frank Begbie's pulse rises and a red mist swamps his brain. Letting the bag drop to the pavement, he spreads his palms and leans back, screaming at the vehicle, — C'MOAN THEN, YA FUCKIN BAMS!!

The limo door opens and Melanie steps out.

36

THE ARTIST IN THE RESIDENCE

Swelling with emotion at the sight of her, Frank Begbie finds it hard not to embrace his oncoming wife. — Melanie, he gasps, but then holds up his hands, urging: — Don't touch me, honey . . . The panic in his gesture and the waft of stagnant urine rising in her nostrils derails Melanie's instinct to hold him and she freezes. — . . . I'm covered in pish . . .

— What the fuck, Jim! Melanie's eyes and nose scrunch up, and she even takes a backward step, as her voice leaps several octaves. — What happened?

He struggles to fight back the annoyance digging into him. *What the fuck is she doing here?* — It's a long story . . . he protests, his eyes narrowing at the sight of Davie 'Tyrone' Power emerging from the car.

Power's face, half lit by the street lamp, has a look of paternal disdain. He reaches back into the vehicle, producing a packet of sanitary hand wipes. He lays it on the bonnet of the limo in front of Frank Begbie. — Do what you can.

Begbie nods, and starts wiping at his hands, face and hair. He feels clean enough to kiss his wife and squeeze her hand. — I got into a wee scuffle wi some bam in the toilets of a pub, and we both landed in the overflowing latrine. He gives a hollow laugh. Then he asks Melanie, while glancing at Power, — You okay?

— I'm fine, she says with reassuring calm, picking up on his reticence in discussing this further in the present company. — What about you?

— I'm okay. I got upset . . . about what happened to Sean. Coming back over here, it really hit me for the first time, he says, and now he isn't lying.

Melanie touches Frank's forearm tentatively. They climb into the back of the limo. As Power starts it up, she looks at the chunky dome and broad back of the man in front of them. Even though he has reunited her with her husband, Melanie is still unable to work out why he fills her with revulsion.

— We've been searching high and wide, haven't we, Melanie? Power sings slyly, as if to help her in her quest, putting on music. As the limo surges up a dark, empty Leith Walk, 'California Dreamin' by the Mamas and the Papas fills the air. — This one is for the California Mama and Papa in the back who'll be dreamin' ay getting hame to their wee yins, he swivels, to display capped teeth. — Three and five, Melanie was saying, eh, Frank?

— Aye, Begbie warily concedes. — So how did you two hook up?

— I was looking for you, Melanie begins, quickly faltering, the look in Frank Begbie's eye again indicating that this story is best told when they are alone.

— As was I, Power continues on her behalf. — A young American lassie asking for you in Leith grot holes, well, that's

246

never going to be off my radar for long. So we pooled our resources, he chuckles, his sturdy shoulders rocking.

Frank and Melanie grip hands in tense silence. In spite of his best efforts with the wipes, the heat in the limo is whipping up a rank smell from him, with Michael's piss drying into his hair and the California flag T-shirt, complete with bear. Power wrinkles his nose in distaste a few times, but only breaks the silence to wax lyrical about the empty roads. —Wish it could be like this aw the time. Driving would be a pleasure.

They reach the approach to the red sandstone mansion, the gravel popping under the wheels. When they step inside the house, Power announces, — I'm going to make a pot of camomile tea for Melanie and myself. Frank, don't take this the wrong way, but not to make too fine a point of it, you are fucking minging, and he hands Begbie a silk robe. — I suggest you go to the basement and put your clothes through the laundry and dryer. There's a shower down there.

Frank Begbie is extremely disinclined to let Melanie out of his sight. But she is urging him to go, and if Power had been intending to harm her, he reasons, he had ample opportunity to do so earlier. He nods and descends the stairs. In departure he can hear David 'Tyrone' Power pompously extol the virtues of Murdo Mathieson Tait.

The basement is a huge, rambling space. It's largely open-plan, apart from the shower and laundry rooms, which lie off a connecting corridor linking a substantial gym to the rear of the house, with a large workshop to the front. Frank Begbie removes his clothes, bundling his jeans, T-shirt and socks into the washer, everything bar his underpants, pouring in the lime-scented detergent and setting the load. Then he heads to the shower, turns on the taps, and washes his son right out of his hair. He thinks of Michael as he scrubs with Power's peach-scented exfoliating gel. Bearing witness to his son's brutal, animal rage was like being shown a 3D movie of his younger self in action. History repeated itself. The 'don't do the things I did' mantra was tiresome pish. The best way to make sure your children don't grow up as cunts is not to be one yourself – or not to let them *see* you being one. This is easier as a sober artist in Santa Barbara than as an alcoholic jailbird in Leith.

Leaving the shower and drying himself off, Frank Begbie pulls on his underpants and gets into Tyrone's silk robe. It hangs so farcically on him he laughs out loud. Then he turns to look around the rest of the vast basement.

The gym confirms that Tyrone obviously pumps iron in bouncer fashion, turning a massive calorie intake into not just fat but ludicrous amounts of chest, shoulder and arm muscle. The Falstaffian figure was a renowned street fighter back in his day, and still reputedly enjoys the occasional busting of chops, but generally leaves the real dirty work to hired hands.

It's the workshop, though, that gives away the darker side of Power's character. Most of it is taken up by two benches, full of all sorts of machine and hand tools. Franco has never taken David 'Tyrone' Power for a DIY enthusiast. The pliers, screwdrivers, but most of all the copious knives – including a throwing set in a box – make Franco decide to get Melanie away as soon as possible.

Frank is relieved to return to her, despite the forty minutes left on the wash cycle. He climbs the stairs, feeling preposterously self-conscious in the outsize silk kimono, wondering if this has been Tyrone's idea all along: to render him vulnerable. Approaching Melanie and David Power, he listens to their chatter about dead painters. Then he gratefully embraces her, this time without any toxic stench, drinking in Melanie's familiar scent, yet aware of Power's sly, rapacious eyes on them. Pulling apart, he looks her in the eye. — Listen, I've a couple of things to straighten out with Davie, he urges, — you should go to the hotel and pack. I'll meet you there as soon as my clothes are dry.

— No way. I'm not leaving you again!

— Ah really owe my old mate an apology, Frank implores, glimpsing Tyrone puffing up in entitlement. — Go and pack. Phone your mum. Find out how Grace and Eve are doing.

Melanie softens at that. Checks her phone for the time. — Will you be okay?

— Well, Frank Begbie laughs, — if I'm not at the hotel within ninety minutes, this time you *do* have my express permission to phone the police.

David 'Tyrone' Power looks hurt, responding with a sour pout.

It doesn't go past Begbie. — Look, he appeals to Melanie, — I want to catch up a bit with my old mate and, as I've said, there are apologies due on my part. I was a wee bit rude the last time I enjoyed his hospitality, he concedes, turning to Tyrone. — What's that auld phrase, Davie? You'd best enjoy my hospitality, because you won't enjoy my hospitalisation.

As Power grins, Melanie looks at them in contempt. Jim seldom talks like this, but whenever he does, coldness locks around her. She shimmies a few inches from him. From *Frank*, as he's called here. — You know, I think I will go, and leave you two with your fucking gangster bullshit.

— Sorry, babe. Franco's brows raise and his mouth tightens in exasperation. — Can I borrow your phone?

Melanie unceremoniously slaps it into his hand, and settles back on the couch, regarding the paintings on the walls. Franco calls Terry, requesting his services. As Tyrone starts talking about one of Murdo Mathieson Tait's *compositions*, Frank Begbie sits in silence until a call comes back fifteen minutes later. It's followed by a cab pulling up outside. Melanie rises to leave.

— I'll be with you soon, Franco urges.

— Right, she says, heading outside. Franco watches her departure from the window, sees her step into Terry's cab.

— She's no happy, Tyrone observes.

— She'll come round. Franco turns to him. — I'm more worried aboot the driver she's got intae the cab wi!

— Aye?

— Mind ay Juice Terry?

— Business Birrell's mate? The fanny merchant?

— Aye.

Tyrone smiles briefly, then Franco registers his expression hardening. — We need tae have a fuckin chat. A chat we should have had a few days ago, he barks, pointing at the empty space on the couch opposite him.

Frank Begbie raises his arms in a surrender gesture and sits down. — Ah wis out ay order on the last visit, he says, shaking his head sadly. — Aw that stuff wi Sean . . . it hit me harder than I thought . . . and that thing wi Nelly. How is he?

— Still in the Infirmary, Tyrone says. — You hit his liver. It was touch-and-go for a while, but he'll live.

Franco lets the concern drain out of his tightening limbs. — So ah decided tae make ma peace by taking care ay your wee problem, he remarks, watching Tyrone's face open up like sunrise on a cold morning.

Then Power's heavy brow furrows, briefly reminding Franco of Chang, the Chinese Shar-Pei dog that belongs to his neighbours in Santa Barbara. — What are ye saying, Frank?

— Anton is no more, Francis Begbie reveals with an understated flourish, enjoying Power's intense absorption of this information. — Aye, poor Larry was collateral damage, but, well . . . he grins and shrugs minimally.

— You've done him? Miller? He's gone? You're joking!

— Your boys should take a discreet wee drive doon the docks. The old dry dock by the abandoned factory units. Anton's in there, and Larry's in the brick howf by the side ay it. His van should still be parked there too.

— How did ye . . . what happened?

— Let's just say they played wi fire and got burnt.

Tyrone starts up a flurry of eager texting as Franco delineates the story, omitting only the details about Michael. His son and former employer are quite able to enter each other's orbits without his assistance. As he listens, Tyrone can't fight the euphoric smile ripping open his face. — Well done, Franco my son! I knew ye'd come roond!

— When I thought it through, I realised it could only have been him, Franco lies easily. — Listen, I was a bit rude with that last drink you offered, he concedes, — but maybe I should have one now, with the missus being away. Californians. He rolls his eyes. — It is a wee bit ay a celebration, after all, and he stands up and moves over to the marble cocktail bar. — Do ye mind?

— Not at all, you've earned it, count me in too! You're a dark horse these days, Franco, Tyrone nods guilefully. — Ah underestimated ye. And as for Melanie . . . well done, he smiles. Then, as he watches Begbie pour the whisky into the gleaming crystal tumblers, Tyrone's tone takes on a peevish hue. — That's where I went wrong; going for the dumber lassies, who ye either get nothing out of, or they just talk boring pish about clathes and families. I always thought that was what I wanted, but when they've nothing of consequence to say, life gets so tiresome.

— Did she like the paintings? Begbie asks, replacing the top on the whisky bottle and settling it down gently on the flecked marble. — She kens a lot mair aboot that sort ay thing than me.

— Oh yes. Tyrone looks around the walls with pride. — She was certainly very knowledgeable about Murdo Mathieson Tait's work; I was impressed. Aye, ye did well for yourself there, Franco.

Francis Begbie beams back at David Power. — You know, you fairly sussed me oot, Davie; that I hadnae really changed. I used to think I was scared that somebody would try and dae something bad tae Mel and the kids. Then I realised that was a lie. Franco hands him the malt whisky. — What I was really scared ay was that *naebody* would try, because ah was desperate for somebody tae. See, ah still enjoy the buzz, but now ah need a proper excuse tae kick off. Like family, he says, moving back over to the chair and placing his own glass on the coffee table, then taking one of David Power's cigars from the box on the bar, waving it at his ex-boss. — This okay?

— Of course it is, Tyrone purrs, nursing his own whisky appreciatively. — Spark up a couple.

— Aye, they call it IED in America: intermittent explosive disorder. Aw the transactional analysis, assertion training, anger management, cognitive therapy, and even the art, it hasnae stopped my urge tae violence. He sticks the cigar in the mini-guillotine and beheads it. Then he lights it up, expelling a plume of blue smoke.

He passes the cigar to David Power, who rises and goes to a small white panel on the wall, pushing a few beeping buttons. — Best pit those smoke detectors off, he explains, as Frank Begbie follows his line of vision to a disc on the ceiling with a blinking green light. Power sits back in his chair, sips at his Scotch appreciatively, as Begbie blazes up a second cigar for himself.

— It just quelled the IED, and made me need that valid reason tae get involved, he continues. — Only family are worth it, even the ones ye dinnae really like that much.

— For sure, Tyrone agrees.

— Funny how a prime minister can condemn a whole generation ay bairns tae a future ay poverty, or gie the order

253

tae wipe out Iraqi women and children in a phoney war, and they cunts get described as *great men ay history*, Begbie muses. Then he laughs. — The likes ay you or me, we take oot a few radges that naebody misses, just fuckin pests tae their ain community, and we're the big villains!

Tyrone looks thoughtful. — Sometimes ah think ah should have gone intae politics. Local, like. That fuckin council. Is it the same where you are in California?

— Dinnae get me wrong, Begbie nods, — ah'm no a social service, any cunt ah've done is only been for ma ain satisfaction. But it jist goes tae show, ay.

— *Slàinte*, Tyrone raises his glass, as Begbie watches him sip at his drink, once, twice, three times.

Slàinte, Frank Begbie toasts, letting the whisky tickle his lips. It is horrible. He realises he never really liked the taste of alcohol, just its effects. Then he smiles across at the fat man, watching him slip into disbelief, then apoplexy, as Franco's cigar again drops into his glass with a dull sizzle.

— What's the fuckin . . . Rage swamps Tyrone, and he tries to stand up, determined to tear Frank Begbie apart with his bare hands.

But he never makes it. Instead he tumbles across the couch. He looks up at Francis Begbie, attempting to speak, but no words will come and only drool spills from the corner of his mouth, as the darkness takes him.

When David 'Tyrone' Power awakens, movement remains beyond him. This time, unlike the effects of Larry's Rohypnol, his bands are external; he can feel his wrists manacled behind his back, and knows that the metal digging into them has to be heavy-duty police handcuffs. Worse, he can't speak, can barely breathe, a ball-and-chain gag having been stuffed into his mouth. To his astonishment, he realises that he is tied down, flat on his stomach on his dining-room table, his head forced upwards by what feels like a block of wood under his chin.

Franco is standing over him, dressed in his freshly washed clothes. He pulls up the gag, another article expropriated from Larry, used for the sex tapes made with Frances Flanagan, and probably the other girls. It allows a sweaty Tyrone to say, with insect coldness, — You've fuckin crossed the line now!

— A line has certainly been crossed, Frank Begbie nods in agreement. — But a wee bit ay appreciation would be good.

— What the fuck dae ye want?

— You're no nice, Begbie says, in faux dismay. — Getting you up on that table was a three-man job. Ah deserve a fuckin medal. Ah nailed yir jaykit and troosers tae it. He flashes a radiant smile, holding up a nail gun, procured from Tyrone's basement, and his prisoner can feel the extent of his restraints. His head movement is minimal as there are two knives stapled by their handles to the wooden block under his chin, on either side of his neck, their sharp edges facing inwards to his flesh.

Then Tyrone sees that Begbie has something in the flat of his hand. It is attached by a length of twine to one of the chandeliers on the ceiling. Begbie holds it suspended in front of David Power's face: a small 5lb lead barbell, taken from downstairs. — This is wee, but it's aw aboot speed. Mind you, ah modifed it a bit. Franco shows him the fattest part, where the weight appears to have cut-up shards of razor blade soldered onto it. He lets it dangle at rest an inch in front of Power's face. The stark blackness of the cast iron and its glinting razors fascinate and terrify the captive gangster. — That's the thing aboot bein an artist, ye get . . . *creative*.

— What the fuck are you –

Tyrone is silenced by a measured jab to his face, framed between the two knives, which cracks his nose. — Shhh . . . Frank Begbie puts a finger to his mouth. — Speed, see. The power comes fae speed. Keep that heid moving, he instructs, and walks away from Tyrone, taking the bladed weight with him. Getting part of the way across the hall, he spins the device on its twisting flex, then turns with a malicious grin, raising it forty-five degrees before opening his palm to unleash it.

Tyrone screams out, — FRRAAANNK, as the barbell hurtles towards him. He tries to move his head but the edges of the knife blades slice into his neck, drawing blood. The twisting iron weight crashes into the side of his face with a dull thud, tearing at the flesh around his cheek. — WHAT ARE YE FUCKIN – Tyrone yelps, then notes that Begbie, rather than preparing to release the barbell again, is detaching it. A flicker of hope in his chest as he briefly imagines that the hideous trial is now over, that Begbie has *made his point*.

But as he removes the load, letting it fall to the hardwood floor with a clunk, Begbie begins attaching something else to the twine: a chisel, weighted at the handle by heavy bolts he's wrapped around it with electrical tape. — This one's different, he explains.

A high screech of dread goes through David Power. — Wait . . . he says.

Frank Begbie looks back at him, snaps his fingers in excited acknowledgement. — Ah was waitin oan that fuckin wurd! Mind we used tae say that, when we talked aboot the debt collection? The part where we got rough, they ey said *wait*. Mind we laughed like fuck at that? No laughin now but, ay-no, mate, Begbie smirks, his mocking lecture sending a shiver through Power's bones, as he walks away before suddenly turning and raising the chisel at forty-five degrees again, like the cocking position an American baseball pitcher would adopt to threaten an opponent trying to steal a base. However, he simply lets it go and watches it fly towards the target.

Tyrone manages to twist his head away, into the blade on his right-hand side, and it sears into his neck, drawing a deep wound. Meanwhile, the chisel misses his eye, spearing into his face under his cheekbone, penetrating the flesh an inch deep and sticking fast. As blood oozes from both wounds he screams out in panic, — FRAANKK!!

— That's ma name, Begbie admits, with a dry chortle. Jim has a nice life, he considers, but sometimes Frank has a hell of a lot more fun.

Tyrone struggles with the agonising pain in his face, trying to fill his lungs with air. — What . . . what the fuck dae ye want?

— This, Begbie says coldly. — Ah dinnae want money. Ah dinnae want favours. Ah want this: you on the table, me wi these blades, and he takes one of the Murdo Mathieson

257

Tait pictures, a smaller study, down from the wall. — Tell me aboot this picture.

— What . . . ?

— Tell ays aboot it.

— Ah no fuckin . . . Power starts, only to scream out in horror, — NO, as Begbie's blade slices through the canvas. He slashes the picture up and tosses the torn remnants under the table.

He then picks another painting off the wall. — Ye might remember mair aboot this yin?

Tyrone focuses, neck straining upwards to see, trying to fight down a new mounting wave of terror. This art collection: *it* is his true legacy. He looks at the picture, then at Franco. — It's the early . . . the early Murdo Mathieson Tait, he says, the digging chisel in his face giving every word a twist of pain, — he'd just graduated fae Glasgow College ay Art . . . then he went away tae Italy . . . Tuscany . . . Umbria . . .

— Fuckin good for him, ay.

— What ah dinnae get, Power pleads, — is why? Ah helped you! At the funeral, wi Morrison!

— He's fuckin nowt. Ye tried tae set me up against Anton. But ah did what ye wanted, cause it suited me. Now this suits me, Frank Begbie declares. — See, ah nivir really liked you that much.

Rage swirls through Tyrone like a venomous tide, overwhelming the creeping fear and the sickening pain. — Ah fuckin took you on! Gave ye work, when ye were just a brainless clown.

— You hud ma missus here. That was an error, bringing her intae it.

— Ah helped her! Ah never touched her!

— Disnae matter whether ye helped her or no. Begbie holds the picture at arm's length, screwing up his eyes. Something in his gesture reignites the foreboding in Tyrone. — When ye brought her here, ye brought her intae it. Ah cannae huv that.

— Ah tried tae help her find you! The lassie was in distress! Ah treated her right, Frank, he begs.

To his relief, Begbie lowers the picture, placing it underneath the table. — See the worst thing in life? When ye git accused ay something ye didnae dae. Ye did that wi perr wee Anton. Ye did it tae me.

— Whaaa . . . ah nivir, Power blubbers, the blood dripping from his neck and face onto the table below him, pooling dark and sticky on the polished mahogany surface. He now seems diminished by terror: regressing, Begbie realises, to the fat kid who was a victim of bullies, probably, before he became one himself.

— You said that ah cut off somebody's hand; that cunt Seeker's. It wis just a fuckin bit ay finger, he stroppily advises. — And you fuckin set us up, oan that job in Newcastle. Ye kent we'd hud a run-in.

Power's overheated brain feverishly grasps the opportunity to correct Begbie's misapprehension about this old affair. — Did ah fuck . . . that wis Donny Laing organised that . . .

— He's no here, though, and naebody kens what happened tae um, Begbie says, unclipping Power's hands, grabbing his right one and pushing it palm-down onto the table.

— You've goat it wrong, Power roars, fighting for leverage, but before the big man can make a fist, Begbie wrenches out

259

one of the blades by the side of his neck and slams it through the back of his hand, pinning it to the wood.

David Power feels no pain in his hand, only a storm of broken glass blowing through his chest. He tries to react, swinging vaguely at Frank Begbie with his other hand, but his mobility is constrained by the nails fastening him, chest-down to the table.

Begbie has picked up a huge cleaver and brandishes it above Tyrone's head.

— NAW . . . FRANK . . . PLEASE . . .

He smashes it down into Power's wrist, severing it; the stump flies upwards, now detached from the hand pinned to the table, and a scarlet rope of blood shivers across the room. Begbie manages to jump back to avoid its trajectory. He moves behind David Power, who then feels his right leg being lifted up and his shoe and his sock being removed.

— Stop . . . Power groans in misery, and turns his head from his sundered wrist and hand, electing to shut his eyes rather than contemplate the puddling of his own wet, warm blood, running from the wooden block onto the table, the metal scent of it thick in his nostrils.

— Why would ah fuckin well stoap? Cause it's wrong tae hurt another human bein? You dinnae believe that. Cause you've goat money? Aw the mair reason.

— Frank . . . we were mates . . . Tyrone lashes pitifully against the bonds. His eyes are rolled back to twitching, vein-threaded whites. — What the fuck are you doing . . . ? He hears his voice reduced to a hysterical fluting, his eyes now closed, trying to block out everything.

260

Franco ignores him, pulling out a lighter. Shines the flame against a canvas on the wall above a walnut sideboard. He recalls Tyrone saying it was Murdo Mathieson Tait's finest work, *The Woods Above Garvoch Bay.* — Oil paint, and probably made fae quite combustible materials, he speculates. — Aye, ah'll wager this boy'll go up, be a fat congealed heap ay shite before long, and he looks at Tyrone maliciously. — Especially as ah've soaked the cunt, and the rest ay this room, in petrol.

But the sense that several more of his paintings have been removed from the walls compels Tyrone to open his eyes and look around, confirming his ghastly fear. — Naw! Dae what you like tae me . . . he gasps, his chest convulsing and hiccuping in acid reflux, — but no the paintings . . . no these works . . . they have tae be enjoyed by future generations! You're an artist, he pleads, — ye surely huv tae get that!

— Naw, Franco's eyes are coloured stones, — the fun is in the daein ay them. Ye dinnae really care what happens eftir they're done, you're already workin on the next yin, ay.

— YOU FUCKIN –

Davie Power never gets to finish the sentence as Frank Begbie replaces the ball gag, and watches his old boss's bloodstained face redden and bloat further. The stump is still bleeding; oozing thick claret onto the table, gathering and dripping down onto the polished floorboards in a steady trickle. — Breathe easy . . . through the nose, he advises. — Mibbe too much ching up the hooter, mate. Anywey, the air's gaunny git a bit thin in here soon. Mind ay Mousetrap? A bairns' game? Played it recently, pit ays in mind ay it. Couldnae be too elaborate, time constraints, ay, but no a bad wee effort under the circumstances, Franco explains brightly, moving over and digging out some of the nails that pinned Power's leg, lifting it up and wedging it under a small stool he puts on the table, as he tightens the string around his foot. — Be still, Franco instructs, coming back round, pointing behind Tyrone. — You cannae see it but there's a string attached tae your big tae. If you move it . . . Tyrone – bilious vomit rising from his gut, hitting the gag and heading back down in a burning trail – follows Franco's gaze to a series of eye hooks screwed into the wall. The string seems to be going through them all. The other end is tied to a burning candle, which sits in a dish of petrol. It is placed on the sideboard, directly underneath *The Woods Above Garvoch Bay*. — Dinnae move.

But that is impossible: David Power's leg is uncomfortably raised at forty-five degrees. He has to keep his foot awkwardly bent to hold the stool in place. But he can feel it sliding away by the angle of his leg pushing on it, the pain and stiffness growing exponentially. He could never keep it there. Power wriggles and flexes his prone upper body against his restraints, glimpsing in horror his dribbling wrist and pinned hand, though they are partially obscured from his view by the chisel handle that juts out from his face. He emits a groan – a miserable, muffled sound somewhere between a plea and a curse – to the receding back of Frank Begbie, who is putting a CD of *Chinese Democracy* into Power's expensive sound system. It blasts out at full rattle. — A wee pressie, he smiles. — Dinnae say ah'm no good tae ye!

Then Frank Begbie removes the ball gag, to the relief of David Power, but this is short-lived as he replaces it with a long, broad knife, plunging this into Davie Power's mouth, hearing a tooth cracking. Power squeals: a sharp, concentrated whine, mostly seeming to Begbie to be coming through his nose.

— Workin wi clay, fuckin shite, Franco says. — This is gaunny hurt, but stey wi ays, buddy, he urges, ripping the knife upwards, tearing Power's face like it's paper, as his other hand pushes and twists at the embedded chisel. — Thaire's the grand finale, he says, in the tone of a host about to offer his guest a quality dessert.

No more sound comes from the fat man, but Frank Begbie can see that his eyes are screwed tight shut. He looks at Power's shoeless foot, and it's still unwavering, remaining propped up on the stool. — Good on ye, Davie, Franco says in brisk sincerity. — Ah'm no sure it's that much consolation tae ye, but you've went up in ma estimation, mate. And ah lied aboot no liking ye: never really hud *that* much against ye, ay-no, he concedes.

With that, Frank Begbie turns and exits, just as the exhausted, mutilated and deranged Davie Power feels the stool slide out from under his leg. And a few painful seconds of fearful anticipation elapse before the patron of the arts witnesses, through a curtain of his own blood, the candle drop and *The Woods Above Garvoch Bay* explode into flame as loud rock music fills the air.

Outside, Franco calmly watches through the bay window, breathing steadily, the flames licking around Tyrone's paintings, the blaze gathering force, spreading through the lounge. He can see his former boss, and remembers that old office in George Street, and the safe that Power would fill with the collections from the fruit machines. The way his eyes swivelled in his head as he made the deposits, like a bloated squirrel furtively hoarding nuts for winter. Now he observes the sweating, grimacing, fat man straining against his bonds, the flames lapping up around him on the pyre of the mahogany table, the missing paintings stacked underneath. Then Power's eyes flitter and spin into his head. His tongue spills out from his face, like a fatigued slug escaping from a cracked wall. When the fire finally obscures the wreckage of Power's body from his sight, it's time for Frank Begbie to slip off down the driveway and along the quiet, darkened, tree-lined street.

Marching in the shadows, his leg holding up, Begbie enjoys the scent of apple blossom in the air, strangely complementing the synthetic lime aroma of Tyrone's detergent, which still emanates from his clothes.

It isn't till he's worked his way onto the main Dalkeith Road some ten minutes later that Franco can hear the fire engines blaring, in all probability bound for David 'Tyrone' Power's red sandstone mansion.

He elects to walk to the hotel, where he finds Melanie waiting for him in reception. It's dark inside, apart from a warm, pastel-green light coming from a lamp on a bureau. The chubby night receptionist emerges from the darkness to give him a lingering accusatory stare.

Terry, who has been loitering in the cab, drives them both to the airport. Franco asks him to make the journey *via* the town rather than the city bypass. Oblivious to the cabbie's constant chat, but aware that the conversation is directed largely towards Melanie, Franco looks out at the city in the darkness and the uplit castle, realising, without sentiment, that this might be the last time he'll ever see it. Of course, there was the likelihood of his exhibition coming here, but in spite of the promises he'd made to John Dick, he might have to throw a sicky for that.

They are both so tired from being up all night, but happy to beat the morning traffic. — Ye might be gittin a wee visit soon, Terry advances mischievously as he drops them off. — Goat offered a wee bit ay work oot in the San Fernando Valley, he chortles, shaking Franco's hand and tipping Melanie the wink.

The airport is deserted at the early hour, bar a couple of package flights, with nothing open except one Costa Coffee chain. He'd read that they were one of the companies who had issued dire warnings of what would have happened had the most unbendingly pro-austerity party failed to win the election. He listens to the dull, slithering clatter of cups and saucers on veneered tables, his head throbbing with excitement and fatigue as if hung-over. A red-eye full of worn-out, desperate-looking business travellers takes them to London, with little more than an hour layover before they board the connecting flight to LAX.

37

THE FLIGHT

The incongruence of fine tailoring matched with ruddy disheve-lment and a stumbling gait indicates an archetypal amateur airport drinker: the nervous flyer who can't manage to get on a plane unless totally wrecked. He returns unsteadily to his seat, from the rear of the London to Los Angeles British Airways flight, clutching the small bottles of red wine he's secured from a sympathetic stewardess who knows his type. As he frantically opens one on the way to his seat, the top slips through his fingers onto the floor. It rolls under a chair, so he presses on, burping, trying to keep down a sudden reflux, stumbling right into a passenger seated on the aisle: Frank Begbie. The claret from the bottle splashes over Begbie's white T-shirt like an opened wound. — Oh my God, I'm so sorry . . .

Franco looks at the mess, then to the drunk. — Sorry isnae gaunny git ma –

He feels Melanie's grip on his wrist, and he draws in a breath as he smiles first at her then the terrified drunk. — No worries. Accidents will happen.

— I'm really sorry, the drunk repeats.

— No worries, bud, Franco insists, as another stewardess materialises, already assisting the man to his seat.

— Ah wisnae gaunny touch the guy, Frank says to Melanie.

266

She gives him a doubtful look. — So you were in control?

— Of course, he declares. Her eyes widen, to indicate that this response isn't sufficient. — Look, as I've said, the most important thing is us and the kids. I'm never going to compromise that.

Melanie's voice, when it comes, is hushed by incredulity. — I love you, Frank, I really do. But you live in a parallel moral universe to the rest of us. It's one where everything you do is justified in some way or another.

—Yes, he nods, in that disarmingly heartfelt way of his, — and I want out of it. I'm working hard to get out. Every day. For us. If you still think there can be an us?

Melanie knows the answer, and it isn't an unambiguous one. In Scotland's and California's prisons she's seen all those pathetic women who stood by their damaged men, and vowed she would never be one. But you had to put children first and, more dauntingly, you had to allow that when you committed to a person, you did it because, on some level, it was what you required. And rather than dig up the psychological roots of her own needs for self-examination, Melanie Francis accepted this. Facts are bigger in the dark. But there are still things she needs to know. And to say.

So she tells her own story. The tale of her betrayal of him with that call to the police, Harry Pallister's disturbing intervention, and the dead man, Marcello Santiago. Only for a very brief moment does she detect a flash of anger in his eyes, when she mentions Harry's troubled phone calls. Then it's gone. — I was wrong, she concedes. — It wasn't the best thing to do. I'm sorry.

— It's okay. He squeezes her hand. — I know you did it with the best of motives. You were right, we should have gone tae the police straight away. Me and my jailbird nonsense, he attempts to admonish them both, — I feel bad that you had to face that Harry creep on your own.

Melanie is not looking for his absolution, though. She has bigger concerns. — Those men on the beach. Did you hurt them?

Breathe, breathe, breathe . . . Franco regards his wife, his lip turned down. — As I told you, I did their van. I would have *loved* for them to have been in it, but they werenae. So I got out of there, as it would have been unwise to stick around, for all sorts ay reasons. I knew those guys wouldnae be far away, but I didn't trust myself to go after them. If they didnae kill me, I would have smashed them to pieces. They would have been found mashed on that beach, and students would have been filming it on their phones and putting it on YouTube.

In massive relief, Melanie sucks in the dry, recycled cabin air. Frank had stayed out of bother because he had managed to control his darker impulses. Santiago had been found snagged on the oil platform; Coover was still missing: Melanie has no doubt about her husband's capacity to be violent towards those men. However, disposing of their bodies in that manner was way too premeditated. It was simply beyond him. — I had to ask. Harry made all sorts of inferences.

Francis Begbie strokes her arm. — Polis are the same everywhere; it's all about clearing the books, he smiles grimly. — I wouldn't worry about him, with his mentality and skill set. He seems to have got obsessed with you and made a bit of a cunt of himself. Not that I can blame him. He raises an eyebrow.

His trivialising flattery doesn't sit well with Melanie. She keeps a pointed gaze on him. Her husband is composed and seems genuine, but she can't shake off the dark sense that he's done *something* terrible.

He reads the dreadful concern in her eyes. — Look, I don't want to hurt anybody, good or bad, Franco stresses. — I just want us to get on with our lives. I've the exhibition coming up –

— Fuck your exhibition, Melanie snaps, to the extent he almost flinches. — Bottom line: I need to know, first and foremost, that I and the kids and my friends and family are not only protected *by* you, but also safe *from* you. Because if you can't look me in the eye and really guarantee that, then we are done.

Frank Begbie doesn't think. He doesn't even breathe. He lets his instincts operate, because part of him knows that if he can't be honest here, for the sake of the ones he loves, then he *will* have to walk away. — Of course you are. I would die before I'd hurt any of you. I'd treat myself in exactly the same way as anybody else who tried to harm you.

He sees a tear rolling down Melanie's cheek. But her breathing stays even, as he feels her great strength and is nourished by it, as he always was. In her absence, he'd let himself get weak again, get drawn into old feuds. But it had served a purpose. Then Melanie's hand goes to his face. He feels a hot wetness on the side of it. It astonishes him. — So I'm not living with a monster, she smiles, a lift in her eyes, and kisses his wet cheek.

— Nope. Franco finds his breath catching. — A human being. Quite a fucked-up one, but one who's trying to be better.

Melanie shakes her head and gazes deeply into his eyes. — Well, maybe you gotta try a whole lot harder.

Her tone makes him feel like a rescued pit bull, a much-loved but dangerous family pet. And, he realises, that's exactly what he is, and he has to earn the right to be more. — For you and the girls I will. I'll do whatever it takes.

— I must be as crazy as you, but I believe you, she says, and they share an embrace.

When they pull apart, he looks at Melanie gravely, punching anxiety back into her frame. — There's something I need to tell you.

Melanie Francis can scarcely breathe. She feels her shoulders sag. *He has done something terrible. I knew it.*

— I know who killed Sean.

— David Power told me. It was that young guy, Anton.

— It wisnae him. Power tried to set me up against Anton.

— You have to go to the police this time!

— I can't.

— You promised you would! Why the fuck can't you –

He grabs both her hands in his. Lowers his voice. — It was Michael, he tells her. — My other boy. He killed his big brother, and she sits in silent horror, agog, as he tells her the story. — So I can't go to the cops.

— No. Of course, she agrees, feeling exhaustion eroding her at the edges.

And then he explains to her why he believes Michael did this, and how he can never absolve himself, because of all his contributions to his son's bad education. Melanie listens patiently, until he's done. Then she curls into him and, emotionally drained, falls almost instantly into a deep, grateful slumber on his shoulder.

Frank wipes his face with his sleeve, opens his laptop, puts his headphones on and lets Mahler flood into his brain, relaxing him. He can feel his breathing regulating deliciously, slow and even.

One . . . two . . . three . . . who . . . are . . . we . . .

His thoughts drift off into the realm of half-dream, half-memory. A boy at the bottom of that old dock with broken Johnnie Tweed looking up at him, as young Francis James Begbie holds the boulder, ready to execute the deliverance. What was that one word Johnnie had mouthed again? It might have been 'wait', but he couldn't be sure.

What he was certain of was that it was Johnnie's last word.

We are the mental Y-L-T . . .

A bump of turbulence. Melanie's eyes flick open, and she squeezes his hand as the plane rattles a little, before finding smoother air.

Now Frank Begbie sits contentedly, anticipating the sun, as *Chinese Democracy*, which he can't remember putting on, segues back into Mahler.

The stewardess approaches and offers them a selection of drinks. — Just water for me thanks, he says. Then he regards Melanie, coming out of her slumber, and kisses her on the cheek. — It's so good to be with you. You know what I'm really looking forward to right now?

— What?

— You, me and the girls, trekking down the beach. We have to take them right down to Devereux Slough, for the marine wildlife an aw they species ay bird. Those terns are gaunny be nesting soon.

— I'm looking forward to salsa dancing again, Melanie smiles, her tone dropping enigmatically.

Franco's face creases in a grin. Succumbing to a nag in his bladder, he rises and heads down to the front of the plane. Loitering in the galley, he nods at a middle-aged woman as she vacates the cramped capsule of the lavatory. She turns away, pretending the acknowledgement hadn't happened. As Frank Begbie pishes precariously he considers the nature of the etiquette of a unisex toilet in the sky. Should he have ignored the woman, spared her obvious embarrassment? A life of jail taught you little about protocol outside it. He'd discuss this with Melanie.

It feels liberating to be heading away from Edinburgh, and all its negative associations. He will never experience any of that nonsense again. When the exhibition comes, he concedes to himself that he will probably go, but just to open it, see John, and possibly Elspeth and her family, and then he'll get the fuck out of Dodge. He shakes, zips up, washes his hands and examines the red wine stain on his T-shirt. It approximates the shape of Ireland. He weighs up the possibility of tackling it, but it needs more than just water, and he senses that any efforts will be fruitless. Besides, he now finds it amusing.

When he exits, the first thing he sees is the man who spilled the wine, looking fearfully at him. However, Francis Begbie's stare does not linger on him, but rather on the passenger sitting next to him, on his left, whom he instantly recognises, despite the glasses and the thinner hair. The old Fort boy looks like he's aged well: wearing a light blue shirt, open at the neck, with navy trousers, reading a magazine called *DJ*. Frank Begbie looms over the nervous, drunken flyer, then leans across him, as the other man, aware of a lurking presence, lowers his magazine and looks up, his eyes widening in the shock of recognition: facing the dyslexic boy he took that punishment for, years ago, all in the solidarity of teenage friendship. Frank Begbie keeps his breathing slow and even – in through the nose, out through the mouth – as he says, with a smile, — Hello there, my old buddy. Long time no see.

ACKNOWLEDGEMENTS

Thanks to Elizabeth Quinn, Robin Robertson, Katherine Fry, Tom Mullen, Trevor Engleson, Tiffany Ward, Alex Mebed, John Hodge, Danny Boyle, Andrew Macdonald, Robert Carlyle, Grant Fleming and Cely and Cassandra of the Two Hearted Queen coffee shop, Chicago, IL.

penguin.co.uk/vintage